The Fath[illegible]
th[illegible]
an[illegible]
Unholy Ghost

DAVID HOLMES

WINCKLEY PRESS

First published in 1999 by
WINCKLEY PRESS
5 Winckley Street
Preston PR1 2AA

ISBN 0-907769-27-6

Set in 10 pt Bookman Old Style
Designed and typeset by Winckley Press
Printed and bound in Great Britain

About the Author

David and Kathleen Holmes

David John Holmes was born in Hanover, West Germany in 1949. At the age of five he went to live in Jordan, in the Middle East, with his parents and brother, returning to England after three years and eventually settling in Preston, Lancashire.

He was educated at Crookings Lane Junior School, and Penwortham County Secondary School (as it was known then) until he was fifteen, when he enlisted in the Army as an apprentice tradesman in R.E.M.E. Following his time at the Army Apprentices College, Hadrian's Camp, Carlisle, he later served in Germany with the distinguished armoured regiment, 1st The Queen's Dragoon Guards.

At the tender age of twelve, when still at school, David says 'I met and fell in love with a young girl named Kathleen Davies who, in 1968, did me the honour of becoming my wife. Thirty-one years on and three children later, we are still happily married.'

'I began writing at the age of twelve and have always been an avid reader. To date I have six poems published in the UK and one in the USA. *The Father, The Son and Unholy Ghost* is my first novel.'

Acknowledgements

To my wife Kathleen, and my daughters, Donna and Dawn, without whose help and patience this book would never have been completed.

IN MEMORIUM

To my dear Mother, and my darling Son, Lee Anthony

Though the years have come between us,
Like a wall that has no gate,
One day I'll hold your hands again,
But for now, I have to wait.

ONE

IT was a harsh February day in the highlands of Scotland. The snow fell incessantly, depositing a white blanket over the shivering countryside. A cold wind scoured the rocky mountains and glens, sweeping them clean for the approaching summer.

A single shot rang out, frightening the winter birds from their sheltered hideaways. The bullet entered the victims left eye, passing through the brain, and shattering the rear of the skull as it exited. The man was thrown backwards by the impact of the bullet, dead before he hit the ground. The snow became a crimson cushion for his head. Two assassins emerged from their perfectly concealed hiding places, dressed in white hooded overalls. One skied towards the victim's body, while the other ran to the car they had left hidden nearby.

Reaching the body, the assassin quickly and efficiently, hacked off the head, and both hands of the victim, and placed them in a bin liner ready for disposal.

His companion manoeuvred their black Mercedes to a point, as close to the body as possible, without leaving the road. They placed the victim into a body bag, and carried it the hundred yards to the car, dumping it unceremoniously into the boot. It had taken them two minutes and forty-nine seconds, twelve seconds longer than planned. They sped off. The Highlands were left to conceal the evidence of their brutality.

The first day of May was sizzling, so hot, it was more than an effort to do nothing. People at work longed to be elsewhere, anywhere, out of the formidable heat, and stifling atmosphere. Humidity had draped itself, like a thick woollen blanket, over the UK.

Two young lovers embraced on the grassy banks of the River Ribble, just south of Preston, in Lancashire. They were so engrossed in their own new sexual world, that they failed to notice the body as it floated by, borne on the incoming tide. It appeared to wave at them, with a grotesque, rigor-mortised arm, raised above the water. If they had been aware of it, they may have noticed that the head and hands were missing, and the body was completely naked.

A short time later, and further up stream, a mother, out walking with her new baby in his pram, suddenly screamed hysterically. The body had been found.

Within ten minutes the police had arrived on the scene. It wasn't every day that a town like Preston, was host to a murder, although the town still had it's unfair share, of unsolved cases. The badly decomposed body was dragged from the murky water of the Ribble, up onto the south bank. Two, shirt-sleeved constables, struggled to hold back the gathering crowd of onlookers. Thirty minutes had passed since the body had been found.

For Inspector Bell, this had all the signs, of being another drug related crime. Preston had already experienced the horror of a headless and handless corpse, it didn't deserve another. He was annoyed, at having yet another dinner hour interrupted, especially by the 'druggies'.

"Well, what have we got so far?" barked the Inspector, to the posse of constables, as he eased his overweight, six-foot frame, out of his car.

"There's a small tattoo on his left forearm Sir, it looks like it could be a name, quite faded, nothing much else," replied the nearest bobby.

"Nothing much else," Bell shouted sarcastically, "the poor bugger's got no head, and no hands, and you notice a bloody tattoo, brilliant, why is it that the nation's finest, always come to bloody Preston to lose their virginity? Anyway, keep the body and the area neat and tidy until the SOCO's arrive, it's their job to play about with these things, not ours. Secure the area, get rid of the sightseers, I want the banks searching, either side, both directions, there's houses on the north side, get some doors knocked, get onto missing persons, sort it out amongst yourselves, come on, get moving, where's my bloody sergeant? Cordon off the area." Inspector Bell issued torrents of orders as the investigation got under way.

For Scott McLenan, it was just another too hot day, too hot to share with a hangover. He lay in bed, still clad in yesterday's clothes, holding his exploding forehead with his left hand, carefully sipping black coffee, from the mug he held in his right. Overnight, his tongue had grown a fur coat, OK in winter, but not now.

Not that many years ago, Scott had served with distinction with the S.A.S. now he was just another unemployed waster, drinking out his remaining years, the drink, a veil to shroud some awful memories. No wife, no kids, no friends, the biggest arsehole on earth. Could it get any worse he thought. Probably.

He heard the postman rattle the letter box, he was sure he did it on purpose, just to annoy him, more often than not, there wasn't even a letter. Scott slipped back into unconsciousness, his coffee mug dropped to the floor, breaking off the handle. The remaining coffee, seeped into the carpet, the stain uniting with all the other stains, to form an ever-growing patch of sticky nastiness.

The sunlight, shining through the holes in his curtains, burned Scott's head, like a laser beam. He stirred uneasily, one eye partially opened, he realised his hangover was still very much a part of him, like an unwelcome Siamese twin. He fell off the bed and staggered to the bathroom. He emptied the contents of his stomach into the toilet. Bloody coffee, he thought.

Moving to the sink in the corner, he turned on the cold tap, cupped his hands, and splashed the water onto his unwashed and unshaven face. Looking up into the mirror, he noticed a dark-haired, handsome, red-eyed tramp, looking back at him.

Scott left the bathroom. Walking past the front door, he spotted a letter, lying on top of the accumulated newspapers and circulars. Could only be a death threat, no one ever writes to me, he thought. He picked it up at the third attempt. Tearing the envelope open, he carelessly tore the letter in half. 'Pillock.' he muttered to himself. He pieced it back together and began to read.

Dear Scott,

Please don't bin this, read it. I'm sorry we don't get on any more, I do wish we could turn the clock back. One woman, two guys, where did it all go wrong? I'm afraid Lynn is dead, car accident. Accident, I'm not so sure. I'm sorry for what I have done to you, please forgive me.

The letter was signed, Danny.

Scott's mind was a blur. His wife and brother had disappeared ten years ago. He hadn't heard from them since. Sorry, he thought, not half as sorry as he was. Bastards, he thought, why bother me now? A friend in need, is usually a pain in the arse.

There was no date on the letter, but the postmark told him the letter had been posted in Argentina on the fifth of January.

Scott knew perfectly well where it all went wrong, it was when he let his brother move in to his home, the bastard, he thought, as he headed back to his bed.

A loud knocking at the door jolted Scott out of his self-pity. He turned to answer it, and stood on the handle that had broken off his mug. "Bastard." he shouted, his temper beginning to boil over. He hopped to the door, holding the injured foot, his head still throbbing. He opened the door.

"Who are you calling a bastard?" enquired his next door-neighbour, a scrawny man named Spider.

"Anyone ear-holing my front door," Scott growled "Why, what do you want?"

"Just wanted to borrow your car for a minute or two, dam batteries buggered again".

"Yeah sure, hang on, I'll find the keys." "Here." he said limping back to the door. "Don't use all my petrol, and don't flatten my battery."

"OK Scott, thanks a lot, I'll not be more than a couple of minutes."

Scott closed the door quietly and hobbled back to the bed. He pulled the grubby sheet over his head to shield his eyes from the invasive sun. What else can go wrong, he thought, nothing, surely.

A huge explosion shattered the neighbourhood. Every window in Scott's flat disintegrated. His front door had been torn to shreds, as if made of tissue paper. A few remnants of wood, were left clinging precariously to their hinges. Scott eased his head out from under the sheet. His bed was covered in thousands of razor sharp, shards of glass, some of which had gashed through the threadbare material, and had impaled his clothing. His flat had been a mess before, now it looked more like a war zone.

Dazed and in shock, he groped for his shoes through

the smoke and dust, finding them full of glass, he cursed, then emptied the glass onto the floor, before putting them on. Scott made his way slowly to where his front door had been, coughing hoarsely as the acrid smoke attacked his throat. The fire raging outside was almost volcanic in it's heat, and ferocity. Flames were spreading from car to car. Dense black smoke blotted out the sun. Another fuel tank exploded. Scott instinctively protected his eyes with his arm. More windows cracked, shattered by the intense heat. A cascade of glass rained down, shredding the fabric of a baby's pushchair, luckily, unoccupied.

The scene reminded Scott of his tour of duty in Northern Ireland, death and destruction in deadly harmony. He could see one body, smouldering, lifeless, and wondered how many others there would be. It was then that Scott noticed the two jump leads attached to the remains of his car, his neighbours car was on fire, but not nearly so badly damaged as his.

Two fire engines screamed into the parking area, men leapt out of the machines, running to different points, each man seemingly knowing exactly what to do. The police arrived within a few minutes, their sirens adding to the frightening atmosphere. Scott could hear women beginning to scream above the bedlam, as the enormity of the situation began to dawn on them. The evacuation was now in full swing. A policeman came to escort Scott away from the crumbling buildings. He was too shaken to argue. How could one penis of a neighbour, cause so much destruction, trying to start one heap of a car, he thought.

At about this time, Inspector Bell and Sergeant Bennett arrived at the scene, twenty minutes had passed since the explosion. Bell couldn't believe what he was seeing. Burnt-out cars littered the area, now just smouldering shells. Shattered windows wherever he looked. To Bell, the area looked like the Luftwaffe had just bombed it. He walked slowly round the area, trying to take it all in, wondering what the place had looked like earlier that day.

"Excuse me Sir, are you Inspector Bell?" A fire fighter asked.

"Yes, can I help you?"

"Sub Officer Davies Sir, could you come with me please?"

"Certainly."

"Over here Sir." He said pointing to the car park.

Bell followed obediently, he had great respect for the fire-fighters, there's was one job he didn't fancy at all.

"It's here Sir." said the Sub Officer, pointing to the charred remains of a human being, "I'll leave you with it, if you need any help, please just ask for me."

"Thank you, I will indeed." Bell replied, mopping his sweating forehead with a well-worn hankie.

Bell wasn't all that sure there was that much he could do. This was a SOCO problem to start with. He didn't want to go too near the body, it wouldn't be good for his image, if the rookies saw him puke at the scene. The smell coming from the body, was disgusting, he turned away.

"Benny, do we know who it is yet?" he shouted, slightly annoyed with himself for being so weak.

Sergeant Bennett stood at well over six feet three inches tall. He had a full head of worried grey hair, his blue shirt and dark trousers made him look like an old constable. He kept himself fit playing squash. He had been Bell's sergeant for five years now.

"Possibly Sir, this man says it could be his neighbour." He said, ushering Scott towards him.

"Oh, and who might you be?" asked Bell.

"Scott McLenan, hung over, homeless and helpless, news at ten, Preston".

"Very droll Sir. May I remind you that we have a body here, burnt to a crisp, beyond recognition. Women and children injured, houses destroyed, cars destroyed." Bell's voice rose in anger. "Belongings lost forever," he continued, "you may think it's a good laugh Sir, but we are the poor bastards charged with the duty of sorting it all out, and a little co-operation from people like you, might just help, savvy?"

Scott ignored the angry tirade as he replied. "I think it might be my neighbour because he borrowed my car keys, to try and jump start his car." His tone of voice altered as he continued. "And don't you ever raise your patronising, policeman voice to people like me again, you might be able to talk to the rookies like that, but don't try it with me, savvy?" He said, prodding Bell's chest with his forefinger.

The temperature rising between the two men, was equal

to that of the fire, an instant dislike of the 'waster', versus an instant dislike of authority.

"Let me remind you to whom you are speaking young man."

"I know exactly to whom I am speaking. A twenty-five year man, with no further hope of promotion, pretty clever at shouting the odds, at every poor bobby within ear shot, yet not quite man enough to look closely at a burnt body. Well I can, and have, so don't you, ever, use that holier than thou tone of voice with me, do I make myself clear?" Scott shouted.

There was an authoritative quality in Scott's voice that set the Inspector back, how had he spotted his weakness, he was momentarily lost for words.

"What was your friend's name?" enquired Bell, regaining some composure.

"I only know him as Spider, never did know his real name"

"Spider what?"

"I just told you, I never knew his real name, but these are council flats, his was number twenty-four, I lived next door at twenty-three, ask the council".

"So which is your car?" asked Bell.

"Was my car, it's that heap of scrap with the jump leads still attached, Spider's car is the one next to it."

"Thank you. I'll speak to again later, now I suggest you get yourself checked over."

Pillock, Scott thought as he walked away, the Army was full of them, so is civvy street.

TWO

SCOTT surveyed the damage to his flat. It was incredible. How could a few windowpanes, create so many glass fragments, he thought to himself.

"Excuse me Sir." said a young bobby through a hole in the wall, "I'm afraid you can't stop here, the building's unsafe, everybody is being offered temporary accommodation, can you quickly gather a few overnight things together, then come with me?"

"Yeah, give us a minute mate." he said resignedly.

He escorted Scott away from the devastation, Scott repeatedly looking over his shoulder, in utter disbelief.

"Just a moment." Inspector Bell called out, "I would like a little word with you.".

"What about, I've told you everythin' I know?"

"No, I don't think you have, have you?"

"Yes." Scott replied curtly.

"Well, perhaps you could start by telling me, in words of more than four letters, what you have been up to lately, Mr McLenan?"

"I haven't been up to anything that could be of concern to you, and if I had, I wouldn't want to tell you anyway."

"Mr McLenan, it's obvious from your attitude, that you are having some difficulty with the situation, let me try and elucidate, you know, make things a little clearer."

"Let me make things a little clearer for you, Sergeant"

"Inspector" Bell snapped.

"If you say so. As I was saying, I might look like a bag of shit, to somebody as important as yourself, but under this rough exterior, is an extremely pissed off has been, who is on the verge of assaulting a police officer, unless he starts showing a little respect. I've had one hell of a day so far, and my advice to you is, don't push it."

"Well excuse me if I don't take your advice McLenan, but. . ."

Scott grabbed Bell by the shirt collar, forcing him backwards, hard up against a wall, knocking the wind out of him.

"Listen you fat, pompous, bastard, don't talk down to me, you patronising piece of shit, it's Mr McLenan."

The young bobby managed to pull Scott and the Inspector apart, before Scott could really land himself in trouble. Bell was surprised by Scott's strength, he had him down as a layabout, but he certainly recognised brute force when he came across it.

"For Christ's sake." shouted the young bobby. "Calm down will you, both of you?"

"Listen, Mr McLenan." stressed Bell, "I don't give a hog's shit what you think of me, but answer this, smart arse, why was there a bomb planted in your car."

Bell's question knocked Scott sideways. A bomb, in his car. Who could want to blow up a drop out like him? Not the IRA, that was too long ago. He stared at Bell as if he hadn't believed the question.

"You tell me, you reckon you know it all."

"Yes, I will tell you Mr McLenan. Somebody, at sometime, planted a bomb in your car, that bomb, has killed your neighbour, that somebody is going to come back, sometime, to kill you, so perhaps a little more co-operation, might just prolong what's left of your miserable little shit of a life."

"Bollocks."

"Not bollocks, Mr McLenan, bomb, bomb just made for you."

"That's bollocks and you know it."

"Listen to me carefully, I don't know what it is you're hiding, but I don't want any more people being blown to pieces on your behalf, savvy, so let's get co-operative shall we?"

"Look at me for Christ's sake, what have I got? Nothing. I certainly haven't anything worth hiding."

"I don't think you're listening, let me make it clear, someone try to kill you, me try to help you, you, help me. Clear?" Bell said in his most sarcastic voice.

"Alright, just get off my back, but I honestly don't know of any reason, why anyone, would want to kill me, it doesn't make sense."

"Let me just warn you, you, are up to your ankles in the shit, head first, if you think of anything, however inconsequential, please tell me, deal?"

"Deal." Scott answered. "But take a close look at me, I'm

nothing more than a turd in life's toilet, waiting to be flushed down the sewer, a nobody, with nothing, who kills nobodies with nothing?"

Bell didn't answer, he thought for a few moments, staring Scott coldly in the eyes, then he said, "It's drugs isn't it?"

"You're a bright bastard you are, after drink, I can't even afford an Anadin for my hangover."

Bell sighed, "Look, we're getting bloody nowhere, I'll speak to you again when you've had time to think it over, ok?"

"Yeah sure." Scott replied wearily.

The young bobby escorted Scott to the nearby primary school, Scott having refused to go to the hospital. The police had arranged temporary accommodation for the victims. From the rows of beds, Scott selected one in the furthest corner, well away from the door. Despite the noise and chaos of shocked and bewildered people, he soon drifted off into a deep, angry, sleep.

Scott woke with a start. He had been dreaming, but he couldn't remember what about. The school hall clock showed 7.30. Christ, he thought, it's morning. He couldn't remember the last time he had woken without the company of a hangover. He needed the toilet quickly. A policeman guarding the entrance to the hall, directed him, also informing him, that breakfast was being served in the school canteen. Scott thanked him for his help, and rushed off.

He hadn't had breakfast in years, but he enjoyed it so much, that he went back for second helpings. He had been unable to think of a single reason why the bomb had been aimed at him, unless it was something lost in the past, something concerning his S.A.S days, but he thought that was highly unlikely. He made up his mind to get away from Preston as soon as possible, he didn't like the thought of being a target, he didn't like not knowing who the enemy were.

After breakfast, Scott washed and combed his hair, his mouth tasted foul as he couldn't clean his teeth, He left the school hall, and headed for the bank. He had his cash card with him, and was hoping his small Army pension had been deposited, as he was in his usual condition, of being financially challenged.

Thinking over the recent events, he tried to sort things

out in his own mind. First, he receives a letter, from a brother he hasn't heard of in years. The letter informs him of his wife's demise. Then his car is blown to pieces, killing his neighbour. Then some prat of a policeman accuses him of being into drugs. He pulled the letter from his pocket and read it. It didn't say much. He felt no remorse over his wife's death. Her leaving had broken him, he had no feelings left for her at all, or his brother. She had been his first and only love, yet she had brought him to his knees, he had been down ever since.

Where did it all go wrong he thought. That was easily answered, the Rampsbeck Hotel, Ullswater, in the Lake District. The three of them had gone there for a short holiday. He had gone out for a run, but changed his mind when it began to rain, and returned to the hotel. As there was no sign of his wife, Lynn, in their room, he crossed the landing to his brother's room, as the door was unlocked, he walked in. Danny and Lynn were in bed together. There was such frenzied activity going on between the sheets, they hadn't heard him enter, or leave.

Scott collected his belongings and left the hotel. He hadn't seen or heard of them since.

'I wish we could turn the clock back'. Why, so the bastard can do it all over again, Scott mumbled to himself.

He read the letter several times, but it just didn't seem to have any meaning, hidden or otherwise.

Scott arrived at the bank cash point. He typed in his PIN number, followed by the amount, then waited for the machine to tell him to piss off. It didn't, and out came a nice, crisp, twenty-pound note. He clutched it to his chest, like a long lost friend, then pocketed it. The receipt followed. Scott read the receipt and nearly fainted. According to the receipt, the balance of his account now stood at £250.230. and some pence. "Computers," he said to himself, "they're a load of crap."

As Scott stood on the pavement wondering what to do, the bank opened. He decided to be an honest citizen, and go in to point out the error. He was first in. Thank God, he thought, there's always some dithering old fart in front of the queue, holding everyone up. He approached the counter.

"Hi, I've just made a withdrawal at the cashpoint, and

I've noticed, there seems to be an error, with the amount remaining in my account, could you check it please?"

"Certainly Sir." said the very attractive young lady cashier, "Just one moment please." Scott watched her closely, she was too nice to be stuck in a bank all day, she should come out with me, he thought.

"Yes Sir, the account is correct."

"It can't be, I'm supposed to receive £250.00 pension from the Army, you've got too many noughts."

"No Sir, this amount wasn't deposited by the Army."

"What, well can you tell me, who did deposit it then?"

"Yes Sir, it was a Mr D McLenan."

Scott stood opened mouthed, his mind racing. "You're sure?" he asked.

"Positive."

"No wind up?"

"No Sir."

"Well, in that case, I would like to draw five thousand pounds please."

"Certainly Sir, could you fill out a withdrawal slip please?"

Scott filled out the form in record time, before anyone could change their mind, and within a few moments, was leaving the bank, with the broadest grin in England spread across his face.

As there was still about an hour or two, before opening time, Scott decided to go off in search of some new clothes. He hated shopping, but was thinking along the lines of spending some of his new-found wealth, before the bank manager came chasing after him. He visited a number of shops, and finally reappeared to the world, wearing a new pair of black trousers, a new white shirt, a pair of black chisel-toed boots, and carrying a new leather jacket. He looked into the shop window as he left, he thought he looked like an out of work waiter.

Scott had been sharing his money liberally, shopping around the town centre, but by now, it was his favourite time of day, opening time. He headed for the nearest pub. Scott went to the bar, ordered a vodka and orange, and found him self a quite corner. From his seat, Scott could see the two entrances to the pub, if someone was intent on killing him, he wanted to see them coming. He took the letter from his pocket, and read it again. 'Where did it all go wrong?' The Lake District. It was his favourite part of the UK. He hadn't been there since that day. It would be nice to get away from Preston for a while, he thought. A plan was now firmly forming in his mind, buy a car, get away to the Lakes, get away from all this trouble, get away from that big pudding Bell. Perhaps his brother had given him the money, to get him restarted in life. Perhaps, perhaps, perhaps. Scott's mind was swimming with ideas.

His train of thought was interrupted as one of the pub doors opened. A giant of a man entered, he seemed to fill the doorway. He didn't notice Scott, as he walked to the bar, but Scott watched him, every move, the hair on the back of his neck rising, he didn't know why. The adrenalin began to surge through his blood stream. He began to shake. He rose from his seat and stepped forward. He tripped over a stool. Cursing, he made his way to the 'gents'. He slapped his face to calm himself. It didn't work. The door opened behind him.

It was the giant, carrying what to Scott, looked like a British Army bayonet. His heart pumped loudly in his ears, this is it, he thought. After all he had been through, he was going to die in a pub toilet.

Scott's first kick caught the giant in the testicles. As he doubled up in pain, Scott's second kick, took his right knee backwards, snapping the joint, with a sickening cracking sound. The giant howled in pain and fell to the floor. Scott was on him instantly. He smashed the giant's ugly face into the urinal, time and time again, until he felt his body relax, until the face was a bloody, pulpy mess. Scott hovered over his assailant, it took all his self-control not to kill him. He picked up the bayonet, and cut of large tufts of the giant's hair, he knew he would understand. With a final kick to the man's testicles, Scott left the toilet, a feeling of triumph sweeping over him. He collected his new jacket, waved to the barmaid, and made his way out.

Scott left the pub via the rear door, making his way slowly to the main street, he looked left and right. A black Mercedes was parked near the front door of the pub, it's engine running. He thought about cutting the driver, but changed his mind. He went to the rear of the pub and climbed over the wall, running off down the alley.

Five minutes later, Scott was sitting safely in another pub, gasping for air. He hadn't realised how unfit he had become. "Are you alright Sir?" asked the barmaid.

"Yes thanks love, I must be getting old or something."

"Can I get you drink?"

"Vodka and orange please, plenty of ice."

The barmaid returned with his drink, Scott paid, but no tip. The vodka was like nectar to his burning throat. 'Right' he thought, 'get a car, get away, get even.'

The used car salesman recognised Scott as he walked onto the pitch, he had sold him cars in the past, he knew he was hard to barter with. He also knew that Scott wasn't a dreamer, he was more than welcome.

"Hi Scott," he greeted him, "how's the car?"

"Going like a bomb, Arthur, how the hell are you?"

"Excellent Scott, and how's yourself? Hey, don't call me Arthur, it's bad for the image."

"Would Daley be more to your liking?"

"No, you cheeky sod, Aristotle Bermuda Jones will do fine."

"Pillock, how's business anyway Tony?"

"Doing alright I suppose, scratching a living."

"Beats scratching your arse."

"You're alright Scott, are you looking for a change, I've some nice stuff in at the moment?"

"Yeah, I fancy something a bit sporty, with a good body, and not so old, and a car as well."

"What sort of price range are we talking?"

"Three grand, no swopper."

"No swopper, what you have done to it?"

"Nothing really, I suppose you could say it overheated."

"Oh, right, what about the 205 GTi, jet-powered them things?"

"Go on then, let's have a look, has it been boy-raced?"

"No funnily enough, it was one old lady owner, Christ knows what she did with it."

Tony went off to the office for the keys, leaving Scott to poke and prod and kick a few tyres.

"Here you are," he said, handing over the keys, "Take it for a blast, and don't forget to put some petrol in, it's taxed and tested for eight months."

"If you give me the money," Scott said climbing into the car.

"You've always been as tight as a ducks, haven't you?"

"See you later." Scott called as he drove off.

Tony watched him drive away, he wished that all customers were as easy to get on with as Scott.

A few minutes later Scott returned.

"What do you think of her Scott, she fast or what?"

"Yeah, it's fast enough for an old lady, but not a 'he' man like me."

"I bet you couldn't handle her, could you?"

"Joking aren't you, it drives like a slug with no legs?"

"Slugs don't have legs, do they?"

"I don't know, how much for cash, no warranty, no moans, no receipts?"

"Got to give receipts Scott, or I'll have the tax man after my blood, make me a bid."

'A Geoffrey.'

"Two thousand, I said a bid not an insult."

"Come on, the old nag's dead on it's feet, two and a daughter?"

"Two and a half."

"Where's your mask Dick, or don't highway robbers wear them anymore?"

"Alright, two and a daughter cash, no screaming?"

"Done."

"Come into the office while I write it up."

Scott followed him into the office. They talked over old times and old cars for a while.

"Right, well I'd better be getting on Tony, it's been nice to see you again, this car had better be the business, or I'll be back."

"Complaints department has moved to new premises Scott, thanks a million, see you soon, take care."

Scott drove off, the speed of the 205 impressed him. He headed for the M6. He had bought a few things to be going on with, like toothbrush and comb, but decided to buy the rest as he needed to. He had left everything in the flat, someone would have to pay. He hoped the giant from the pub would send a clear message to his bosses, that Scott McLenan was best left alone, or else.

He drove north along the M6, the thought of the Lake District filled him with pleasure. It would be a good place to re-start his life. The quite and the solitude would give him time to think, time to get back in shape, time to re-build the man he wanted to be, the man he used to be, the man he should have been.

It was four-thirty-five in the afternoon as Scott left the motorway. Turning left off the slip-road, he headed toward Ullswater. He loved this part of England. The way of life was so much slower, visitors were forced to take it easy and relax.

He caught sight of Ullswater through the trees, his spirits lifted. Why he loved it up here he didn't really know, he just did. He drove slowly beside the lake, to the annoyance of other motorists, but he didn't care. Yachts manoeuvred to and fro across the water, wind surfers were falling of their boards, like toddlers learning to walk. Even the boats had to go slow on Ullswater, ten miles per hour maximum.

After driving for a few more minutes, Scott spotted the sign. Rampsbeck Hotel. He indicated left and turned into the driveway leading down to the hotel. The view of Ullswater was superb, he thought, who invented towns?

The Rampsbeck stood in all it's glory, a wonderful building, a beautiful location. He drove into the car park, and came to a halt near the main door. He got out of the car and stretched, looking out over Ullswater. Scott stood for a few minutes taking in the view, before turning and walking toward the main door. Just inside the door and to the left, was an enormous mirror, it seemed to have been there forever. Over to the right was an ancient grandfather clock, which had stood sentinel here, longer than the mirror, or so he thought. The clock chimed five as he walked to the reception area, he rang the bell and waited.

"Hello," a voice called from behind, " can I help you Sir?"

Scott turned to see who had spoken. There, stood before him was a beautiful woman, his idea of the perfection, he realised he was stood with his mouth open, slightly embarrassed he spoke.

"I certainly hope so, I would like to book a room, but I'm not exactly sure for how long, would that be a problem?"

"No problem at all Sir." she replied as she came and stood behind the reception desk.

"May I take your name please?"

"Scott McLenan, everybody calls me Scott."

"Oh, Mr McLenan, your room has already been booked."

Scott's brain was searching desperately for an answer. First the letter, then the bomb, now this. "I don't understand, I've only just decided to take a break, are you sure it's for me?"

"Are you Mr McLenan from Preston?"

"Yes."

"Well Mr McLenan, the room has definitely been booked on your behalf, let me see, yes, it was booked for you by a Mr D McLenan, would that be right?"

"That brother of mine." Scott said, "He can read me like a book, well, could I see the room please?"

"Certainly Mr McLenan, would you like to follow me?"

"Please lead the way, I'm in your hands." He wished he was. "I would be a lot happier if you called me Scott, and you haven't told me your name."

"My name is Shannon, Shannon Richards."

She led him up the first flight of stairs, then along the landing.

"This is your room, Scott, I hope it's suitable."

All the rooms at the Ramps' were suitable, but this one was special. It had it's own veranda, overlooking Ullswater. The interior of the room was sheer luxury. Large double bed. Drinks cabinet. Television. All the things most important to Scott's life.

"Have I died and gone to heaven Shannon?"

"No, but your brother did insist on the best room."

"I bet he didn't insist on paying?"

"Yes actually, that's all been taken care of."

"Well, room 21 it is then, it's beautiful Shannon, just like..." Scott stopped himself from completing the sentence. He had only just met her, and didn't want to be too forward, too soon. "Just like they always were."

"Thank you Scott, right, I'll leave you in peace. See you later?"

"Of course. Oh Shannon, when could I get a bite to eat?"

"Anytime really, the lounge bar is open all day, the restaurant opens for evening meals at seven-thirty. We like our gentlemen to wear suits in the restaurant, but you can wear anything in the lounge bar."

"Ok, I'll see you in a while."

As Shannon left the room, he caught the scent of her perfume. Beautiful, he thought. She had a perfect figure, long blond hair, blue eyes and lovely lips, he had fallen for her already. He spent the next few minutes thinking how lucky her husband must be, and wondering why women like Shannon were always spoken for. Lynn had been his one and only love, until now.

Scott lay on the bed and closed his eyes, trying to come to terms with the puzzle of the last couple of days. The letter from his brother. The explosion. The money. The giant in the pub. The room booked. What did it all add up to, he thought, as he drifted off into a peaceful sleep.

Back in Preston, a large black Mercedes drove onto a small, used car sales pitch.

THREE

INSPECTOR Bell." An excited constable called out.

"Yes, what is it?"

"There's been another murder, only this one is different Sir."

"For God's sake what's happening to this town Benny?" he said addressing his sergeant. "What's different?" he asked the constable.

"First reports are that he may have been tortured Sir."

"Christ, do we have a name yet?" asked Bell, almost hoping it was McLenan.

"We're checking now Sir, we believe it may be a used car salesman named Tony Hastings, of Hastings Motors, here in town. His body was found in a small workshop at the rear of the premises."

"Right, tell them I'm on my way. Come on Benny, don't just sit there looking pretty." he said rising from his seat. "If this keeps up, we'll have to stack the bodies up at North End, make the kop look fuller."

"There's probably more life in them, than some of the Preston players." Benny replied dryly.

"What do you mean, it's promotion this season, wanna bet?"

"No thanks."

They reached the car and sped off in the direction of Hastings Motors.

A few minutes later they arrived at the scene. There was no need to ask where the body was, the crime scene team were already buzzing around it, like encroaching flies.

"Can we have a look yet?" Bell asked one of the forensic scientists.

"You can look, but don't touch, and only stand on these sheets of paper." He moved out of the way to let Bell in.

"Jesus Christ," he blasphemed, "What a bloody mess, it's no wonder you're not sure who it is." The victim's face was unrecognisable. There appeared to be stab wounds everywhere. Large tufts of his hair had been very roughly cut from the sides and back of his head. His left ear was almost severed. His left arm had to be broken, judging from the position it had been left in. The guy had suffered terribly. Bell was angry. Things seemed to be getting out of control, in what he believed to be a drugs war. He invited Sgt Bennett to take a look.

"Christ all bloody mighty, he must sell crap cars." Benny said in a dismissive manner.

"Show some respect Benny, come on, let's have a look in the office before I puke."

The SOCO team was busy there as well, so they waited until they were given permission to enter. There were no signs of a struggle in the office, they concluded that Hastings must have been tortured and killed in the garage. The office was tastefully decorated. A computer sat mutely in one corner.

"Do you know how to work that," he asked Bennett, pointing at the computer.

"You must be joking, I bet my kids could though, I struggle setting the video. There's just too many buttons these days."

"Your age is showing. Right then Benny, see if you can find his sales invoices, one of these younger bobbies can have a go at this, who knows what may be hidden in there."

"Sales invoices, they're on the desk Sir." one of the SOCO team told him.

"Oh right, thanks." answered Bell.

"Here you are Sir." said Benny passing them over, "Eh up Sir, look at the top invoice."

"I bloody knew it, I knew that little shit would be involved, S McLenan, Peugeot 205GTi, right Benny, let's bring him in, cocky little sod, wherever there's trouble, his name crops up."

The altercation between McLenan and Bell was the talk of the police station, Sergeant Bennett knew that Bell was itching to arrest McLenan, there was no love lost there he thought.

"Right Sir, I'll get onto it." He noted the registration number and left the office. Bell had never known three days like it. Preston was becoming more like Chicago in the old days, he thought. Looking out of the office window, he noticed the media gathering in ever-increasing numbers. A murder was of little interest these days, but three was bringing them out of the woodwork 'en masse'. Three might even attract the nationals. He wondered if he might get his picture on the front page. If he could solve these murders, with a bit of media attention, he could well put himself back on the promotion bandwagon. He purposely left the office, hoping for a reaction. He got one.

"Hey Dinger, what's the story." called out one of the local press reporters.

"Inspector Bell to you, you cheeky sod. There's not a lot I can tell you at the moment. We've had three murders in three days, as yet unconnected."

"Can you give us any names?" shouted another.

"No, no names have been confirmed as yet." He turned away from the press and headed back to the garage. "Found anything lads?" He asked the team working in the garage.

"I'm beginning to think this is more professional than we first thought Sir."

"Why."

"It's all too clean, no prints, no foot prints, no weapon. These drug fights are a lot messier, and they don't usually torture. They usually give each other a good slapping, then go on there merry ways."

"Yeah, that's a good point, but hit-men, in Preston, it's a bit hard to believe isn't it."

"It's only my opinion, but you do get a feel for it don't you Sir?"

Bell knew what he meant. These forensic guys are pretty good he thought, and if he said professional, then it probably would be.

Scott woke from a deep sleep. For the second night on the trot, he had slept right through. He thought it must be a reaction to the blast, or the shock of it all. It was 8.30am, on the third day of May. He got up, showered, dressed, then went down to the hotel restaurant, in search of breakfast. He hadn't eaten since breakfast the previous day, and was ravenous.

There were a number of guests already seated in the restaurant. Scott found himself a table away from the others. Trying to make small talk at this time of day, wasn't his idea of fun. He watched as Shannon and a younger girl served breakfasts efficiently and quickly.

Shannon looked beautiful, there was a freshness about her, that attracted his attention. He found it extremely difficult take his eyes off her.

Shannon noticed him staring and came over to his table.

"Good morning Mr McLenan, I hope you slept well?"

"Good morning to you Shannon, I slept like a log with no eyes. I promise I won't sulk if you call me Scott."

"I'm sorry Scott, a large number of our guests prefer to be addressed by their surnames only, it's just habit for me."

"Please don't apologise Shannon, you can call me what you like, most people do."

"You missed dinner last night, are you ready to eat?"

"No" he fibbed, "I'm trying to get myself into better shape, that's why I'm here, it's a kind of get-fit holiday."

"Would you like to order your breakfast Scott?"

"Yeah, could I have fresh orange, toast and black coffee please?"

"Ok, are you sure you wouldn't like anything else?"

Scott had many other things on his mind, but he replied, "No thanks Shannon, that's fine."

She went off to the kitchen with his order. Scott followed her every move. He wanted Shannon badly, he wanted her to end his loneliness, but he didn't want to become a wedge between her and her husband. That had happened to him, and he knew how bad it felt. He watched as she emerged from the kitchen carrying his breakfast.

"There you are Scott, if you would like anything else, please don't hesitate to ask."

"Thank you, I most certainly will."

She left his table. He watched her as she went about her work. He was captivated. Her blue eyes were bluer than any blue eyes he had ever seen, her long blond hair hung down below her shoulders, slightly curled, just how he liked it. Every now and then Shannon looked his way and smiled. He was hooked, but what could he do. He had only just met her, but he knew he wanted her more than anything else in the world. He noticed how Shannon managed to keep everybody attended, everyone received a passing smile, it wasn't just him. Her husband wasn't much help, unless he was the chef, he certainly hadn't seen anything of him yet. He finished his meal and went outside for a walk in the hotel gardens. He walked down to the water's edge. The silence was loud to a towny. A hint of a breeze came off the lake, ruffling his dark hair. The Ullswater steamer passed by on the other side of the water, on the first of many crossings it would make each day.

Scott sat on a rock thinking over recent events, trying to come to terms with it all. How did his brother know he would come to the Ramps'. In the letter he asked, "Where did it all go wrong?" It all went wrong here, and here he was. The letter also said, "I'm sorry for what I have done to you." Scott wondered if Danny had inadvertently dropped him into the mire, or deliberately. Whichever, somebody seemed to be annoyed with him. His mind was turning circles before coming back to square one.

"Hi Scott."

He was so startled he almost fell off the rock. He looked up to see who had spoken, then began to laugh.

"Hi Shannon, you gave me a heart attack, I was miles away on that steamer." he said, pointing to the dark silhouette in the distance.

"I'm sorry, I didn't mean to alarm you."

"Well, I'll let you off this time." he said, wondering if she walked here everyday, or had she come looking for him.

"Left poor old hubby to do all the chores have you?"

"No no," she answered quietly, "I'm afraid my husband passed away two years ago."

"Oh Shannon, I'm really sorry, I didn't know, me and my big mouth." He could have kicked himself, he was sure she would be angry with him.

"It's Ok Scott, I'm over him now."

"Shannon, I'm so sorry, I always seem to put my big foot in my even bigger mouth, I'm sure my tongue has never been securely attached to my brain."

She laughed. "No honestly, I can talk about him now, without getting too emotional."

"I'm sorry Shannon."

"If you don't stop apologising, you'll be taking an early morning swim."

"Sorry," he said deliberately.

She raised her hand in a mock slapping gesture. The ice

had been broken.

"Shannon, would you mind very much walking with me for a while?"

"I would love to Scott, where to?"

"Let's go down the marina and look at the boats shall we?"

"Sounds good to me."

They walked across the field to the stile that led to the marina. He helped her climb over, then followed.

Scott was in heaven. Scenery that was perfect, and a beautiful woman at his side. He thought he could easily spend the rest of his life, right here. He watched her as she looked out across Ullswater, and wondered what she was thinking about. "What are you thinking Shannon?" he asked.

"Oh, nothing, everything, I don't know really, I don't get a lot of time to think anymore, the Ramps' keeps me fully occupied, but I was wondering, no, it doesn't matter."

"Go on, what were you wondering?"

"I know it's none of my business, but why didn't your wife come on holiday with you?"

"It's a long story Shannon, I wouldn't want to bore you," he said, as they looked out at the boats moored nearby. "My wife and my life died here ten years ago, as far as I'm concerned. In a way, I'm using my time here to re-start my life, I've wasted too long, self-pity, self-conscious, and probably selfish."

"How did your wife die, Scott, don't tell me if it's too painful?"

"I'm not sure, it was only recently, somewhere in South America."

"I'm sorry, I thought you said ten years ago?"

"Just feeling sorry for myself again Shannon, I found her and my brother together, in bed, here, at the Ramps', I haven't seen either of them since, ten years, give or take a hangover or two."

"That's awful Scott, how did you cope?"

"Very badly. Lynn was my first and only love, I turned to drink for comfort, got myself thrown out of the Army, then concentrated all my efforts on becoming a full-time, waste of time, it's the only job I've ever been good at."

"I don't believe that, but why did he book the room?"

"I honestly don't know, I don't even know how he knew I would come here, but I did." Scott didn't mention the letter or the bomb.

"Perhaps it's a peace offering." The wind caught Shannon's hair, caressing it away from her face. Scott watched her as she looked into the distance, her thoughts unknown. He wanted to take her in his arms and never let go.

They walked along one of the moorings, peering into the unoccupied boats, both lost in their own thoughts and memories, the silence broken only by the sounds of birds, busily chattering from tree to tree, and the small waves as they lapped the shore and slapped the boats.

"Scott, I must get back to the Ramps'." She turned to face him, tears welling in her eyes.

"I'm sorry Shannon, have I upset you?"

"No, you've made me happy, I had forgotten how beautiful Ullswater is, I only seem to work here, I hadn't looked at the lake since my husband died."

Scott reached for her. She put her head onto his chest as his arms enfolded her. Two years of pent-up anger and loneliness washed away on her tears. They stood holding each other as she sobbed quietly, Scott's heart ached for her.

"I'm sorry," Shannon said, pulling away from him as she wiped her eyes. "I shouldn't burden you with my grief, you must have your own to contend with."

"Don't be sorry, I'm glad I was here for you Shannon, a shoulder for you to cry on, if you want to walk and talk again, I would be honoured to be your escort."

"You're so very kind, perhaps it's time for me to let go of the past as well."

Scott offered his hand, she accepted, and they walked slowly back toward the Rampsbeck.

"Shannon, I've not been totally straight with you," Scott confessed, "something strange is happening to my life at the moment, it's as though I'm a puppet, but I can't see who is pulling the strings."

"Why, what's been happening to you?" She stopped and turned to face him.

"Well, first I received a letter from my brother, then my car was blown up, then I come here and find my room booked, I'm just a waster by trade, and now I seem to be being used, it doesn't make sense."

"Your car blew up?"

"No, it was blown up according to the police, a bomb, but I don't believe them."

"Perhaps your brother will meet you here and explain what's happening, did the letter give a clue?"

"Not really, but I suppose it did lead me here, and I'm thankful for that." Scott said, as they walked on again.

They reached the main entrance of the Ramps'.

"It's been lovely walking with you Scott, but I really must go, can we talk later?"

"I'd love to Shannon, just find me when your free."

Shannon turned and entered the hotel, looking back once and smiling as she went. Scott went to his room, changed into shorts and T-shirt, and went for the first of many runs beside the lake.

Later the same evening, Shannon joined Scott in the lounge bar. They sat at the table by the French windows, overlooking the gardens, it was a calm and pleasant night.

"I'm glad you came to the Ramps'," Shannon said, "you have woken me from a bad lonely dream, even amongst all my guests, I still feel trapped, in a kind of public isolation, almost like an exhibit. At times I wanted to give up the Ramps', but felt so guilty even thinking about it, as though I would be letting my husband down."

"I know exactly what you mean Shannon, it's time we both realised that, like it or not, life does go on, we have to learn to let go, start again, the past is exactly that."

"You know Scott, when I first met you, I knew you were different, you spoke to me like a friend, rather than a boarding house landlady."

"That's because I knew you were special, I've only ever had that feeling once before, but I knew there had to be a man in your life."

"To be honest, there still is a man in my life, but I can't bring him back Scott, I think, like you, it's time to start my life again."

"Well, in that case, we'll both start today. When you feel down, we'll walk and talk. My new job is to cheer you up, and you can do the same for me, do we have a deal?"

"Deal." she replied smiling radiantly, the weight of

loneliness had been lifted from her shoulders. She liked Scott, and hoped his stay would be a lengthy one. Scott hoped their relationship would grow much more, but didn't want to push too hard, too soon. He couldn't know it, but Shannon had the same feelings.

Scott reached across the table and took Shannon's hands in his.

Shannon struggled with her emotions. At that precise moment, she was unable to suppress her feelings of guilt, feelings of betraying her husband's love, and of hers for him.

Scott on the other hand, had so many thoughts, he couldn't think coherently. He feared it would all be just a dream, a dream that he would wake from at any moment. Perhaps Shannon was involved in some way, with what was happening to him.

"Sir".

"Yes Benny, what is it," replied Inspector Bell.

Sergeant Bennett approached Bell's desk and sat on the chair provided. His over- sized, ex-boxer's hands, held reams of papers. He began his report.

"No sign of McLenan, he seems to have vanished. We still have no positive ID on the River Man, but we have confirmation on the ID of the man killed in the explosion, it was McLenan's neighbour, James Alan Shephard, known as 'Spider' locally."

"Bloody hell," Bell said, annoyed at such little progress, "I want that little shit finding as soon as possible Benny, and I think it's time we used the media, to help with the River Man, issue photographs of the tattoo, we're getting bloody nowhere at the moment. Any joy with the car salesman, Hastings?"

"Possibly Sir, several witnesses noticed a black Mercedes in the parking area, at roughly the time of the murder, but nobody noticed any people, and nobody noticed the reg'."

"Bloody marvellous, well we know the little shit didn't have a Merc', he went to buy a car."

Bennett had an idea. "Sir, what if McLenan was the target, not the suspect?"

"It's a good point Benny, but why him, he's a nobody, you could try checking his relatives, perhaps somebody is trying to get at them through him."

"I've already done that Sir, just a mo." Bennett flicked through the pages of his notebook. "Yes here we are, parents deceased, brother and ex-wife last heard of living in South America together, that's what turned him to drink."

"Bloody brilliant, his brother and his wife at it, they obviously couldn't stomach the little shit either." Bell couldn't help laughing.

"You're not nice, not nice at all." said Bennett.

"Anyway, keep digging, let's hope the photo' gets things moving, what do you think of it all?"

"Do you mean, do I think all three deaths are related?"

"Could be."

"If the people who planted the bomb, realised they had missed McLenan, found out about the car, tortured Hastings to find out where he intended going, he didn't know, so they kill him anyway, that still leaves the River Man unconnected."

"Bloody hell and buggery, where's that sales invoice Benny?" shouted Bell excitedly.

"You've got it somewhere."

"Christ" exclaimed Bell searching in the draws of his desk. "Here it is." He read the invoice. "I bloody missed it, look Benny, 'paid cash'," he said pointing to the bottom of the invoice. "Two-thousand, two-hundred and fifty pounds, he told us he had nothing, lying little bastard. I'm more convinced than ever it's drugs or drugs money, what if McLenan killed the River Man Benny?"

"The River Man's friends realise McLenan is the killer, and go after him."

"Exactly, so now we have a possible link, find him before there are any more killings, let's get into McLenan's bank, find out if he's stashed any large amounts recently, more likely to have hidden it though."

FOUR

IT was May 10th. Scott rose early, put on his tracksuit, and left the Ramps'. He had jogged every day of his first week, using the roads around Ullswater as his tracks. His body was beginning to respond to the training regime, the aches and pains of the first few days, now a fading memory. He also spent two hours each day in the Ramps' gym, mainly weight training. Every afternoon Scott would walk in the hills, the freedom giving him time to think, the solitude and quite giving him time to look at himself.

He had realised just what a fool he had been. Meeting Shannon had shaken him back into reality. For Scott it had been love at first sight. He knew that to win Shannon's heart, he would have to rebuild Scott McLenan. The waster had to go. The drunkard had to go.

His relationship with Shannon had grown a little stronger each day. He allowed Shannon set the pace, he didn't want to rush her, he knew she had to overcome the love that she still shared with her husband, and the guilt, as she realised that she could have feelings for another man. They had spent many hours during the evenings talking, analysing their respective pasts. So far, they had only held hands while walking, but for Scott this was sufficient. Following the traumatic experience with his brother and wife, he had no confidence with women, for him, holding hands was the first step, he still wasn't sure if he could ever trust a woman again, but he really wanted to try with Shannon. While Scott ran he would think about the letter, and how it had been responsible for him coming to the Lakes. He pondered over each sentence, trying to gain some insight, trying to find some hidden meaning.

Scott arrived at the yacht club directly opposite the Ramps', across Ullswater. He stopped there every morning for a short breather. He would walk among the yachts, watching their owners hard at work, keeping their craft shipshape. Life was so much slower here, he wondered if he could settle in the area. He wondered if he and Shannon would become an item, and if they did, would her husband's memory haunt her, would the Ramps' itself be a constant reminder of her lost love. Would she be willing to leave it all for him? Was she interested in him anyway? Was he reading too much into their talks? So many unanswered questions filled his head, and then it dawned on him. 'I wish we could turn the clock back'. What if this meant the clock in the Ramps' entrance hall, he thought, could there be some sort of message for him, perhaps another letter. He began to jog back to the Ramps'. Was he being ridiculous or not, after all, the letter did guide him here in the first place.

Scott arrived back at the Ramps', the return run seemed to have taken much longer than usual, but in fact it hadn't. He walked into the entrance hall. There it stood, as always, the pendulum swinging from side to side, the comfortable, warm click clock emanating from deep within. Yet now the clock seemed threatening, if there was no message, he had been a fool, if there was a message, perhaps he wouldn't want to read it. He stood looking at the clock, as if waiting for it to invite him to make the next move.

He leaned forward and opened the front casing carefully, like an unexploded bomb. He peered inside. Behind the pendulum, something white was attached to the body of the clock. As his eyes adjusted to the darkness within the clock, he could see it clearly. It was the makers label.

"Scott"

He jumped back like a naughty schoolboy caught in some naughty act.

"What on earth are you doing?"

"Oh hi Shannon, I was just watching the workings." he lied. He instantly hated himself for lying to her. "No, that's not true," he confessed, "this may sound ridiculous, but I thought I might find another message from my brother inside your grandfather clock, but there's nothing of course."

"Has your brother been here?"

"I don't know Shannon, it was just a stupid thought, perhaps when he booked the room."

"Wouldn't he have left a letter at reception?"

"Probably, but I did say ridiculous."

"What made you think there would be a letter in the clock Scott?"

"Well, it's another of my long stories, but I received a letter from my brother, which I believe has led me back to the Ramps', how, I don't know, but here I am. I think I'm supposed to find clues in the letter, which wouldn't mean anything to anyone else. Part of the letter says, 'I wish we could turn the clock back', so I thought I might find the next letter here, but I haven't."

"Scott, tell me to mind my own business, but if the letter says turn the clock back, why did you open the front?"

"What do you mean?"

"Surely it means turn the clock, look behind it?"

"Shannon, you're either a genius, or you're as daft as me, can I look?"

"Certainly, be careful, it's heavy." she warned.

Scott stood up to the clock, trying to get a good hold on it. With a heave, he managed to move it away from the wall. He peered behind. There was definitely something there.

"Shannon, you're a genius."

With another heave, he managed to move the clock far enough from the wall, to get his arm round behind it, and tear the envelope of the wooden casing. He and Shannon struggled to push the clock back into position. Scott looked at the envelope, his mind full of trepidation.

"Aren't you going to open it?" Shannon enquired, "Or are we going to die of suspense?"

"I don't know Shannon, the last letter caused a lot of trouble. I think my brother may be in danger and wants me to help, but can't tell me why, it doesn't make much sense."

"Do you mean you want to be alone to read it?"

"No no, Shannon, I just don't want to bring my brother's troubles to you and the Ramps'."

"Perhaps you already have?"

"Oh God Shannon, I hope not."

Scott decided to tell her the story, as he knew it so far. She listened intently. When Scott had finished, there was silence while she thought.

"But why should that bring trouble here Scott?" she asked.

"I really don't know love," Scott said without realising it,

"But I would rather be safe than sorry, I think I had better leave."

"Oh no Scott, please don't,"

Scott was surprised, he hadn't realised she had become so fond of him.

"Shannon, slap me if you like, but I think I am falling in love with you, I just don't want you getting hurt."

"Mr McLenan."

Scott thought he was about to be slapped. "Yes."

"I just want you to know, that I think I am falling in love with you too, I want you stay, I want to help you with your problems," she laughed suddenly, "after all, you couldn't even find the letter without me could you?"

"No, that's true, and thank you for caring about me Shannon, it's been a long time since anyone did, but I'm so frightened, because I don't know what's happening, or who to be frightened of."

"A trouble shared is a trouble halved Scott, perhaps here in Ullswater, the problems may pass you by."

Taking Shannon in his arms Scott said, "I really want to stay with you Shannon, just being near you has completely changed my life. A few days ago I was a nobody, and I didn't care, now I want to be a somebody, somebody good enough for you."

Shannon ran her fingers through her golden hair, interlocking her fingers behind her head. She looked at him, saying nothing, just thinking. Then she smiled. "Mr McLenan, you're staying, and that's an order." She wrapped her arms around him.

Scott kissed her passionately. He hadn't felt so happy in years. As they kissed, tears rose in his eyes. He had forgotten how good the warmth of a woman could feel, pressed against his body. A snigger from behind them broke their embrace, it was the child of a guest. They both laughed.

"Ooh, I like a dominant woman."

She laughed, "Warts an' all?"

"Warts an' all."

Scott opened the letter, and read it.

Dear Scott,

If you are reading this, it most probably means that I'm dead, or at least captured. Everything you are about to read is true, I realise you must hate me, but you must also believe me. I work for a department of the British Secret Service, known as A1. I was assigned to Lynn all those years ago, it was my job to take her from you. I even had to marry her, in order to stay with her. It was Lynn's idea to go to Argentina, to carry on with her work, I just tagged on. Her work was the problem. A1 needed to know what it was, but even after all this time, I have been unable to find out very much, she has been so secretive. Over the last few weeks of her life, she changed, agitated, depressed, hard to talk to, I was convinced she had found out about me. Perhaps she had been ordered to kill me. Maybe she refused, so they killed her, I just don't know. What little I do know is as follows: Lynn's grandfather wasn't English. He was a Nazi named Pappine, he disappeared just before the end of the war, and has never resurfaced. He served with the Lufftwaffe. We know a large number of Nazis fled to South America before the capitulation, most, we believe, headed for Argentina, although that isn't proven.98% of gold and art treasures stolen by the Nazis, has never been recovered. The scientists captured by the Allies, were few in number, and not the most senior. Most of these spoke of Hitler's secret weapon, which he boasted would win the war, yet none of them were aware of what it was, or where it was being developed. There are a number of rumours circulating, suggesting that not only is Nazi party alive, it's alive and kicking, and ready to rise again. All this is fairly common knowledge, what it adds up to is anybody's guess, if it adds up at all. Scott, I want you to find out if Lynn was murdered, this may lead you to more answers. Call this contact number 0171, your birth date, my birth date, Lynn's birth date. Your code word is Amazon. Scott, please remember that this has become a highly dangerous game, you must play to win. Good luck brother, I'm sorry for bringing you in, I know you wont let go.

Danny

"Scott."

"Sorry Shannon, I was miles away," he said, "I can't believe this letter." He passed it to Shannon.

She read the letter carefully, then read it again. "What does it all mean Scott?" she said, handing the letter to him.

"I honestly don't know Shannon, but I'm more convinced than ever, that I should leave, I don't want to place you in any danger."

"I thought we had discussed that?"

"Yeah, I know love, but we are talking murder. Shannon, my life has been nothing but trouble, I don't want to be a blemish on yours. Whatever this is, it's serious, when it's over, then we can start afresh."

Shannon's face said it all. She wanted him, and nothing else. "I'll speak to you later Scott." she said. As she turned and walked away, tears filled her eyes. She thought she had had her share of misery, now it had returned.

Scott went to his room. He showered, then lay on his bed, reading the letter over and over. It occurred to him, that the last few weeks had almost been planned for him. Was he that predictable he thought. What was all this about Nazis and A1, and Lynn being an assignment. Scott dialled the number. It rang.

"Yes."

Scott paused, he felt embarrassed about the code word, it was a bit too James Bondish for him.

"Amazon"

"Listen very carefully. There is a letter at reception addressed to B J Charlton, get it, read it, destroy both letters, clear?"

"Yes."

"Good luck, oh, by the way, watch the news." The line went dead.

At twelve-thirty Scott switched the television on in his room. He was a little reluctant to follow orders given by a stranger, but he did appear to be trying to help him. The news began. The first ten minutes were the usual, politics, disasters, scandals, but his attention was grabbed by one word, Preston. The cameras switched to a reporter standing on a bridge.

"Murder squad detectives in Preston, have released a photograph of a tattoo, found on the left forearm of a man's body, recently pulled from the river Ribble, up stream from where I'm standing." Onto the screen came a picture of the tattoo. "Anybody with any information, is asked to..." The screen went blank as Scott switched the television off. He sat in stunned disbelief. The tattoo used to say 'Trouble', it was Danny's nickname for him.

Everything was becoming horribly true. He phoned directory enquiries and asked for the number of Preston police station. He then dialled.

"Police, how may I help you?"

"Inspector Bell please."

Scott left his room and went looking for Shannon. He found her behind the reception desk, catching up on some paper work.

"Hi Shannon, I bet you haven't got a letter for B J Charlton have you?"

"Just a moment Scott, let me see," she said, as she stood to start searching through the stack of uncollected mail.

"Can I take you out for a meal tonight love?" he asked, "I'm afraid I'm going to have to leave soon."

"But Scott, I don't want you to leave, can't you stay for another week, for me, please?" she begged.

"Shannon, I would stay here for the rest of my life, but I have to go."

"Why, what's happened?" she said, handing him the letter.

"It's my brother, he's been found dead."

"Oh Scott, I'm so sorry, is there anything I can do to help?" She said, as she came out from behind the reception desk and took him in her arms.

"Yes, you can cheer me up tonight over dinner, and I'll pay."

"How can I refuse then, aren't you upset over your brother?"

"No Shannon, all my upset has been used years ago, but I do have to find out who killed him."

"Scott, I don't want you to go love, just stay here with me," she pleaded.

"Shannon, I'm going to have to leave in the morning, but I promise, when I come back, I will never, ever leave you again, cross my heart." he said, making the sign.

"I'll hold you to that S McLenan, about eight o'clock then?"

"Excellent, I've all sorts to say, but don't know where to

start, I'll see you later then," he said as he turned and left the hotel. He put the letters in the glove box of the 205, he had more important things on his mind, like a present for Shannon. He drove of towards Penrith.

Scott returned from Penrith full of mixed emotions. The present he had bought for Shannon was superb, he could hardly wait for the evening to arrive, so that he could share his joy with her. Yet he also knew the evening would be their last together, until all the problems were sorted and buried.

He went to his room and began to pack. He had spent lots of his unearned income on new clothes. People who knew him from Preston, probably wouldn't recognise him now. He chose clothes for the evening, and for the day after, and decided to leave out his running gear, he wanted one last run around Ullswater before leaving. He took the suitcase out to the 205 and put it in the boot, then returned to his room. He lay on his bed thinking of Shannon, finally drifting of into a dreamy sleep. When he woke, he showered and shaved, he wanted to be looking at his best tonight, he wanted to be sure that Shannon would remember him, he still hadn't fully regained his confidence with women, he still believed she might forget him the moment he left. Finally he decided he could do no more, it was now or never. He left the room, and went looking for Shannon in the lounge bar, suddenly having doubts about his appearance. He stopped, had one final check, still wasn't sure, so he went and stood in front of the gigantic mirror in the entrance hall. Facing him was an extremely well dressed young man, gone the red-eyed, unshaven, hung over tramp. He marched proudly into the lounge bar, like a soldier on parade.

Shannon looked up as he marched in. Her face told him she was impressed. She stood to greet him. She looked absolutely stunning. Her golden hair fell over her shoulders like a waterfall. Her black halter-neck dress hugged her body. She wore just enough jewellery to enhance the picture. Scott stood with his mouth open, frozen in an eternal gape. His own mental image of the perfect woman now stood before him.

"If you don't close your mouth soon, something is going to build a nest in it," she laughed.

"Oh Shannon, you're absolutely beautiful," he purred,

"I can't tell you how proud it makes me feel to be taking you out."

"Flattery will get you everywhere, you're looking particularly handsome yourself Mr McLenan, would you care to escort me to your horseless, fossil fuel burning carriage, or should we stand here for the entire evening exchanging pleasantries." she said in a mock, posh accent. Inside, Shannon felt a pang of guilt, she hadn't been so dressed up in a long time. She tried to pack the guilt away for the night.

"After you Madam," he said, waving his arm in an arc in front of her. Inside, Scott's stomach had turned to jelly, he just knew he would make a mess of the evening.

Scott turned the car key in the door lock, the central locking whined into action. They sat looking out of the front window. Scott spoke first.

"Where would one care to be entertained this evening madam," he said copying her posh accent.

"One is in one's capable hands." Said Shannon.

"Hows about Pooley Bridge for a starter?"

"Drive on my good fellow," said Shannon, still using the posh accent

The 205 eased out of the Ramps' car park, sunroof and windows open, the evening breeze cool in their hair. They talked incessantly, as if they were making up for so many missing years.

Scott slowly drove over the narrow bridge leading into the village. There were still hoards of tourists milling about aimlessly, the few shops were still open, still selling the usual tourist junk.

They drove into the car park of one of the village pubs. Parking spaces were at a premium, but Scott spotted one and headed for it. They left the car walking hand in hand.

"I think I've done something stupid Shannon," Scott said crossing his eyes, and rolling them upwards.

"Why, what's the matter?" Shannon asked, a note of concern in her voice.

"Come with me," he said, turning her around and walking back toward the car.

"Oh I see, what were you thinking of?"

"You." He said re-opening the car door. From the driver's seat he closed the sun- roof and both door windows. "You're so beautiful you're distracting me, anyway, you didn't notice either, what were you thinking of ?"

"I was miles away Scott, it seems so long since I've felt this happy, I was just riding along with it."

"Right, let's see if we can increase your happiness, you deserve it, you've earned it, and I want to help you find it right now, let's go."

He took her hand and set off running across the car park. Shannon squealed as he pulled her along. After three or four strides she lost a shoe and stumbled. Scott stopped running.

"I'm sorry Shannon, I didn't mean to embarrass you."

"I'm not embarrassed, if you apologise once more tonight I'll hit you with my handbag."

"Sorry."

Shannon swung her handbag towards him. He ducked and grabbed her around the waist before she could get another shot in. He kissed her lightly on the cheek then ran off.

"Sit." She shouted after him.

Scott stopped in his tracks, like an obedient dog.

Shannon walked towards him.

"You bad boy." She laughed.

She took his hand and they walked of, looking in the shop windows, but not bothering to go in. They looked like a couple in love. They both felt warm in each other's company. They behaved like a couple in love.

They entered the pub at the other end of the village. Scott fought his way through the crowd, making a way for Shannon.

"What would you like to drink Shannon?"

"A sweet white wine please Scott."

"Sweet white wine and a vodka and orange please," he called to the barman. The barman brought the drinks over. Scott passed him a few pound coins and told him to keep the change. There was nowhere to sit, and hardly anywhere to stand, so they went outside. Scott was proud at the envy he could see on the other men's faces, wishing they could exchange places with him. Their conversations ranged from topic to topic, as they slowly unravelled each other's innermost thoughts. They left their empty glasses on the window ledge of the pub, and walked back to the pub where the car was parked. They went in. This pub was a lot quieter than the other, but there was still no really quiet corner. Scott noticed that this pub had a restaurant annexed to the main building.

“Would you like to eat?” He asked Shannon.

“As long as I’m with you, I don’t mind what we do.” she replied.

“Ok then, it looks nice in here.” He said looking through the restaurant door, “Come on, let’s find the best table.” Scott held the door open for Shannon. She touched his cheek as she passed him. Shannon selected a window table.

Their conversation was perpetual, like two long-lost friends. Scott had ordered a bottle of Asti Spumanti, knowing that Shannon loved sparkling white wines. The meal went by almost unnoticed as they chatted, both of them revealing their likes and dislikes, their hopes and fears. Neither of them ordered dessert. Shannon could feel the effects of the wine, she was relaxed and fully at ease in his company. Scott wasn’t a wine drinker, and he too could feel the wine working on him, mixed with one or two vodkas. He had fallen head over heals in love with Shannon, and didn’t want tomorrow to come.

“Scott.”

“Shannon.”

They laughed as they both spoke at the same time.

“Ladies first.”

“Well, I just wanted to say how happy you make me Scott, what were you going to say?”

“I was just going to say how much I love you, but I don’t like being interrupted, so I won’t.” Scott turned away from her in a mock sulk.

“Oh please don’t sulk, talk to me.”

“Shan’t.” he said turning further around.

“Please, Scott talk to Shannon or I’ll cry.” she sniffled.

“Go on then, just this once.” He paused. “Shannon, I love you more than I’ve ever loved anyone before, and I know I will never feel love like this again as long as I live.”

“Oh Scott, please don’t leave me tomorrow, you have given me a new reason to live, I love you too, and I want to be with you, always.”

“Shannon, wherever this problem takes me, I know you will be with me, and I promise, that when it’s over, I will come back to you, and never leave you."

"But Scott, what if you get hurt?"

"Don't worry about me, I'm fireproof, nothing ever happens to me, honest."

"Scott, can we go now."

"Sure, anything you say, I'll just settle up, I don't think I had better drive, shall I call a cab, or would you prefer to walk?"

"I would love to walk, is that alright with you?"

"Sure, the exercise will do me good, if I tire, you can always piggy-back me."

"Get lost," she said, the smile returning to her face and voice, "I think you might be carrying me, that Asti has gone right to my head."

Scott called the waiter over and asked for the bill. Shannon offered to pay half, but Scott refused. He paid the bill, and they left.

Outside, the day had turned into a beautiful, calm, moonlit evening. They walked slowly, their arms around each other, stopping here and there to kiss. Ullswater, bewitching in the moonlight, captured their mood, the stillness only broken, as night birds called to each other across the darkness. A shooting star sped across the sky ahead of them.

"That's a sign of true love." said Shannon.

"Well, it must be a true sign Shannon, because I know I will love you forever."

"Scott, I love you so much, I just don't want tonight to ever end."

"Nor do I, but I've promised you, I will come back, then we can start over."

They had arrived back at the Ramps'. The glow from the interior lighting, shone out over the car park, silhouetted the lovers as they embraced. They stood facing each other, silently, gazing into each other's eyes. They kissed with wilful abandon. Suddenly a round of applause pierced the night. They turned to see guests standing at the restaurant windows, some clapping, some waving, all smiling.

"Well, I guess it's goodnight from me." said Scott.

"But not from her." Said Shannon. "Would you like to come to my rooms for a coffee?"

"I thought you would never ask."

They returned the waves, took a bow, and went into the hotel.

"Come on then, before the staff notice I'm back, and start handing over their problems to me."

Scott followed her quietly up the stairs. Shannon giggled like a naughty schoolgirl.

"What's tickling you?" he asked

"I've just realised, I'm sneaking into my own home, like a naughty teenager."

They laughed together. Shannon unlocked the door to her apartment.

"Come in, make yourself at home."

Scott entered. The apartment was beautiful. Spotlessly clean. He was glad he hadn't invited her back to his flat at Preston. He had never seen luxury like this. He began to feel out of his depth, conscious of the gulf between them. He stood statuesque, afraid to touch anything, in case he broke it.

"What's the matter?"

"Shannon, I think I had better go."

"Why, what have I done?"

"Nothing, it's just me, I couldn't keep you in this sort of lifestyle," he said, waving an arm aimlessly round, "I'm just not good enough for you, I'm sorry."

"Oh Scott, you are a one aren't you?" she said, "All this was here when we bought the place, it's not the real me, besides, I love you for being you, don't try and change yourself into what you think I want you to be."

"What?" he said screwing up his face.

She slapped him playfully on the shoulder

"You know what I mean McLenan, I just want you to love me the same."

He took her in his arms and kissed her passionately. He pulled away slightly and looked at her, cupping her face in his hands.

"Shannon, I'm so afraid that I won't live up to your expectations, and that while I'm away, someone else will come along, somebody more than I will ever be, somebody I can't compete with."

"Mr McLenan, you can compete, just be you, that's all I ask."

"You make me feel so special Shannon, I don't deserve you."

“Don’t be silly, look, there’s a drinks cabinet over there, help yourself, I just want to go and freshen up, back in a moment, OK.”

“OK.”

Shannon went off to her bedroom, while Scott did as he was told. He poured himself a glass of Mosel wine. Although he was not a wine person, he loved the German wines, so fresh and fruity, nectar he thought to himself. He reached into the back pocket of his trousers, and pulled out the present he had bought for Shannon, it was a silver friendship ring.

He heard a noise from behind him, and turned. Shannon stood in the bedroom doorway. Scott almost dropped his glass. Shannon was wearing a very short, see through nightie, the soft light from the bedroom illuminating her nakedness. She held out her hand for him.

Scott put the wine glass down on the cabinet, and moved towards her. His heart pounding so strongly, he thought she must be able to hear it. He took her hand gently in his.

“Will you wear this for me, and remember me while I’m away?” he asked, as he presented her with the ring.

“Oh Scott, it’s beautiful, I will wear it forever, for you, thank you for giving me my life back, I love you Mr McLenan, and I always will.”

She turned and led him into the bedroom. His eyes were drawn to the magnificent four-poster bed. They stood and kissed as she opened his shirt. Her hands wandered over his pounding chest. Scott felt his body responding, but a latent fear prevented him from touching her. As if guessing his dilemma, Shannon took his hands and placed them on her breasts. The flood gates of their frustrations opened. There was an urgency in their movements, as they began to explore each other’s bodies. They removed their clothing and lay down on the bed, their nakedness a symbol of their honesty and openness to each other. They held each other closely, silently, the perfection of her body, warm against his, the years of loneliness they had both endured, now forgotten, they made love. Afterwards, they lay talking of the future, lost in a guiltless tranquillity. Later they made love again, eventually falling asleep in each other’s arms.

Outside, a black Mercedes quietly drove into the Rampsbeck car park.

FIVE

SCOTT woke early, it was five-forty-five. Shannon lay beside him, sleeping peacefully, her body warm against his skin. She looked as lovely asleep, as she did awake, he thought. He kissed her tenderly on the cheek, she turned towards him, and he kissed her forehead. Scott managed to get out of bed without waking her. He slipped his clothes on and quietly left her apartment. He went back to his own room, where he changed into his running kit, having decided to have one last run before leaving. He was thinking of proposing marriage to Shannon before he left, but the fear of rejection was firmly in his mind. He knew also, that by not proposing, would give him something to cling to, in the days or weeks that lay ahead. As he left the hotel, he realised he had forgotten his car keys and credit card. He returned to his room mumbling to himself for being so absent minded, but really it was because Shannon was the only thing on his mind. He set off again. He ran to Pooley Bridge and found the 205 untouched in the pub car park. That wouldn't happen in town, he thought to himself. He put the credit card into the glove box, the fuel gauge had been showing empty when they had arrived last night, so he would go for petrol when came back from his run. He hid the car keys behind the front tyre, so that he wouldn't have to carry them, then continued his run.

It was another glorious morning. Ullswater looked like a skating rink, as yet, no boats had disturbed her waters. The morning chorus of the wild life was the only sound, mixed with the steady patter of his trainers. The morning jogs had paid off, Scott felt better and fitter than he had for years. The cobwebs of decline, had well and truly been cleared from his system. He really did feel fighting fit, perhaps, he thought, he needed to be. His love for Shannon, and hers for him, had finally been sealed last night. Looking over Ullswater, he knew he could live here, hopefully for the rest of his life. Shannon had changed that life, from nothing to live for, to everything to live for. She had shown him what a fool he had been, now, with Shannon, he couldn't go wrong. He came running into the yacht club car park, stopped and checked his watch. His time had improved again. He felt pleased with himself as he walked to the water's edge. He looked across the lake. There stood his future. A morning mist draped itself over the Rampsbeck, like a bride's veil. The early sun rays caressed the hotel, dispelling the night's cold shadow. The Rampsbeck exploded like an angry volcano. Flames and debris shot hundreds of feet into the air. Thick black smoke began to spiral skywards. The lake began to erupt as large pieces of masonry crashed downwards from the sky. Sheep grazing in the fields close to the Ramps', were killed as the debris came thundering back to earth with a vengeance.

Scott's heart missed several beats as he bore witness to the terrible event. He sank to his knees screaming, "No, no, no."

People came running from the yacht club. Women screamed in horror as they realised exactly what carnage had been reaped upon their neighbours.

Another huge explosion razed to the ground, what little of the Rampsbeck had survived the first explosion. Scott cried out loud, inconsolable in his grief. Two elderly women helped him to his feet, wrapping their arms around him, trying to comfort him, but he was beyond that. His body shook, his hands trembled, he felt so weak, so useless. He couldn't bring himself to look at the destruction again. He knew it had been him that the bombers were trying to kill.

Shannon, and everyone at the hotel, was dead because of him. He wondered how many more had to die because of him. Slowly his sobbing subsided, and he began to regain his composure. He thanked the women for their kindness, and walked unsteadily back to the road.

His thoughts turned to vengeance. His finely honed, killer instinct had been re-awakened in him. Whoever was responsible for this atrocity, had re-kindled the fire of the trained killer, that had lain dormant in him for so many years. He vowed to Shannon's memory, to punish the culprits. It was time to turn the tables. The hunted had become the hunter. Scott had been good at his job with the S.A.S., the murderers would find out just how good.

He ran back to the pub car park at Pooley Bridge, retrieved the keys, started the 205, and drove off at great speed.

It was almost nine on the morning of the Rampsbeck bombing, when Sergeant Bennett entered the office. " 'Scuse me Sir."

"Yes Benny, what's to do?"

"We're getting reports of a huge explosion in the Lake District, it occurred to me, that there may be a link to our explosion, what do you think Sir?"

"Well, it's not everyday we have bloody explosions, mind you, if this keeps on it will be, give the locals a call, and see what they've got."

"Right Sir." Sergeant Bennett rang the police headquarters at Penrith. They told him of the total destruction of the Rampsbeck hotel, and that there were no survivors as yet. "Sir, no survivors as yet, and not much detail, they are going to keep me updated."

"Ok Benny, keep on it, how are we doing with our other little problems?"

"To be honest, not very well. There seems to be a wall of secrecy wrapped around McLenan's brother and his ex wife since they left England, it's as though they went to the moon. I think the car salesman may have been in the wrong place at the wrong time. McLenan is the only link, until we get our hands on him, we're struggling, oh, a black Mercedes was seen near McLenan's flat and at the car sales pitch."

"I wonder if it would be worth your while having a day in the Lakes, I'm sure I can smell McLenan above all the other sheep shit, yes, perhaps you might see something there to connect it to us. Right Benny, you said you wanted a holiday, find out where this hotel is, or was, and off you go, keep in touch."

"Right Sir."

The Rampsbeck was addressed as Watermillock, beside Ullswater. Bennett located it on a map of the Lakes and set off. It was roughly seventy miles. The drive would give him time to think about his inability to catch one little loser. That was a problem on it's own. Who would want to kill a loser so desperately, apart from Bell, who had an almost passionate hatred of the man. Perhaps he knew something about his brother that he shouldn't. Yet by all accounts he hadn't seen or heard of his brother in ten years, and the two would probably kill each other, if they ever met. If the Lakes explosion was linked to McLenan, how had the bombers known where to find him, nobody else could. These thoughts, and many more, helped the journey pass quickly.

About ninety minutes after leaving Preston, Bennett pulled up beside a policeman, standing at the entrance of the drive, leading to the Rampsbeck. After producing his I.D., he was waved through. He drove slowly down the drive. A heavy black cloud hung in the still air, refusing to leave its place of origin. The smell of burning flesh, was one he had smelt too often recently. Fire fighters raked the rubble, searching for evidence, finding the pitiful remains of personnel possessions.

Sergeant Bennett stood beside his car. The explosion in Preston was bad, but this was a lot worse. Although he had never seen the hotel, it was obvious to him, that this was a major disaster. What had been once a proud building, was now no more than a heap of smouldering debris. After many years service, Bennett thought he had seen it all, but this really choked him up. He made his way towards a uniformed police sergeant. "Hello there, my name is Bennett, I'm up here from Preston, basically to see if there are any connections with our explosion."

"Ah, right, we've been expecting you. Welcome to the peaceful Lakes, where nothing ever happens. The guy you are looking for is the big fella over there, Inspector Hawkes." he said, pointing to the Ramps' gardens.

"Thanks a lot," he said, "see you later."

Bennett carefully walked toward the Inspector, trying to keep out of the way, eventually entering the garden through a hole blasted in the privet hedge.

"Inspector Hawkes?"

"Yes."

"Sergeant Bennett from Preston. Pleased to meet you." he said, offering his hand. Inspector Hawkes shook his hand.

"Nasty business this, I don't like it on my patch, I don't like it at all, how can I help you?"

"Well Sir, we've had a similar incident in Preston, mainland bombings aren't exactly commonplace, so we thought there may be a connection, I'm here to see if I can find one, in particular, a certain Scott McLenan, is one possible link."

"Well, it's early days yet, we're still looking for the register, if it hasn't been destroyed."

"These cars in the car park, are they all linked to the hotel?"

"We think so, why?"

"McLenan recently bought a 205 GTi, and I noticed that it isn't here, have any been moved?"

"No, this is how we found it, perhaps his car is in a garage for repair, maybe your man isn't here."

"Is it Ok if I have a nosey round, I won't get in the way?"

"Certainly, give me the details of the 205, and I will see what we can do for you.

"Bennett gave the Inspector the information he required, then went for a walk around the grounds, the devastation was complete. Without the car or the register, there was little he could do. He found Inspector Hawkes, gave him his contact number, and set off back to Preston. He had only gone a few miles when his mobile phone began to ring.

"Bennett."

"Inspector Hawkes, we have located the register, your man's name is here alright, S McLenan, Preston."

"Brilliant, thanks for your help, please keep me informed of any progress you make, and thanks again."

"Glad to help, all the best." the line went dead.

Scott had driven off on the B5320, out of Pooley Bridge, heading towards Penrith. He had found a quiet spot, beside the river Eamont, where he was able to change out of his running gear. He stayed hidden for some time as he tried to calm himself down. There was nobody to share his grief with, making it all the harder. His tears flowed like the river. The anger raged within him. It was his fault that Shannon was dead, he had led the bomber to the Rampsbeck. Their short time together had been heaven for Scott. He began to realise the enormity of his situation. To kill so indiscriminately, takes a special kind of professional. He was pitted against a merciless hit-man, it had to be a fight to the death, but whose.

He remembered the letter in the glove compartment. He hadn't had a chance to read it previously. Perhaps, he thought, it may shed some light on his present dire situation. He reached in to the compartment and removed the letter. He opened it. There was a note with a key tucked inside it

The note read:

Carlisle main, box 63.

Scott realised that the key obviously belonged to a left-luggage locker, and that he was being directed towards it for information. This was the start of his new agenda, he would not rest until the killer, or killers, lay at least six feet underground. He made a silent promise to Shannon. From his hideaway near Penrith, Scott headed for Carlisle. The city had changed considerably since he had last visited. He parked the 205 in a multi-story car park, he seemed to remember there had been a bus station on the site, years before. He walked through the shopping mall, making his way to the railway station. He constantly looked over his shoulder, eyeing everyone with suspicion. He came across a Yates's Wine Lodge and went in. He ordered a vodka and orange, and took it to a corner seat. From there, he could see most of the bar. He felt calmer now, his anger under control. He thought about the left luggage, and what would be waiting. It might be another bomb, he thought. Scott had one more drink then left. The railway station was just a short distance from the wine bar. He asked a porter for directions to the left luggage department. Standing in front of the lockers, he located number 63. Looking around him all the time, he moved towards it. He placed the key into the lock. His hand began to shake.

"Sir."

"Yes, is that you Benny, it's a bloody awful line?"

"Yes Sir, McLenan's name has been found in the register, but there is no sign of the car."

"Benny, I want that little prick catching and fast, he's too dangerous to be running about without a leash."

"I'm on my way back at the moment, or do you want me to stay up here?"

"No, the little shit will be long gone, leave the locals to find him."

"OK, see you later."

McLenan was getting right up Bell's nose. He couldn't believe that one nobody, could give him such a run-around.

Scott finished another vodka. He had to open that locker. The message had been from A1, surely they wouldn't blow-up innocent people. He went back to the railway station. For the second time he put the key in the lock. People passing by, laughed at the man with his head turned away from the locker, holding the key. He turned it. Nothing. Very slowly he began to open the locker door. Nothing. He turned to look. He saw a brief-case, nothing else. He removed the case from the locker and left the station. The perspiration dripping off his chin, the only clue to how frightened he had been, not so much for himself, but for everyone in the station complex. Scott could tolerate fear, he knew it kept him alert, and alive.

He returned to collect the 205. He drove north at speed out of Carlisle. The sign post indicated Gretna Green. He turned left off the main road, and drove into the village. Behind the Old Blacksmith's Shop, he found the car park had been enlarged, coaches on one side, cars on the other. He parked in the furthest corner from the shops. It had occurred to him, that the briefcase could contain an explosive device, he didn't want any more deaths on his conscience. Unfortunately there was only one way to find out. He remembered from a Bond film, that his briefcase had to be opened correctly, or it would blow. He pressed the two locks. They sprang open. It was now or never. He raised the lid. The gun caught his attention immediately, the black metal dull, and cold to touch. His tension eased knowing that there was someone helping. There was also an envelope taped to the lid of the case. He removed it, and opened it. The letter read:

Scott, Your brother has disturbed a wasp's nest. It would appear that the enemy believe he has passed on vital information to you. We want you to take over your brother's role. Our problem is based in Argentina. In the case you will find a gun, false passport and car keys. You will go to Kippford, Galloway, and book in to the Anchor hotel, using the name Tony Hewitt. You will await further orders. The car is parked in the Carlisle multi-storey, it is a white BMW, registration number, H363 DKH. Destroy this letter. Good luck.

For Scott it was like going back in time. Covert operations were a speciality of the S.A.S. If this was to be his chance to avenge Shannon, he would grasp it firmly with both hands.

He destroyed the letter and headed back to Carlisle. He quickly located the BMW. He cleared the 205, putting both cases into the boot of the new car. He felt more comfortable now that he possessed weapons. He had kept the bayonet, preferring it to the gun. The bayonet had the advantage of being a silent killer. Scott had had time to mull things over. Time and time again he had gone over the last weeks. He now drove at speed toward Preston.

Inspector Bell arrived home late. There had been little progress on any of the murders. McLenan was still missing.

He and Sergeant Bennett had spent the evening at a local hostelry, discussing the cases, and imbibing copious amounts of the amber nectar, as they called it. They failed to reach any sensible conclusions. By the end of the evening, Bell had decided to bring back the death penalty just for McLenan, and Bennett had decided not to holiday in any of the Lakes hotels, as long as McLenan was at large. At closing time, they bade each other goodnight.

Bell was a bachelor. He had almost married on two occasions, but the job had intervened on both occasions. He lived in a three-bedroomed semi, on the outskirts of Preston. He had hailed a taxi after walking a short distance, which now disgorged him at his front gate.

After a brief struggle with the key, he opened the front door. He reached in, and flicked the hall light switch. The light remained off. “Bloody bulbs,” he muttered to himself. He flicked the landing light switch, that light stayed off. “Bloody bugger and dam,” he cursed. He tripped on the bottom step, steadied himself, then made his way carefully upstairs. He flicked the bathroom light switch. “Bloody marvellous,” he cursed again as it came on. He relieved himself in the toilet, gracefully splashing the seat. “Bloody marvellous,” he cursed yet again. He looked into the mirror, and saw a fifty-five-year-old, looking more like a sixty- five-year-old. “Bollocks.” He cursed once again, turned and headed for his bedroom. Bell undressed in the darkness. He hadn’t even tried the bedroom light. He fell heavily into bed, and within seconds was snoring like a bloated warthog. Downstairs, a dark figure silently opened the French window, and entered the house.

He stealthily crept up the stairs. He knew which lights wouldn't work, as he had removed the bulbs earlier. He had watched as Bell arrived home, his inebriated condition being a big plus for his plan, even missing the bathroom light worked well, it had meant that Bell hadn't become too suspicious. He stood statuesque on the landing, listening to Bell's snores, his heart beating faster than normal, his adrenalin flowing rapidly through his veins. He moved silently into the bedroom, and paused while his eyes re-adjusted to the darkness. A glint of moonlight reflected off the blade of the weapon he held. Bell grunted and turned over, unknowingly facing the intruder, his large mouth agape. Suddenly Bell was fully awake and terrified. One of his own socks had been roughly jammed deep into his mouth. His feet and hands had already been secured with plastic ties, he couldn't shout for help. He pulled against the ties for a few seconds, before realising the futility of his efforts, his body went limp as he surrendered. Out of the darkness, and behind him, a man spoke.

"Listen you fat ugly bastard, and you might be able to save your miserable little shit of a life."

Bell recognised the voice, but was unable to put a name with it.

"Tonight, you are going to answer the questions, if you don't, you die, savvy."

Now he knew who it was, it was McLenan, and he was more terrified than ever.

"Savvy." Scott repeated the question.

Bell nodded.

"Do you know who blew up my car?"

Bell shook his head. He felt the cold steel of a British Army bayonet, as it was pressed firmly into his cheek.

"Well I think you do fatty, and I think you will want to tell me soon. Scott pressed the bayonet harder into Bell's cheek. Bell's eyes widened, he fought against the restraints, but again had to give up.

"I think you know lots of things fatty, and I'm sure you want to tell me everything, so, either tell me or die, the choice is yours." The bayonet penetrated Bell's cheek, a small rivulet of blood wound it's way downward, until it began to drip off his chin, and on to the white sheet.

"Whoops, that was careless of me, I didn't want you to

bleed yet, I always was clumsy with knives, you know who blew the Rampsbeck don't you fatty?"

Again Bell shook his head.

"Listen fatty, I'm trying to be friendly, and you're not helping. Do you think you can stand a lot of pain, I bet you can't?" Scott turned him over, so he was face down on the bed. "I don't like torture, I prefer a straight fight, man to man, do you want to talk to me?"

Bell shook his head again, certain that McLenan wouldn't go any further.

"OK, then I shall begin. Where would you like me to start fatty, how about your feet, then work upwards?"

Bell lay motionless.

The bayonet cut deeply into the soul of his left foot. Blood gushed onto the bed. The scream in Bell's throat, stifled by the sock.

"Whoops, I've done it wrong again fatty. I meant to cut your toe off, better luck next time, are you ready to talk?"

Bell nodded, he wasn't loyal enough to anybody to suffer like this.

"Good, I'm going to remove the sock, you won't shout or scream will you?" he said, pressing the bayonet firmly against Bell's jugular vein. "Will you?"

Bell shook his head. Scott slowly removed the sock.

"You baboon's arse." Bell shouted.

"Shut your mouth fat boy, speak when you are spoken to. I don't like murderers, but in your case, I wouldn't mind becoming one, who do you work for?"

"Nobody."

"But we both know you do." The bayonet entered his neck, just enough to hurt and make him bleed. "I don't know how many people you have killed, but tonight, you, are going to pay."

"I didn't do it."

"Maybe not, but you give the orders, don't you, but you've made some mistakes haven't you?"

"I don't know what you're on about." Bell mumbled.

"First mistake, you had me down as a nobody, some piece of crap that you could kick around at playtime, well fatty, you were wrong, very wrong. Second mistake, I phoned you from the Rampsbeck, but the police didn't come, the bomber came, who is he?"

"I don't know, honestly."

"Honest, you murdering bastard." The bayonet described a red line across Bell's throat. He screamed. Scott punched him hard in the mouth, splitting both of his lips.

Bell fell silent.

"Who do you work for?"

"They'll kill me."

"I'll kill you, now if you insist." he said wielding the bayonet close to Bell's eyes.

"No, please no, I'm begging you, it was orders, I had to obey orders."

How many times throughout history has the same excuse been offered. Orders. To Scott it was still murder.

The bayonet sliced through the skin of Bells back. He howled like a wolf. Scott stuffed the sock back into Bell's mouth.

"You will tell me who you work for, from here on, the pain increases, are you ready to tell me?"

Bell nodded.

"I'm going to remove the sock, you're next scream will be you're last, I promise." He removed the sock. "Talk." He ordered.

"No names, just numbers."

"Bollocks."

"It's true, 4185938, they call me, say their number, I say mine, they give orders or ask questions."

"You're lying fatty."

"That's all I can tell you, kill me if you like, I can't tell you any more."

"How much do they pay?"

"Nothing."

"You useless fat bastard, are you telling me you killed people for nothing?"

"They threatened to kill my relatives."

Scott ignored his reply. "Where can I find a pen fat boy?"

"Top drawer, bedside cabinet."

"Right, tell me that number again."

"4185938."

"That a phone number?"

"No, it's my identity number."

"How long have you worked for them?"

"January this year."

"Right fatty, sit up. I'm going to remove the ties, so that you can write your confession do not try anything that we both might regret, I'm even more clumsy with guns." he said, pushing the barrel of his pistol into Bell's ear. "Now write. I, Inspector Bell, have passed information to a secret organisation, leading to the bombings at Preston and Ullswater. Now sign it. Now write another, and sign that. He watched over him as he did as instructed.

When Bell had finished writing, Scott read it through.

"Hands."

Bell held out his hands while Scott secured them with a new plastic tie. He pushed the sock back into his mouth. "It's funny, fat bastard, all these people dead, and you haven't apologised once. We have another problem, don't we fatso? You killed the lady I love, that has made me very angry, what would you do in my shoes?"

Scott paced back and forth across the bedroom, wielding the bayonet where Bell could see it. Now Scott's survival instincts came into action. There could only be one answer.

SIX

SERGEANT Bennett sat at his desk, his annoyance at Bell's absenteeism growing.

"Harry," he shouted to his colleague in the adjoining room, "could you call the Dinger residence, I think he might have overslept, we did have one or two to drink last night?"

"OK Sarge'."

Bennett pondered the cases, they were in need of fresh leads. He felt a pang of guilt at his impotence as a police officer.

"No answer Sarge', what do you want me to do?"

"Never mind, I'll go round to his house myself and dig him up."

It was a good excuse to get away from the office, the bigwigs wanted results, and they weren't forthcoming, away from the station he was safe from their criticisms, if only temporarily. He tidied his desk and left.

"See you later Harry, don't mention where I've gone will you?"

"OK Sarge'."

Bennett arrived at Bell's house a short time later. He noted the curtains were all still closed. Lazy bastard, he thought to himself.

He walked along the garden path to the front door, and knocked loudly four times. After waiting for a reply, and not getting one, he knocked again. There was still no reply. Out of curiosity, he pushed against the door. To his alarm, it opened. He stepped into the small entrance hall.

"Sir, it's Bennett, are you awake yet?"

Still there was no reply. Bennett's concern was growing. He had a quick look around downstairs. His anxiety grew even more on discovering the French windows open. He finished his search downstairs. He went up the stairs, taking one step at a time, listening as he went. On the landing he paused. The bathroom light was on. He looked in, it was vacant. He went towards what he thought would be Bell's bedroom. Through the gap in between the door and the architrave he could see Bell on the bed. He moved into the bedroom, immediately noticing the plastic ties that bound Bell's hands and feet.

"Oh my God, what's happened?" he called to Bell.

Bell didn't answer. Bennet noticed the wounds to Bell's feet and back, he realised he had been tortured. He rolled him over onto his back. The stab wound in Bells cheek, an angry looking mess of skin and dried blood. His throat had been skilfully cut, just deep enough not to be fatal, yet deep enough to inflict maximum pain.

Bennett radioed for assistance and an ambulance. He ran downstairs to the kitchen to find a knife. Running back up to the bedroom, he quickly cut the plastic ties. The ties had cut deeply into the skin of Bell's wrists and ankles, as he had struggled for freedom. The bed sheets bore testament to the suffering he had endured. Bennett felt for a pulse. There was one, but very weak.

"Hang on Sir," he said, bending closer to Bell's ear, "Help's on the way, you're going to be alright, I'll get the bastard that did this to you, promise."

Within a few minutes, the sirens outside announced the arrival of the ambulance and the squad cars. From the top of the stairs, Bennett called out to the ambulance to hurry.

They ran up the stairs, the distress in Bennett's voice, enough to convey the seriousness and urgency of the situation.

"Shity death, what the bloody hells been going on here?" asked the first ambulance man into the bedroom

"Jesus H Christ, did he upset someone or what?" asked the second.

"Just hurry up will you, I think he's had it?"

They did as ordered, attempting to stabilise Bell, before moving him.

Bennett spotted the note on the bedside cabinet. He picked it up and read it. He pulled a plastic evidence bag from his pocket, and put the note into it, then put it back in his pocket.

The ambulance crew had to manhandle Bell down the stairs, then onto a trolley to the ambulance. They sped off, sirens wailing.

Bennett ordered the constables to cordon off the house and wait for S.O.C.O.

He was an angry man. He was sure McLenan was involved, but couldn't understand how he could come and go unnoticed, when everyone was supposed to be looking for him.

He was also frightened. His investigations into McLenan's background had shown him to be anything but an ordinary citizen. From the military, he had learnt what McLenan really was. McLenan was nothing less than a highly-skilled killer, trained to work alone under the most arduous of conditions, once given an objective, there was only one way to stop him, and that was to kill him. The S.A.S. had trained him well, too well. In their opinion, he was a natural. He had always trained harder than the others. His self-motivation was 110%. If there was such a thing as a perfect killer, it was Scott McLenan.

Bennett wondered if he would be the next to receive a night visit from McLenan. He drove off to the hospital.

Scott had left Bell barely alive. He hadn't enjoyed torturing him, he would have prefered to kill him. He had been responsible for Shannon's death, as surely as if he had planted the bomb himself. Scott now felt guilty for failing Shannon, but consoled himself with the thought, that he, and Bell, would cross swords again one day, and when they did, he would show no mercy.

Scott had driven through the remainder of the night, heading for Scotland. The BMW was a superb machine, a definite step up from the 205.

The sun was rising on a new day, the golden red orb, promising new life, but not for Shannon.

At this time of day, the roads were very quite. Scott slowed the BMW. There was no particular rush. He wished he could share the sunrise with Shannon. In his rear- view mirror he saw the Mercedes, black and ominous. Could it be tailing him, he thought. No, he answered himself, how could they have found him, they couldn't have known about the BMW, could they. He watched as he drove. There were two men in the front seats, he couldn't see any others in the rear. He began to increase his speed. The Mercedes stayed with him. He was travelling at 80 mph as he passed the Lockerbie turn off, on the A74(M). Lockerbie had been the scene of a bombing tragedy in 1988, where a PAN-AM flight, was blown out the sky, killing all on board, and some of the villagers. Scott hated bombs. They killed indiscriminately. They killed Shannon. Both cars occupied the outside lane as they sped north. There could be no doubt now, Scott thought, it was the Mercedes from Preston.

Scott jammed the brakes hard on. The Mercedes swerved to miss him, passing him on the inside. Scott took the left turn onto the A701, the Mercedes overshooting the turn by fifty yards. Scott sped off towards Dumfries, hoping to put enough distance in between them, so that he could lose them in the town. Unfortunately he soon met with slower moving traffic, and the Mercedes was soon back on his tail. The traffic was still light in Dumfries, as Scott headed west on the A75. The sign said 'lay-by 1/2mile ahead', he had had an idea, but would it work. He indicated and pulled into the lay-by, the Mercedes following, keeping it's distance. The passenger door opened. A bullet shattered the rear screen of the BMW.

"McLenan, get out and stand by the car."

Scott reached into the briefcase and removed the gun, flicking the safety catch off.

"McLenan, get out now."

He opened the door of the BMW, as he did, he swivelled in his seat, firing four rounds off at the Mercedes. The first two rounds hammered into the passenger, taking him out of the chase, the other two shattering the front screen of the Mercedes, but missing the driver. Scott sped off. The Mercedes driver punched the shattered glass outwards, then accelerated after Scott, his rear wheels crushing and tearing his partner's legs, as they tried to gain traction on the tarmac.

Scott had gained some thinking distance, now all he had to do was use it. He could see the Mercedes in his rear-view mirror, but at these speeds it was hard to plan. He turned right onto the A712 at Crocketford. After a couple of miles he came to a sharp left-hand bend. He slammed the brakes on and came to a halt. He leapt from the car just as the Mercedes came into the corner. The driver swerved to avoid the BMW, lost control, and veered across the road, his left front wheel clipping a mile marker. The car went into a 180 degree spiral, crashing through the hedge at the other side of the road, and sliding across the field on it's roof top. The engine screamed, the rear wheels clawed the air. Petrol from a fractured fuel line ignited, turning the Mercedes into a fireball. The car came to a halt. As the fuel tank exploded, the driver crawled out through the front windscreen aperture. His clothes were already well alight, the heat of the flames already blistering and tormenting his skin. He screamed in agony, as he ran off across the field. Scott chased after him. He finally collapsed, as the flames ate into his body. He rolled around, unsuccessfully trying to smother the flames in the damp morning grass.

Scott stood and watched. The driver begged him to help. Scott aimed the pistol. The driver begged for mercy.

"Mercy you bastard, what about mercy for all your victims, who do you work for?"

"Piss off." he screamed.

"Certainly, have a nice day," he said turning away. "Oh, I nearly forgot," he said turning back. The shot rang out above the roar of the flames. The Mercedes driver's agony was over.

Scott walked back to the BMW. The fight was dirty, and getting dirtier, and he still had no idea who he was fighting. He was convinced that these two had bombed the Rampsbeck, but he wanted the man that gave the order.

"Sarge."

"Yeah."

"There's reports coming in, of two more suspicious deaths in Scotland, involving a black Mercedes, do you think it could be our one from the pitch?"

"Good thinking Harry, see what you can find out about it." The phone on his desk rang.

"Sergeant Bennett."

Harry waited for further instructions

"Oh no." said Bennett. "Right, thank you." His face went ashen.

"What's up sarge?"

"Bell's dead, ten minutes ago, it's a murder hunt now, get the little bastard, and get him quick." he shouted, slamming his fist into the desk. "I hope I get to him first, I'll kill him myself."

"How come we're having so much trouble finding him sarge?"

"I don't know, it's as if the bastards invisible, we must get him Harry, he's killed one of ours."

"Right, I'll get on to Scotland, see what they have."

At about 12.30 Bennett went home for lunch, although he wasn't hungry. He hadn't been home long when the phone rang.

"261,223."

Bennett answered. "418,5938."

"Report."

"Number 2 dead, two more dead in Scotland, no further information.

The line went dead. Bennett replaced the receiver and waited.

The phone rang again. He lifted the receiver.

"261,233."

"418,5938."

"Is McLenan alive?"

"Yes, the force is searching for him, he's vanished."

"He must not leave the country."

"I understand."

The line went dead.

Bennett was a frightened man. Two years previously he had been lured into a compromising position. The photographs were obscene. He had been blackmailed ever since. He wished he had confessed to his superiors. Now, with the body count growing almost daily, Bell dead, McLenan still at large, the whole thing was getting out of hand. He wondered where it would end, if ever.

He went upstairs to the master bedroom. It was tastefully decorated, but ordinary. He walked over to the built in wardrobe, which faced the bed. He opened the doors, and reached up for an old shoebox, that languished on the top shelf. He lifted it down. He opened it. Inside were some old press cuttings, stories from his career in better times. He took them out. Beneath them, was a loaded gun. He took the gun out of the box, and sat on the bed. He read some of the cuttings. How did it all go wrong, he thought, how could his life be totally controlled by someone he didn't even know. Tears welled in Bennett's eyes. So many dead, all because of his weakness. He raised the gun, and placed the barrel into his mouth. He flicked off the safety catch, and squeezed the trigger.

Scott's first priority had been to distance himself from the Mercedes. Having done this, he searched for a garage where he could have the damaged screen repaired. Deep in the wilds of Scotland, hadn't been the best place to have the repair carried out, Scott had had to wait for two hours. Once the repair was complete, he headed further into the lonely countryside of the Galloway Forest Park. From the A712 he drove along the A713, passed Drumjohn to Mossdale, where he took a left turn, heading south back to Loch Doon until the road ended. He remained here, watching the birds in their tireless quest for food, listening to the stillness, the pressure off, thinking of Shannon, and what might have been. He wanted to have a family with her, two daughters would have been perfect, maybe a son as well. Now it was all a dream. He listened to the local radio broadcasts. The deaths were reported, but no mention of his white BMW. Feeling safe he set off for his destination, Kippford. He went a long way for a short cut, going via, Girvan, Newton Stewart, Kirkcudbright, crossing the Army ranges at Dundrennan on the A711, taking a right at Dalbeattie, the A710, until turning right on a B road to Kippford. He drove into the car park at the rear of the Anchor Hotel.

Scott sat in the car as he surveyed the area. Opening the door, he got out, and had another look around. All appeared to be clear as he walked to the hotel's front door and entered. He rang the bell at reception and waited.

"Good afternoon young man," the old lady said, in her deep Scottish accent. She was overweight but pleasant enough, somebody's grandma no doubt.

"And a good afternoon to you, I'm after a room, preferably a double, have you any available?"

"How long will you be staying Sir."

"I'm not sure, is that a problem?"

"No problem, would you like one overlooking the harbour?"

"That would be excellent, could I see it?"

"Of course, would you follow me please?"

"After you." Scott said politely.

She led him up a flight of stairs, and along a narrow corridor.

"Here it is Sir, room 14." she said opening the door.

Scott looked in.

"It's beautiful, I'll take it."

"Thank you Mr."

"Hewitt, Tony Hewitt, please, call me Tony."

"OK Tony, when you have settled in, we can book you in properly, I'll see you later."

"Sure, see you later."

Scott stepped over to the window. The view was excellent. Boats leaned to one side, waiting for the tide to return and lift them. Other boats in the centre channel of the river, faced the incoming tide, like soldiers on parade. It was like a picture postcard, he felt relaxed and easy, time for a drink.

First, he brought his luggage in from the car, had a shower, shaved, and fell asleep on the bed.

He woke at 7.30. After brushing his hair and putting on his after-shave, he went downstairs to find the bar.

In the hotel lounge bar, each table carried a menu. He chose a table in the furthest corner from the door, and sat down.

The barmaid appeared behind the bar, but hadn't noticed Scott.

"Can I order?" he asked.

She dropped the glass she had been cleaning.

"Oh, you startled me, I hadn't seen you there."

"Sorry, I didn't mean to."

"No no, don't apologise, it's just me, I'm a bit edgy."

"Could I have the steak and chips please, with a few mushrooms, and a dollop of English mustard?"

"Certainly, how would you like your steak Sir."

"Well done please."

"OK well done it is."

Scott liked her. She had long black hair and very dark sultry eyes. She didn't speak with any trace of a Scottish accent.

She returned to the rear of the bar.

"Would you like a drink Sir?"

"Yeah please, vodka and orange, easy on the ice."

"Are you a guest at the hotel?"

"Yes, I'm in room fourteen. Is it always this quite?"

"Yes, it will liven up a little, later, if you call fishing stories lively."

"My name's Tony, by the way."

"Well Mr Bytheway, my name is Angela."

"Pleased to meet you Angie, can I buy you a drink?"

"Thank you, I'll have a coke."

Scott went to the bar to collect his drink. He took it back to his table. He watched as Angie busied herself behind the bar. She was beautiful, with an athletic build, her body looked hard, whereas Shannon's body was soft and cuddlyable, as he called it. Her eyes fascinated him, almost Egyptian in colour and shape, more piercing than Shannon's.

"What are you staring at?" she asked.

"I'm sorry Angie, I was wondering how I ever became a serial rapist."

"Get lost, come near me and you'll get a bucket of ice cubes down yer trousers, followed by a swift kick in the jewels." They both laughed, easy in each other's company.

"You've got a nice tan Angie, have you been on holiday?"

"Sort of, more a working holiday."

"Where did you get to then."

"Travelling in America."

"North or south."

"North," she lied, "we did route 66."

"What, north to south."

"No, west to east, there is no north to south."

"Isn't there, I've never been, so I wouldn't know." Scott's trick question didn't catch her. "I bet it's a bit of a bummer coming back here after a holiday like that, what's it like working for the old dragon that owns this place?"

"It's not that bad, she is my mum."

"Whoops, sorry, I didn't mean to sound nasty."

"It's OK, she can be a little fiery at times, she makes a good friend or a bad enemy, depending upon how she takes to you, so be careful, you have been warned."

"Thanks, warning accepted, I'm just nipping out to my car, cold you give me a shout when my dinner is ready, if I'm not back?"

"Yeah, no problem."

Scott went out to the car, removed the gun from the briefcase, and cleaned it. It had saved his life earlier in the day, he was in debt to whoever had provided it. He replaced it in the briefcase, put the case into the boot, locked the car, then returned to the bar.

Angie was just serving his meal to an empty table. It was the first time he had seen her from the waist down, he was very impressed. He noticed that he was still the sole customer.

"Great I'm starving."

Angie was startled.

"Oh, I didn't hear you come in." she said apologetically.

"Us rapists always sneak about, you had better tie a bell to my ankle."

"I think I had better tie one somewhere, but not your ankle," she laughed, "enjoy your meal."

"Thank you, I'm sure I will."

Scott ate the meal quickly, and returned the now empty plate to Angie, as she stood behind the bar.

"There you go, all gone, as my mum used to say. I could have eaten that twice. Trouble is, I have to watch my figure." he said, patting his stomach.

"Your figure looks alright to me."

"When you have a perfect body like mine, you have to look after it."

"Who mentioned perfect."

"You did, didn't you?"

"No, I don't think so." They both laughed.

Scott stayed at the bar talking with Angie, they were becoming good friends, he thought. Angie seemed to Scott, to be a lovely young woman, he liked her a lot. However, she didn't have that something special that Shannon possessed, he knew they would only ever be friends.

He missed Shannon terribly, he was glad of Angie's company. He had become accustomed to their long chats, talking of their future together, talking of their love for each other. Now there was only one future, one of revenge.

As the evening wore on, the bar began to fill. Angie's attention was now elsewhere. Scott called her over.

"Angie, I'm going to take a walk around the village, is there a curfew?"

"Well, we usually lock up at about midnight, but I can let you have a key."

"That would be excellent."

Angie went to find a key.

"Here you are, now try not to get lost, and are you sure you won't be frightened in the dark?"

"I hadn't thought of that, if I am, I'll come running back, don't you worry."

"OK, I'll see you later Tony." she smiled as he left the bar.

Outside it was quite dark. The sea breeze swept through Scott's hair, like an invisible brush. The tide had returned, now all the boats faced into the current, like an armada at anchor. There was stillness and quite, a loneliness that he felt he could lose himself in. His thoughts turned again to Shannon. Tears filled his eyes. She was dead because of him. Their love had been so special, yet so cruelly swept aside. He cried openly, his pent-up grief and anger finally bursting from him. His utter loneliness without her, suddenly realised. His deep sobs carried on the breeze, as if searching for Shannon, to beg for her forgiveness.

When Scott had regained his composure, he continued with his walk, eventually returning to the hotel. The bar was still open, so he went in for a drink. As he entered, every head seemed to turn to see if the newcomer was a friend, or a stranger. They quickly looked away, they didn't like strangers. Scott walked over to the bar.

"Hi Angie, large vodka and orange please."

"Hi Tony, did you enjoy your walk, you look a bit red-eyed?"

"The wind blew sand in my face," he lied, "and yes, it's a beautiful part of the country isn't it."

"It's double edged, it can be beautiful in summer, yet so savage in winter."

"Yeah, I bet, there was a bit of a bite in the breeze, unless I'm getting soft."

"Where are you from Tony?"

"I'm a Lancashire lad, red rose county."

"Whereabouts in Lancashire?"

"Preston."

"Oh yes, I passed through there once on a train." she lied. She handed him his drink. "Don't bother paying, I'll put it on your bill.

They spent the remainder of the evening talking, whenever she could, slowly probing, getting to know each other. A little after eleven-thirty, Scott said goodnight and went to his room.

Lying on his bed, his thoughts returned to his task. He wondered how long he would be kept waiting, how long he would have to keep up his pretence. He had only just met Angie, but he didn't like lying to her.

Although Scott hadn't realised it, his contact had been in the hotel that evening.

SEVEN

SCOTT woke early. The radio alarm beside his bed indicated 6.00am. He donned his jogging gear, washed the night's sleep off his face, combed his hair, and left the room.

He went downstairs to the front door of the hotel, which he found to be locked. He walked back through the hotel to the kitchen area, where he found Angie's mum preparing the breakfasts.

"Good morning Mr Hewitt," she said, making it sound almost like an order.

"And a good morning to you to, please, call me Tony."

"And what can I do for you?"

"Is there a way out through here, I found the front door locked?"

"Certainly, that door leads out the rear of the hotel." She said pointing to a white wooden door behind her, "It's open."

"Thanks a lot, I'll see you later, I'm just off on my morning run."

"Just a moment, I think Angie's going for a run today, she can show you the way."

Scott waited as she went in search of her daughter, the smell of breakfasts being cooked tempted him not to bother. He sneaked a slice of toast out of the toast rack, and was still eating it when Angie and her mother appeared. They both gave him a wry look, like two headmistresses at a bum-smacking contest.

Scott swallowed the toast quickly.

"Hi Tony, do you mind if I join you?"

"It will be nice to have your company, I usually run alone, you know, lost in thought, today I would probably just be lost, come on."

They left the hotel at a steady jog. The early morning sun promised yet another wonderful day.

As they ran, Scott thoughts turned once again to

Shannon.

"Penny for them."

"What? Oh right, I was just thinking about a friend."

"Male or female?"

"Female, she died recently."

"I'm sorry."

"It's OK, it's just that I was out jogging the morning she died."

Angie let it go at that. She was running slightly ahead of Scott. In her shorts and T- shirt she looked a picture. He could tell from her figure, that she was the athletic sort, she obviously took great care of herself, he thought that she must at least be a kick boxer or something.

"Tell me if I'm going too fast, won't you?" he said cheekily.

"I bet I could out run you wearing a pair of wellies." she joked.

Angie suddenly sprinted ahead. Scott chased after her.

"Wait." he called.

"What's up?"

"Hang on," he caught up with her, "You didn't say how much the bet was."

"Tenner."

He rubbed his chin as if deep in thought, then suddenly set of at a sprint shouting "You're on." as he went.

"Cheat," she screamed, as she set of after him.

Angie soon caught up with him, and they ran on at an easy jog. They talked, covering a whole variety of subjects. Scott found her very easy to talk to, as if he had known her for years. She led him through some beautiful countryside, enjoying his company. She found herself thinking about love, and how she could easily fall in love with such a vibrant young man, so different from the local men. He hadn't talked to her as a barmaid, as most men would, more as an old friend, and she liked that.

They had entered a densely forested wood, following a well worn path, used by joggers, walkers and riders, at this time of day it was deserted.

"Tony, can we stop for a few minutes?"

"That'll be a tenner."

"No it won't, we didn't shake on it."

"You're not going to welch on a bet are you, I might never

speak to you again?"

"Well, I'll have to save up then."

"I can lend it you if you like."

"OK, deal, and there is something I wanted to ask you though."

"Go ahead, ask, but I can only lend you a tenner."

She laughed. "Does the word Amazon mean anything to you?"

Scott was stunned. Surely Angie couldn't be mixed up in this mess as well.

"Yes."

"What word is tattoed on your brother's right arm?"

Scott stared at her. She knew he had a brother, what else?

"There isn't a word tattoed on his right arm."

"On the left then."

"Trouble."

"What's your real name?"

"What's yours?"

"My name is Angie, now what is yours?"

Scott made a grab for her but missed. She seized his arm, and thrust it upwards behind his back. The pain was excruciating, but he didn't show it.

"Now tell me your real name," she said giving his arm an extra push.

"Tony Hewitt."

"Pillock, down on your knees."

He did as instructed. She pushed him face down into the undergrowth, and sat on his back. She pulled a plastic tie from her knickers, and bound his hands.

"Who do you work for?"

"I'm unemployed, if you're so dam clever you should have known that."

She stood beside him. She gave him a swift kick in the ribs, just to let him know she was serious.

"Well done old girl, are your brains in your trainers, or vacationing in your knickers?"

She gave him another kick.

"Name."

"Piss off lady, it's a man's job."

"Get up, and don't try to be clever."

Scott struggled to his feet, his mind working overtime. He had set out to avenge Shannon, and had failed already.He wondered how she would kill him. He was powerless with his hands behind his back. Then he remembered. He had seen it in a film, lay on your back, bringing your hands up under your legs, easy.

"Walk."

She pushed him in the direction she wanted him to move, heading deeper into the forest.

Ahead of him, Scott noticed tree roots growing across the path. As he strode over the roots, he pretended to stumble, crashing down on his back. As Angie bent to help him up, he kicked her hard on the hip, sending her staggering and falling to his left. He quickly brought his arms forward, the tie catching momentarily on the heel of his trainer, then he was on his feet. Angie tried to stand, but Scott kicked her hard again, sending her reeling. She lay prostrate. Now Scott sat on her, taking her neck in his hands. He squeezed, hard.

"Now little lady, not so clever are you. You can tell me who you are, and who you work for, or you can die here, understand?"

Angie nodded.

The gun crashed down on Scott's head, he toppled over, unconscious.

"I'm at sergeant Bennett's house," the beat constable said into his radio, "I've had a look round, everything seems locked and quiet, what should I do now sarge, over?"

"Wait there, have you checked his garden shed, over?"

"He hasn't got one, over?"

"Right, well ask the neighbours if they've seen anything of him, and wait for assistance, out."

Sergeant Bennett hadn't been seen for twenty-four hours, following recent events, there was a genuine concern for his welfare.

The constable went to the house next door, where he had noticed a neighbour watching him curiously through the curtains. He knocked. After a few seconds the door opened.

"Sorry to trouble you madam, have you seen out of Benny, I mean Sergeant Bennett, in the last twenty-four hours?"

"Yes, I saw him come home yesterday, about lunchtime I think."

"But not since?"

"No, but there was a funny noise, no, it doesn't matter."

"Go on, what noise?"

"Like a car back firing."

"From his house?"

"I'm not sure."

"Ok, thanks for your help."

The constable walked down the garden path back to the road.

"PC 1124 over."

"Receiving."

"Lady next door to Bennett's think she heard a noise like a car back-firing, I'm really worried sarge, over."

"Right, help should be with you any second, just stay calm and wait, out."

A police Metro pulled into the kerb outside Bennett's house.

"Hi there Harry, what do you think's going on?"

"I don't know Mick, let's hope it's nothing, come on."

They went round to the rear door of Bennett's house.

"Do you want to do it, or shall I?"

"No, you do it Harry, he's your mate."

Harry smashed the window of the door, reached in, turned the key, and tried the door. It still wouldn't open.

"Bollocks, it must be bolted."

Harry carefully reached through the broken glass, and gingerly felt his way round the door case, feeling for the bolt. He found it and pulled it open. The door opened. They crept into the kitchen.

"Why are we creeping Harry," Mick whispered, "you've just made enough noise to wake the dead?"

"I don't know, why are you whispering then?"

"I don't know." Mick said, pushing the back of Harry's head.

"Oh my God, oh no, quick, look at this Mick."

"What, what, what is it." Mick said excitedly.

"He didn't wash the supper pots." Harry said, pointing into the sink.

"You're a bloody pillock, I nearly wet me-self then, pack

it in."

"Come on soft lad, let's have a look round, and don't touch."

They searched the downstairs and found nothing.

"Come on hero, let's go up." Harry said, leading Mick out of the sitting room.

"You first."

"Why?"

"Your senior." They had actually been recruits together, but Harry had arrived at the training college five minutes earlier than Mick on their first day. They had gone through training together, but didn't see all that much of each other now, although they would remain friends for life.

"Prat."

They went slowly upstairs. Harry didn't know why, but he had an uneasy feeling gnawing at his consciousness, the cheeks of his bum began to tighten, biting into his Marks and Spencer underpants

"Mick, take a look in there." He said, pointing to the bathroom.

"Get lost, you look."

"You big Mary, how did you ever get on the force?"

"I aint seen a dead 'un before."

"What. Who said he's dead?"

"There's been bodies all over bloody Preston recently, I wish I was back on motorbikes, nailing the arses of poor defenceless motorists."

Harry checked the bathroom, nothing. The room next to it appeared to be the master bedroom. Harry entered cautiously.

"Oh my God no."

"Piss off, you can't catch me twice, pillock."

Harry turned in the doorway, looked Mick in the eye, and spewed his last two meals over the landing.

Mick pushed past him.

"Oh Jesus Christ Almighty." He said, barely able to control himself.

Sergeant Bennett's brains were adhered to the back wall of the bedroom. Blood had run down the wall in lines, like a deathly, macabre bar code, and covered the headboard in a crimson, sticky shroud. Bennett lay face up on the bed, his eyes looking at the door, as if seeking help. He still held the gun barrel into his mouth, as though smoking his favourite pipe.

"Sarge, get help urgently, Benny's dead, he's been shot, there's blood everywhere, what do we do?" Harry almost screamed into his radio.

"Get a grip of yourself for a start, you're supposed to be a policeman, now start acting like one, seal off the house, CID should be there soon, and don't touch anything, do you understand?"

"Yes sarge, but it's horrible."

"I know, I know, but you must get a grip Harry, you can't help him now, seal the house, right?"

"Right Sarge, understood."

They both went downstairs and out of the back door. Harry was close to tears, Bennett had become a good friend and confidante, in the short time he had known him. Mick had never seen anything like it in his life, and was in a state of shock.

"I'll hang that McLenan myself one day, the bastard, Dinger and Benny hated the little prick, I'll kill him, if it's the last thing I ever do, I'll kill him, and that's a promise."

Mick nodded dumbly.

Scott's consciousness began to return, the pain at the back of his head, worse than any hangover that he had ever paid for. He slowly opened his eyes.

"Don't talk." ordered Angie, "Just get up, and shut up."

He could see the impressions of his fingers on her neck, he could also see the gun she held in her right hand. He eased himself into a sitting position.

"Get up." she said angrily, as she kicked him hard on the leg.

"Do that again lady, and I promise you, you will eat shit before this day is out." he said through gritted teeth. He rose slowly to his feet.

"Move."

"Which way, or is it a guessing game?"

"To your left smart arse, and don't get clever, or you will have two headaches."

"Yes Sir, did anyone ever tell you how sexy you look,

with your hand firmly gripped around a weapon?"

"You're annoying me, don't."

She led him to the rear of the hotel, and ushered him towards the hotel garage. There were no windows, and Scott found it difficult to see, after being in the bright morning sunlight. He realised the conditions must be the same for Angie. As she prodded him in the back with the gun, Scott spun round, knocking it from her grip. She tried to punch him, but missed. He kicked out wildly, catching her on her left knee. She screamed in pain, and slumped to the floor.

"Now you bitch, time to eat sh. . ."

Half of the word went unspoken, as the rope tightened around his neck, cutting off any further tirades.

"Kneel, foul mouth."

Scott knelt.

"Now for God's sake, tie his wrists and ankles." It was Angie's mum.

Angie did as instructed.

"Well Mr Hewitt, what shall we do with you?"

"Do what you like lady, I really don't give a shit."

"But you should foul mouth, or you may end up dead."

"I am dead lady, you can't kill me again."

The statement meant nothing to Angie's mum. She switched the garage light on.

"Now Mr Hewitt, I want you to look at this photograph." She said as she held it in front of him.

The photo' was of him, as he jammed Inspector Bell up against a wall, shortly after the explosion outside his flat.

"Very nice, which one is you?"

"You are not helping yourself with this attitude, Mr Hewitt, the young man in the picture is Scott McLenan, so who are you?"

"That is me, or are you blind as well as bloody stupid?"

The kick in the ribs sent him sprawling.

"What have you done with Scott McLenan?"

"Are you deaf as well?"

Angie kicked him hard in the stomach. Scott lay on the floor gasping.

"I hope you like the taste of shit lady?"

"It must be an acquired taste, you're the only one in it." answered Angie.

"Shut up children for God's sake, where is Scott McLenan?" She asked him again

"I am Scott McLenan, you're in charge, check it."

"I will Mr Hewitt, I will."

She questioned him for what seemed like an eternity. He ached in all the places that had been kicked, and some that hadn't. During the interrogation, his frivolous answers had been greeted with more kicks, his body was weakening, but not his spirit. When she had finished, she gagged him. As they left the garage, Angie gave him one last kick, like a memento, just to remember her by.

Scott lay still on the cold concrete floor of the garage. The plastic ties had cut into his wrists and ankles, as he had struggled for freedom. He wondered what James Bond would have done in a similar situation, but unfortunately, he had no secret weapons, no hidden gadgets, no beautiful girl to come to his rescue. There was only one thing he could do, he drifted into unconsciousness, a merciful release from the pain.

"Wake up." Angie shouted as she shook him. "Wake up."

Scott's head ached more than ever now, his neck had stiffened through lying at a funny angle, he felt like a worn out old punch bag.

"Is it room service?"

"Hands."

"What?"

"Hands, let me see your hands."

The sunlight now shining through the garage door, silhouetted Angie and the gun she held.

"I'm going to cut the ties, don't be a hero, the gun is loaded, and yes, the safety catch is off, and I'm nervous, so don't push it, right?"

"Right."

The knife cut through the ties effortlessly, and his hands parted. He could see the blood on his wrists. The tie on his left hand had stuck deeply in the cut. He pulled it off.

Someone switched the garage light on.

"Right palm." she ordered.

He did as ordered without comment. He couldn't comment, as the noose had been placed around his neck, and tightened again.

Angie stepped forward and looked at the palm.

"It's there mother."

The rope eased on Scott's neck.

"Pleased to meet you Scott, or should we still call you Tony?"

Angie's came and stood in front of him, and proffered her hand. Scott took her hand in his, and squeezed as hard as he could, she didn't flinch.

"Is this how you welcome all your guests, or am I privileged?"

"Scott, sorry, Tony, we thought you were an imposter, it's our job to get you out of the country."

"What, dead or alive?"

"We have had to be extra careful, so many people are dead, we don't want to be next. They think your brother has passed information to you, are they right?"

"Is who right?"

"We don't know that."

"How do I know I can trust you?"

"You don't."

"Great."

"The enemy have been trying to kill you since Preston, we caught you and you're still alive, so you decide."

"Ok, so you're my guardian angels, so what next?"

"Nothing, we all wait."

"For A1?"

"It's not A1, it's AI."

"Aggro international?"

"Alien Intelligence."

"You're kidding, not little green men?" Scott said.

"Yes, well no, so far there are no little green men, but because so many people believe the government are withholding information, AI was set up to find out what really was happening."

"What did you mean, so far?"

"We believe Danny discovered something in South America, and he was killed to keep it secret, terrestrial or extra-terrestrial, or a combination."

"A combination?"

"Yes, if an alien race wanted to come here, the first priority would be a safe haven."

“Just a minute, an alien race, isn’t this getting a little ridiculous, surely if an alien race came here, they could land where ever they bloody well wanted?”

“Well, like I said, we just don’t know anything, we hope you are going to find out.”

“Me?”

“Yes you, that’s why you have been brought here.”

“Great.”

“But for the time being, we must wait for orders, Angie, it’s time you were working, Tony, may I apologise for the rough treatment, and suggest you make the most of your time here, relaxing.

“Ok, that’s fine by me. I’m relaxed.”

“Right, I’ll see you both later.”

Angie’s mum left the garage.

“I’m sorry too Tony.”

“Forget it, you had a job to do, whenever I look at my bruises, I’ll think of you.”

“Come on, I’m going to the bar, I’m sure you could manage a drink.”

“Force me.”

They left the garage and went into the hotel. Scott settled on a bar stool, while Angie served the drinks. He had two vodkas then left, promising to see Angie later.

He went to his room, filled the bath with water hotter than he could really stand, and got in, hoping to soak away the aches.

Scott woke with a start. The bath water was now cold, he had lost track of the time. He climbed out of the bath, aching more now than when he got in. He showered in cold water to wake himself. It was early evening. He dressed and went down to the lounge bar. Angie was serving evening meals.

“Hi Tony, would you like to eat?”

“No, just the usual please.”

“How are you feeling?”

“I feel like I’ve been kicked by a five legged mule.”

“I hope you’re not name calling?”

“Not me.”

“I hope you’re going to enjoy your stay here.”

“Of course Angie.” he leaned over the bar and whispered.

"Or should I say 008 and a bit?"

"Watch it, or I'll set my mum on to you."

"Oooh ecstasy."

Scott finished his drink.

"See you later Angie." he called as he turned and left the bar.

"See you."

Scott went outside and stood looking about, it was quiet. The evening was warm, yet the sea breeze was doing it's best to cool things down, He walked down to the moorings. The boats bobbed on the restless water. Seagulls dived like Stukas on bombing raids, then soared away, their constant, chattering shrill voices, like a gang of argumentative women.

He walked down a concrete slip way to the water's edge. His eyes slowly filled with tears as he thought of Shannon. She had lost her life because of him. Their life together had been destroyed because of him. All those dead people, all those grieving families. His fault. He felt desperately sad, desperately lonely. He cried deep sobbing tears. His thoughts turned to suicide. The cold of the water would take him quickly. Would anyone notice? Yes, the bombers would. He realised that he had to live. He had to take revenge on behalf of the dead. He would take revenge. AI was his way forward.

Scott regained control and headed back to the hotel. Angie turned as he came into the lounge.

"Can't stay away can you?"

"No, it's either you or the vodka that's attracting me."

"Cheeky, would you like a drink?"

"Are you buying?"

"I suppose so."

"Then I'll have a large one, if you'll pardon the expression?"

"Coming up, if you'll pardon the expression, where did you get to?"

"Not so far, I just needed to sort things out in my mind, I think I'm ready to go now."

"Can I help?"

"Yes, just point me in the right direction, it's time I made waves."

"Remember Tony, nobody has ever got near this, it's not a game, it's deadly serious."

"So am I."

EIGHT

TONY."

It was Angie's mum.

He had sat at the bar through most of the evening, talking to Angie whenever he could. He had disposed of quiet a few vodkas during the course of their conversations.

"Yes."

"Could I have a word?"

"Sure." He left the bar and followed her into the kitchen. She beckoned him into a small office at the rear. There was a large desk taking up most of the available room, it was totally covered with invoices and files. She sat in a large leather chair behind the desk.

"Would you like to take seat Tony?"

"No thanks, my bumb's numb from that bar stool."

"Ok, your orders have come through. Tomorrow night you will be going on a fishing trip. You may take a suitcase. I suggest that you rest as much as possible during the day."

"Is that it?"

"Yes"

"Oh, I thought there would be more."

"No, only good luck, and God bless you, and I sincerely hope that you will return safely to us."

"Thank you, I'd better say goodnight to Angie, see you tomorrow."

"I hope so Tony, I want you to promise me that you will take great care, remember that you are up against a highly-trained and motivated organisation, whatever they are up to, so please take care, and be sure to come and see us when you return."

"I promise I will, well, goodbye, and thanks for the kicking."

"Go on, before I give you another." She said, as she waved him out of the office.

He went back to the bar. Angie was collecting empties and tidying the furniture.

"Well, that's it, I'm leaving tomorrow, will I see you before I go?"

"Definitely, I'm having a couple of hours off in the afternoon, fancy a walk?"

"That will be great, right, I'm off to bed, I'll see you tomorrow then, goodnight Angie."

"See you tomorrow Tony."

She watched him as he left the bar. He wasn't like other men, he didn't push it all the time. He talked to her as an equal, none of the macho innuendo that she was forced to listen to on a daily basis. She could talk freely to him, without the need to be on guard. She liked him, she liked him a lot, and hoped he would return. She wanted to know him even more. She knew she could easily fall in love with him, but not now, not until he returned, if he returned.

Scott woke slightly after eight, showered, dressed, and went down for breakfast. As he walked along the narrow hotel passage, he felt a metamorphosis occurring in his stomach, as the pupa tuned to butterflies. He had a sudden urge to visit the toilet.

"Morning Tony, would you like to order?"

"Morning A.M." he smiled. "Yes please, poached egg on toast and coffee should do the trick."

"A.M?"

"Angie's mum, you haven't told me your name yet."

"I'll tell you when you come back safely."

"Deal."

She went off to the kitchen. Scott could hear voices coming from the kitchen, it was Angie talking to her mum. After a few minutes, the kitchen door opened, and Angie came to his table, carrying a tray holding a coffee pot and two cups. She was wearing a long nightie that he could see through. He could see sufficient to know she had a beautifully proportioned body.

"Hi Tony, can I share a coffee with you?"

"Of course you can, take a seat."

"Did you sleep well?"

"Like a bird in the bush."

"What?"

"I always sleep after a good kicking," he replied, "don't you?"

"We did apologise."

"Oh, well that's alright then, are we still on for the walk later?"

"Definitely, it's not every day I have somebody to walk with."

"Who was the last one, Master Spy?"

"Danny."

"Danny was here?"

"Yes, we brought him back into the country, we thought he was safe, so did he. Then he went missing. The next thing we knew, was when his body turned up in Preston, AI believe he was trying to reach you, Tony, we don't know what, or who you are up against, but they are obviously powerful, and international."

"I'd better make the most of my breakfast then, it might be my last."

"Don't even joke about it Tony, we want you to come home safely." She took his hand in hers. "Tony, I think I'm. . ."

The lounge door opened, stopping Angie in mid sentence.

"Morning all." It was one of the guests.

"Morning." they replied in unison.

Angie rose from the table, the moment lost. She went to the kitchen.

After breakfast alone, Scott returned to his room to pack. He packed the minimum for a few days. The remainder of his belongings, he stowed in the boot of the BMW. He decided against a run, opting for a drive instead.

During the drive, Scott's thoughts ranged from Shannon to the task ahead. He hoped he would be successful in his mission. Somewhere out there, somebody was responsible, not just for the murder of Shannon, but a lot of other innocent people as well. If it befell him to avenge them all, then so be it. In his mind, he promised all the victims, that he would fight hard, and he would fight to the death.

Scott returned to the hotel at lunchtime. He ordered lunch, but in truth, he was not feeling particularly hungry, he sat at a table with Angie, pushing his food around the plate, much to her annoyance.

"If you don't stop that, I'll hit you with it." Angie said.

"I'm sorry Angie, I guess it's getting to me."

"Don't apologise Tony, I was only kidding, I know you must be under a great strain at the moment."

"Wanna walk?"

"Yes, I'm not that hungry either."

They left the hotel, taking the same route as their run.

"I hope I'm not in for another kicking? I'm ready for you this time, I'll try not to hurt you."

"I don't think so." she laughed. Suddenly the smile deserted her face. "Tony, I'm really sorry about Danny, I don't know what went wrong.

"It's ok." he said, putting his arm around her. "If this organisation is as dangerous as you say, then you can hardly blame yourself. We are up against a force that nobody knows, but when I find them, I can promise you this, they will find out what force really means."

"Tony, just remember to be more like my mum and me, don't trust anyone, promise."

"I promise."

"Whatever they're up to, it must be big, big enough to go to all this trouble in the UK."

Scott agreed. It was obviously a large international organisation that he would be fighting. Perhaps the best way to kill it, was to cut it's head off, he thought to himself.

He realised he had put his arm around Angie, and suddenly felt so guilty, although it was only a friendly gesture, nothing more. The brief love he had shared with Shannon, had changed his life. She had become everything to him, his reason to live, breath, and be.

Angie was happy to have his arm around her. In her job, she couldn't get close to the men she met. With Tony it was different. He had an air of easiness about him, a carefree attitude that she found so alluring. She prayed he would return safely to her arms, more, she did not want him to leave. She put her arm around him as they walked on.

They arrived back at the hotel. Scott thanked her for being such pleasant company, gave her a quick peck on the cheek, then went up to his room to rest, as ordered.

Scott woke at five-thirty. He felt like he had been on hunger strike. He freshened up, then went hunting for food.

Angie was cleaning behind the bar in the lounge.

"Hi Tony."

"Hiya Angie, I'm ravenous, what you got to eat?"

"Well Mr Ravenous, this is today's menu." she laughed.

"I hope it's not my last supper."

"Please don't talk like that Tony."

"Sorry, I didn't know how much you cared?"

"I don't." she lied. "You just don't know who's listening."

"There's nobody else in here."

"Walls have ears."

"They have sausages as well."

They both burst into fits of laughter.

Angie came to the table with his meal.

"Are you sure?" she said.

"Yeah, why?"

"Steak, scrambled eggs, and mushrooms?"

"What's wrong with that?"

"Nothing, if you're a gorrilla?"

"Hey, I hope you're not calling me, I usually have onions as well."

"Ugh."

She left him to go and serve other customers.

When he had finished the meal, Scott passed the time playing darts with the locals. He lost most of the games. The locals liked that, and queued to play against him. They found his Lancashire accent a source of great amusement. The ale flowed swiftly all through the evening, by closing time Scott had made many new friends.

Angie cleared the pub and locked up. Scott had gone to his room to pack his last few items.

"Angie."

"Yes Mum."

"Where's Tony?"

"He went to this room."

"Can you go and get him please, it's time?"

Angie went up the stairs to his room. She knocked on the door. There was no reply. She knocked again. There was still no reply. Something was wrong. She tried the door handle. The door opened. His room was in darkness. Her heart began to pound. She reached for the light switch and turned it on. Scott's body lay half on, half off the bed. Angie rushed in.

"Tony, Tony." she called.

There was no response.She shook him.

"Tony."

He grunted as he regained consciousness.

"What?"

Angie was angry. "You're drunk Tony. It's time to go, and your drunk for God's sake. Tony, get up, now."

"Sorry."

"You will be if my mother sees you, get washed in cold water, quickly."

"Sorry."

"Shut, up, and get a move on." she said sternly.

Scott did as ordered.

"I thought we agreed this was deadly serious?"

"It wasn't me, it was your regulars, I don't drink, honest."

"Shut up. Never mind your inane excuses, Mum will be furious."

"Sorry."

"Shut up."

She led him out of the room, down to the office at the rear of the kitchen, carrying his case for him.

Angie's mum was standing there, her face was a picture. A picture of a rabid bulldog mauling a trainee postman.

"What's the hold up?"

"It's him Mum, he fell asleep."

"Sorry."

"Shut up." they said in annoyed harmony.

"Now listen Tony, go with Angie, do exactly as she says, don't argue, try and stay awake, it gets really serious from here, I mean it, life or death. Anyway, God bless you, and please come home safely to us.

"I will, promise, better keep my room tidy, or else."

"Of course, now off you go, and Angie, you be careful too, and come back safely."

"Don't worry mum, I will." She bent forward and kissed her on the cheek. To his surprise, so did Scott.

They left the hotel through the back door, coming around the side, then crossing the road that passed by the front door, and walked of towards the quays.

A boat was waiting for them, engine ticking-over, lights dimmed. It looked like a tugboat to Scott, but he couldn't be sure in the pitch black of the night. They boarded. A member of the crew, pulling the gangplank in after them. Within minutes they were underway.

They had been ushered into a tiny cabin. Through the porthole, Scott could see the occasional light on shore, after a time, there was nothing but waves.

They talked constantly about the task ahead, Angie trying to ensure that he really did realise the enormity of the situation. For his part, Scott tried to sound cool, but inside he was becoming very nervous.

Eventually they fell asleep, the motion of the boat as it rode the waves, and the long day, affecting them equally.

Angie woke with a start. The engine tone had altered. She left Scott asleep, and went up on deck to check.

The captain was at the wheel. He wore a captain's hat and smoked a captain's pipe, the smoke of which had turned his captain's beard and moustache, an awful amber colour

"Any sign yet?" Angie asked him.

"No luv, don't worry, she'll find us."

"Ok, call us when it's time please."

"Yes luv."

Angie returned to the cabin. She opened the door. Scott's bunk was empty. There was nowhere to hide in the cabin, so she went back up on deck.

In the wheelhouse she could see Scott and the captain. Scott held a British Army bayonet firmly against the captain's throat.

"Tony, what the bloody hell do you think you're doing?" She swore at him.

"You tell me lady."

"I thought you were drunk?"

"You were supposed to lady, now tell me what in Christ's name is going on?"

"We are here to meet the Royal Navy, a submarine to be exact, you're going to South America."

"Oh, of course, why didn't I think of that." he said sarcastically. "Now tell me the truth, or your friend will be breathing without using his nose."

"That is the truth for God's sake."

As she spoke, an eerie shape broke the surface on their starboard side.

"Look." she shouted. "What do you think that is, an overgrown dolphin?"

Scott released the captain.

"Sorry mate."

"No problem, I'm glad you're beginning to take it seriously, you owe me a pint."

"Deal."

The captain steered his boat nearer to the submarine.

They watched as a small dinghy bounced it's way towards the tug. Angie went to the cabin for his case. She came back on deck and handed the case to Scott.

"Well Tony, please be careful, for me and mum." She kissed him full on the mouth. She made the kiss last longer than it should have.

"I will, don't worry."

With that, he passed his case over the side of the tug, to the waiting sailors. Scott followed, and with one last wave and smile, he disappeared into the blackness of the night.

Tears welled in Angie's eyes. She had fallen deeply in love with Mr Hewitt, even though she had tried not to.

Scott climbed down the ladder, into the bowels of HMS Valiant, the Royal Navy's latest nuclear submarine.

"Tony Hewitt, very pleased to meet you." said the captain smiling broadly.

"Pleased to meet you too, Sir."

"I'm Captain Henry Bowler, Tom to the crew."

"May I call you Tom?"

"Of course, come on, I'll show you to your bunk. It's a bit cramped down here, but we manage."

Scott followed him through the control rooms. There were dials and computers, switches and levers, he wondered how they ever got the thing to move.

The knife thrust expertly inwards and upwards beneath the rib cage, until it punctured the heart. The lifeless body crashed to the floor, it's dead eyes still staring at the killer, it's mouth still wide open in surprise. The four-man team had searched the building silently, stealthily, seeking out their target. The duel, when it began, lasted less than three seconds She might have shot the first two, maybe all four, but in her panic, she had forgotten to switch off the safety catch of the gun. The mistake had cost her, her life. The team leader bent over the inert body of Angie's mum, then shot her through her gaping mouth.

NINE

THE Atlantic appeared to seethe and boil as HMS Valiant surfaced, the journey of eight thousand miles, completed with faultless precision. The coastline of Argentina lay in the distance, illuminated only by the borrowed light of the moon. Scott had not enjoyed his enforced submergence, he much preferred to have both feet on solid ground.

"Well Tony, it's been nice having you along." said Captain Bowler. "I hope you will be making the return trip sooner rather than later."

"So do I Tom, but I think I will walk home, if that's alright with you?"

"Why, what's the matter with my nice little boat?"

"Well, it sinks for a start off, I always thought boats could swim."

"By the time we get you home, you'll be used to it."

"I don't think I could ever get used to these things, you can't even look out the window, or go for a walk."

"Landlubber, right, it's departure time, look after yourself Tony, we'll be waiting for your signal, stay lucky."

"Thanks Tom, I hope to be back soon, preferably in one piece, two at the most."

They shook hands. The two of them had become good friends during the course of the voyage. It had been Tom's job to brief Tony and provide him with as much information as possible, which had been precious little in the circumstances. Tom had been involved once before in a mission designed to find out the truth concerning Argentina, the last agent, Freddie (Whispering) Williams, had never been seen alive since being put on the beach by dinghy. Tom had never met Scott's brother, and knew nothing of him, and had been unaware of his mission here.

"Right, off you go, and good luck Tony."

"Thanks, I'm sure I'll need it, thank the crew for me, there's not much room down here, I'm sure they didn't need me taking up their valuable space, and asking questions all the time."

"I will, goodbye, and good luck again."

With that, Scott climbed the metal ladder of the forward hatch. The cold sea wind hit Scott full in the face, but he was pleased to find that it wasn't raining. He looked back along the hull of the Valiant, as she lay in the water like a gigantic metal whale, he hadn't enjoyed being pent-up deep within her bowels, but now, as the reality of his lonely mission began to encompass him, she appeared almost inviting.

The sailors helped Scott into the dinghy, then passed him his suitcase, none of them volunteering to take his place. The small craft edged away from the Valiant, before picking up speed towards the shore. The sailors in the dinghy didn't speak, they could think of nothing useful to say, that would make him feel more at ease. After a few minutes at full speed the engine was cut, and the two sailors began to row quietly in towards the beach. In total silence the dinghy hit the beach of the Rio de la Plata. Across the water from his position lay Montevideo. Scott clambered onto the sand, shook hands with both men, then turned and walked towards the lights of La Plata, the uncertainties he felt, eased by the comforting feel of his Smith and Wesson, and his favourite weapon, the bayonet.

The sand of the beach gave way under Scott's feet, making his stooped walk toward the sand dunes more laborious than he would have prefered. Within a few minutes, he reached the comparative safety afforded by the dunes. He found a sheltered hollow on the leeward side of the sandy mounds, and took time out to gather himself, and figure out exactly where he was. From his hideout Scott could see the lights of La Plata off to his right, knowing this, he knew there should be a coast road directly ahead of him. It was here that he would be making contact.

When he felt rested and sure of his position, he set off in the direction he hoped the road would be.

He had only walked about one hundred yards, when a noise to his right made him freeze. His eyes strained through the dark, another noise, like a groan. His former training now took over. He crept silently toward the noise, through the darkness he made out two shapes. He remained motionless, like a big cat stalking, waiting for the exact moment to present itself. Yet another groan followed. Now he understood. Two lovers had also found a sheltered hollow. They had no idea of his presence. He waited while their love-making grew louder, then quietly slipped away into the darkness, replacing the bayonet in it's scabbard as he went. It was midnight.

As the headlights of an approaching car stabbed through the darkness, Scott realised he had located the coast road. He now sought another refuge, his contact would not be until first light. His main concern now was to remain invisible. He found another natural hollow and lay in it, burying his suitcase beside him and covering his protruding legs with sand. He knew he must remain awake at all costs. For him to be discovered now would be disastrous. His thoughts returned to Shannon. He remembered their last night together, and the horror of the following morning, his memories only served to intensify his feeling of utter loneliness. He knew nothing of Argentina, other than the Falklands war, and his briefing on the submarine. His thoughts now turned to vengeance, he pondered the question, could he find and kill the person responsible? Others had failed and died. Death didn't concern him, without Shannon, he felt dead already.

The sound of approaching footsteps snapped him back to reality. His left hand withdrew the bayonet by instinct. The footsteps stopped. Scott felt his heart beating against his chest. It sounded so loud to him, he felt sure it could be heard for miles around. His ears heard every noise of the night. His eyes saw imaginary attackers. His breathing sounded like a tornado whistling through a wind tunnel. He still couldn't see the person responsible for the footsteps, but he knew that to move would be fatal.

The girl giggled and squealed as she ran from her lover. He chased after her, almost standing on Scott's outstretched legs. Scott could see them now in silhouette, as they ran towards the road. He lay motionless until they reached the road. He watched as they walked along the road in the direction of La Plata, until they disappeared into the night. A few moments later he heard the noise of two car doors as they were slammed. As the vehicle's lights were switched on, he could see it was parked in a lay-by, no more than two hundred yards from his position. At last he relaxed. Without realising it, he had arrived at almost exactly the correct location. From his hideaway he could watch the lay-by, waiting for the correct vehicle to arrive, only then would he break cover.

The hours of darkness dragged on interminably. He drifted into sleep on many occasions, only to be cruelly woken as his head slumped forward, or as cars sped past. Slowly but surely, night turned to light. From his vantage, he could see the lay-by clearly, now all he had to do was wait for the correct vehicle. In the darkness he had chosen well, he couldn't be seen from the road, even in daylight.

His watch showed 07.45, fifteen minutes before his contact was due. At precisely 08.00, a black taxi pulled into the lay-by. Scott's pulse rate quickened again. This, he hoped, would be the vehicle he had been waiting for. He slowly rose from his sitting position, his legs stiff from their hours of inertia, and started toward the taxi, keeping the sand dunes between them. The noises of the breaking Atlantic masking any sounds his footsteps made.

The driver of the taxi was completely unaware of Scott's presence, until she felt the cold, sharp blade of his faithful companion, pressing hard against her jugular vein. Scott was not expecting to meet a woman.

"I want you to take me to the airport." Scott said.

"I prefer to fly by night." she answered.

"Out."

She opened the door of the taxi and climbed out. She wore a battered straw hat, that looked like it had seen active service in two world wars, a black crop top, and tatty blue denim shorts. Her plimsolls looked like standard British Army issue, tied with ordinary string.

"Now put your arm around my waist, we're going for a little walk, like lovers, ok?"

"Ok." The young woman replied.

They walked across the sand, following the footprints Scott had made earlier.

"Where are you taking me, please don't hurt me?" She begged him. Her words held only a slight trace of a South

American accent.

"Be quiet, just walk, and you won't come to any harm, upset me, and you will."

They walked on, back to Scott's overnight hide.

"Brush the sand away there." he said, pointing to an area of sand that had obviously been disturbed. She did as instructed, revealing Scott's suitcase.

"Now pick it up."

She obeyed without hesitation.

"Right, we're going to walk back to your cab, like lovers, you can carry the case, ok?"

"Ok."

They walked slowly back along the sand dunes. A passing car with four men in slowed down as they spotted them, and gave a series of rude hand signals, before laughing and driving off. Scott felt a little embarrassed.

"Sorry about that."

"It doesn't matter."

As they arrived back at the taxi, Scott tightened his grip around her waist.

"Don't do anything silly, just put the case in the boot, then slowly walk to the driver's door."

She did as he requested. Scott eased himself into the car through the driver's door, making her follow. As she entered the taxi, she felt the cold bayonet pressing into her side.

"Where is he?"

"Who?"

"The driver, what have you done with him?"

"I am the driver, you are Tony Hewitt, am I right?"

"Listen lady, I don't know who you are, and it doesn't matter who I am, but you are within moments of losing your life, now where is the driver?"

"I'm telling you, I am the driver."

Scott pressed the knife harder into her ribs, until she reacted to the pain.

"I am your driver, you tell me what I must do, and I will do it, I know nothing else."

"I'm expecting a male driver, who are you?"

"My name is Georgetta Cardoba, all my English friends call me George."

Scott removed the bayonet from her ribs.

"Unless you're lying, nothing has changed, there seems to have been a cock-up, I was told I would be contacted by George, they didn't say it would be a lovely young woman."

"Thank you for the compliment, I'm glad I didn't meet you when you were really angry."

"I'm sorry, may I call you George?"

"Of course, and you are Tony, aren't you?"

"Yes."

"What must I do next then?"

"Take me to Buenos Aires, the Hotel De Las Americas, in downtown Barrio Norte."

"Sure, I know it."

She started the car, indicated, and pulled away. Scott kept the bayonet at the ready, still not entirely convinced of her identity. She was a lovely woman, he sincerely hoped she was telling the truth. They drove through La Plata, the morning traffic beginning to build. The time had been chosen specifically, there were hundreds of taxis operating at this time of day, it would be easy to lose one. Scott kept a wary eye on the following traffic, but there was no apparent tail, he now felt more relaxed.

"Who do you work for?"

"A.I."

"Have you worked for them long?"

"About five years, my brother worked for them before me."

"You say worked, has he resigned?"

"No, he went on a mission for them five years ago, nobody has seen him since, that is when I became involved. Unfortunately, I was becoming a nuisance in the search for my brother, so they employed me, it is easier for them to keep me out of trouble."

"Where do you think he is?"

"I do not know, they will not tell me the nature of his mission, but they have promised me, that by working for them, I am helping to find him."

"Five years is a long time to be missing, perhaps I will find him for you."

"Are you going on the same mission?"

"I don't know what I'm doing yet, nobody has told me." he lied.

Scott took in as much as he could as they drove. He had often wished he could have visited North America, now here he was in Argentina, a country he had never wished to visit, especially after the Falklands war. As far as Scott was concerned, if ever there had been a complete waste of lives, on both sides, the Falklands had been it. After all of the killing, nothing had changed, businesses on both sides, still did business. The generals all retired, keeping their ranks, drawing their pensions. The higher-ups still played polo. The only difference was felt by the families of the dead and maimed, the ordinary soldiers and their loved ones. Buenos Aires was nothing like Scott had been expecting. For some reason he had it in his mind that the city would not compare favourably against the cities of Europe. He was wrong.

"Tony." she said for the third time.

"Sorry, I was miles away."

"We are nearly there, better tidy up a little, you still have sand on your trousers and shoes."

"Ok George, sorry, I haven't been very good company have I?"

"No you have not, do not let it happen again."

"I won't, promise. It's just that there is so much to see, and I'm not sure how long I will be here."

"There."

The Hotel De Las Americas loomed before them. Scott was impressed by George's handling of the rush hour traffic, he was a bad back-seat driver, but on this occasion had kept quiet. She drove the taxi onto the hotel forecourt, stopping in front of the large main entrance.

"Thank you George, you have been a great help, I'm sorry our introduction was not so friendly, would you allow me to take you out for dinner this evening, to make up for it?"

She thought for a moment. "If my knife wound has healed, I would love to, what time?"

"I thought about eight would be ok."

"Then eight it is." she replied with a smile.

"Great, right." he said a little nervously. "I'd better check in, see you later then."

He opened the taxi door and clambered out, and with a wave, headed towards the hotel.

"Tony." she shouted after him.

He stopped. "Yes."

"Suitcase."

"Oh yes."

He came back to the car and took his case from the boot.

"Sorry George, I'd forget my bal. . ." He cut the sentence short. "Sorry."

"Bye Tony, see you tonight."

Scott watched as she drove away. What was a nice girl like that, doing mixed up in a dirty business like this, he thought. He turned and entered the hotel foyer, making for the reception desk.

"Good morning, the name's Hewitt, I believe there is a reservation for me?"

"One moment please Sir." said the receptionist, a man with dark greasy hair, stocky build, in his early thirties, who looked more like a bouncer, than a desk boy He checked the bookings.

"Ah yes, room 63 Sir, second floor, en-suite, very comfortable, these are for you Sir." He said passing three letters to Scott.

"Thank you."

"The boy will show you to your room Sir. With an almost unnoticeable nod of his head, he summoned a pageboy.

"Room 63 Juan."

"Ok, would Sir like to follow me please?"

"Sure, you speak good English"

"Thank you." He led Scott into the elevator, pressed the number two button, the doors closed. The hotel boasted one hundred and fifty, air-conditioned rooms, large enough for Scott to be invisible, just another tourist. Juan looked him up and down as the lift rose steadily.

"American."

"British."

"Oh." Juan's smile vanished.

"Does it matter?"

"No."

"You?"

"Argentinian."

"Oh." Scott let his smile vanish.

"Does it matter?"

"No."

The elevator shuddered to a halt, the doors opened, they both waited for the other to move first, then both moved together, colliding. They laughed loudly, the ice broken. Scott ruffled Juan's hair, and lightly pushed his head.

Juan led him to room 63, opened the door, and took Scott's case in. He looked Scott straight in the eye, waiting. Scott pretended not to notice the stare.

"Thank you, you can go now."

Juan coughed twice.

"If you're ill, you shouldn't be working." Scott teased.

Juan turned and walked to the door, silently cursing the British.

"Just a minute, haven't you forgotten something?"

Juan turned in the doorway, his smile returning.

"The case should be in the bedroom."

Juan's face dropped again. He carried the case into the bedroom under protest. He returned to the lounge, walking past Scott without looking at him.

"Just a minute, haven't you forgotten something."

"No."

"So you don't want this?" he said, offering a tip.

"Yes please Sir, thank you."

"Call me Tony if you like."

"Thanks Tony, see you later."He took the tip before Scott had the chance to change his mind. He turned and left the room, silently praising the British.

Scott undressed and headed for the shower, the night on the beach hadn't left him feeling over fresh. After his shower he went to bed, falling instantly into a deep sleep.

He woke at around 5.30pm. He slowly climbed off the bed, and stretched. Going to the window, he looked out over Buenos Aires. The feeling of being alone, so far from home caught up with him again. He still had not made his mind up concerning George, whether she was friend or foe.

The city was buzzing. He took a clean shirt from his suitcase, dressed and left his room. He took the stairs to the ground floor, and left the hotel through the main entrance. Buenos Aires was a bustling, cosmopolitan, urban conurbation, situated on the western bank of the Rio de las

Plata. A population of about three million, with a definite hint of European influence, but a far cry from the peace of the English Lake District.

Scott felt a rush of nervous excitement course through him. Maybe, somewhere not very far from where he now stood, lurked the man responsible for Shannon's murder. Maybe he was looking for him. Maybe he already knew which hotel he was staying at, maybe he knew the room number. His head filled with a myriad of maybe's.

Scott walked for an hour, taking in Florida Street and Santa Fe Avenue, window- shopping, but not interested in buying. During his wanderings, he changed direction regularly, sometimes doubling back on himself. There had been no apparent sign of anyone tailing him, so either they weren't, or they were very good at it, he thought. Eventually he arrived back at the hotel, and went straight to his room.

He sat on his bed wondering what would happen next. How could he find a killer in this huge country, or even in this large city. He had come here for revenge, and, live or die, he would go after the killer, somehow.

His thoughts turned next to George. She was a lovely girl, and he sincerely hoped she was to be a friend. She had been at the right place, at the right time. She did know his alias. She had brought him to the correct hotel. Yes, he decided, she must be friend. He looked forward to her company that evening, if she appeared.

He busied himself preparing for the evening. He hoped his second impression on her, would be better than the first. Very soon the time had arrived at 7.45. After one last look in the mirror, he left his room and headed for the hotel restaurant.

"Table for two please, somewhere secluded if possible." he instructed the headwaiter.

"Certainly, would Sir like to follow me please?"

"Sure."

The headwaiter led Scott to a window table, in a quiet corner of the restaurant, overlooking the city.

Thank you, this is perfect, my name is Tony Hewitt, if a young lady asks for me, could you please show her to my table, and could I have a beer please?"

"Yes to both Sir."

Within a few moments a waiter brought his beer. He drank it too quickly. Perhaps he was nervous, he thought.

Eight came and went, with no sign of George. Scott was now slowly drinking his third beer, and feeling very hungry.

The wall clock showed 8.45, and Scott was about to order a meal for himself, when the headwaiter appeared, escorting the most beautiful woman he had ever seen. Scott stared, he couldn't prise his eyes off her, as she walked towards his table.

"Hi Tony, I'm really sorry I'm late." she said, as the head waiter held the seat out for her.

It was George. She stood facing him.

Scott's mouth moved but didn't say anything, then he felt foolish, he had forgotten to stand.

"George, I had almost given up on you, you look absolutely beautiful."

"Thank you Tony, you do not look too bad yourself.

Tony sat looking at her, as did the other male guests in the restaurant, she was stunning. A torrent of jet-black hair fell to bellow her shoulders. Her white, low cut evening dress accentuated her figure, yet without being too revealing. She wore just enough jewellery, in no way ostentatious. Gone the lovely young taxi driver, now, a beautiful young woman, in full bloom.

Scott stood.

"Please, take a seat George, you're annoying the other lady guests."

She thanked the waiter and ordered fresh orange to drink.

"I'm sorry I'm late, the taxi got a puncture, and the spare tyre was flat."

"Please don't apologise, I can assure you it was well worth the wait."

"I bet you say this to all the girls."

"Only when I mean it."

"I thought you might have already eaten, or left the hotel before I arrived."

"I was about to order, I haven't eaten since yesterday, would you care to order?"

"Yes, could I see the menu please?"

Scott passed the menu over the table. He watched as

she studied it, fascinated by the depth of blue of her eyes. Her beauty was beyond him. He knew his place in life, and he knew a woman of such beauty, would never look twice at a man like him. He was almost afraid of her. She was the type of woman every man wanted, but most could never get near.

He smiled to himself as he watched other men in the restaurant glancing in her direction, much to the annoyance of their wives. But her's was a beauty that could not be ignored, and she was at his table. He felt sure his face wore a smug expression, he wanted them to believe she was his and his alone. Shannon had meant the world to him. Shannon was beautiful in her own way, not just facial. But George was mesmerising.

"Why are you smiling?"

"Nothing George, just thinking, are you ready to order?" He fibbed.

"Yes, I think I will have the chicken salad."

Scott beckoned the headwaiter.

"Are Sir and madam ready to order?"

"Yes, chicken salad for the lady, and I would like the T-bone steak please, well done, no dressing."

"Thank you, would Sir like to order wine?"

"Not for me. George?"

"No, a fresh orange though, with ice, thank you."

The waiter departed, obviously impressed by George's appearance.

"Where's the boyfriend tonight George?" Scott asked, hoping she didn't have one.

"I have no boyfriend Tony, I am dedicated to finding my brother, nothing must come in the way."

"You must love him dearly?"

"I do, we are all we have, our parents died when we were young, then our grandparents cared for us, since they have died, we only have each other, it is so lonely without him."

"I'm sorry George, I know all about loneliness, it hurts, it depresses, it saps your self confidence."

"Why are you lonely?"

"I had all I ever wanted, then had it taken from me, I've never felt such loneliness."

"Was it a woman."

"Yes."

"Did you love her?"

"More than I've ever loved before."

"What happened."

"I would rather not talk about it, if you don't mind." Scott knew that Shannon's murderers, probably worked for the same organisation that had taken George's brother, he didn't want to be the one to tell her how ruthless they were.

"It is ok, I should not have asked."

Their meal was served. Scott's steak was a monster. Being frugal, he ate the steak first, then couldn't eat anything else, being full. George didn't really eat, she appeared to pester the food rather than bite it.

"Is everything alright?" Scott asked her.

"Yes, why?"

"You don't seem to be eating very much."

"Oh, I am always like this. When I eat, I think, and when I think, I forget to eat."

"If you don't stop thinking, you will die of malnutrition."

"I do not care."

"Come on George, that's not the way to talk."

"I am sorry Tony, it is just that I miss my brother so much."

"Right, then you must let me cheer you up, I would tell you a joke if I knew a clean one."

"You are cheering me up Tony, just being with you is making me feel better."

Scott was pleased to hear her say that, she was definitely making him feel better.

They finished their meals and decided to go for a walk. George retrieved her jacket from the cloakroom, and they left the hotel. George delighted in showing the way, Scott, swept up in her beauty, would have gone anywhere, just as long as she was there.

"Where are you from Tony?" she asked as they walked along Santa Fe Avenue.

"I'm from Lancashire, England."

"Lancashire?"

"Yes, have you heard of Blackpool?"

"No."

"Manchester?"

"No."

"The Beatles?"

"Yes, from Liverpool?"

"That's right, well Liverpool is in Lancashire, and I'm from a town named Preston, which is near Liverpool."

"My father was a Beatles fan."

"So was mine, are you from Buenos Aires?"

"Yes, I have lived here all my life."

"Ah, that explains how you knew the streets so well this morning."

"What do you think of my city?"

"It's odd really, I always think of South American towns as a collection of straw huts, with men sat outside of them wearing sombreros, taking siestas, this has been a shock for me."

"A nice shock?"

"Oh yes, definitely, your transformation is the greatest shock of all."

"Thank you Tony, you are very kind, but I do try to look the part."

"Are you just playing a part this evening?"

"Of course not, you are with the real me."

"I'm sorry, I'm not used to this cloak and dagger stuff, I don't seem to trust anyone at the moment."

"You can trust me Tony, my orders are to look after you during your visit, nothing more."

"So is it a real taxi."

"No, it's owned by AI, that is why you got off without paying this morning."

Scott was annoyed with himself. He had completely missed that one small detail, perhaps the next mistake would cost him his life. He realised that he still wasn't match fit.

They were slowly making their way back towards the hotel. The time had rushed around to midnight, as they questioned each other, as if both were suspicious of the other. In fact they shared an affinity, and found themselves being unavoidably drawn to each other. They also shared a common enemy.He didn't want the evening to end, if there was one woman on earth who could help him get over the loss of Shannnon, and get on with his life, it was her.

"What do you know of this organisation George?"

"Like everyone else, almost nothing. AI cannot

understand how everything is kept so tight, no leaks, no one ever leaves, they must demand and receive total loyalty."

"Do you know where they are based?"

"Near a town named Bariloche, it is a tourist resort built by European immigrants, sometime around 1895. It is situated in what is known as the Argentine Lake District, near the Andes. Not far from the town, is a small mining company, that is where my brother was sent."

Scott knew of Bariloche from his briefing on the sub'.

"Who owns the mine?"

"We do not know, it appears to be a small part of a major conglomeration."

"What about tax records?"

"The Argentine government won't allow AI access to investigate them."

"Did your brother apply for a job at the mine?"

"That was the idea, there must be something going on down there, or we would have had contact, the only good thing about his disappearance, is that it seems to confirm their location."

"Yes, my ex-wife worked at the mine, but she is dead now."

"Oh, I am sorry Scott."

"Don't be, I haven't seen her in years, my brother used to be with her in Bariloche."

"Used to be?"

"Yes." Scott realised he had said too much. "Yes, he turned up in the UK, didn't have a lot to say for himself though."

"Perhaps they will send you to Bariloche?"

"I don't know."

"If I give you a photograph, would you look for my brother, for me, please?"

"Sure, if I go."

George linked her left arm through Scott's right as they walked. He noticed how often passing men, would turn for a second look at her. He knew even the most faithful husband would be tempted by her beauty.

"Tony."

"Tony."

"Sorry George, I was miles away."

"Pardon?"

"Oh, I mean I was lost in my thoughts."

"What about, or do you not want to tell me?"

Scott decide to tell her his story, from the bombings in Preston, his love for Shannon, her murder, and how he had come to be in Argentina.

"I am so sorry Tony, these men are more ruthless than I have been told, do you think they have killed my brother?"

"I really don't know, perhaps he is being held captive, somebody has to do their work for them.

George appeared to be happy with his answer.

They arrived back at the hotel forecourt. A taxi waited impatiently for it's next fare.

"Tony, I must go now, will I see you tomorrow?"

"George, if I don't see you tomorrow there had better be good reasons."

They walked over to the taxi. She kissed him lightly on the cheek.

"Thank you for a wonderful evening Tony, talking with you has helped, I hope I did not bore you with my troubles?"

"Not at all, it's been a pleasure, are you working tomorrow, or can you spend the day looking after me?"

"I do not know Tony, I will call you in the morning."

With that, she boarded the taxi and was gone.

Scott watched the car until it's rear lights had disappeared into the fussing night traffic. He felt he should have said so much more, yet the memory of Shannon and the love they shared, had become an obstacle. He knew life had to go on. He had only ever loved one woman before, now his life seemed to be overrunning with beautiful women, it was a problem that he had never had to deal with in the past.

Would she see him tomorrow, or had it all been an act, only time would tell.

TEN

SCOTT woke later than he would have liked to the next morning. His first thoughts were of the previous evening, especially George. She was, without a doubt, the most beautiful woman he had ever met. He was convinced she had been telling him the truth, and hoped sincerely that he wasn't being blinded by that beauty.

He showered, then dressed in a short-sleeved shirt and chinos, before going down for breakfast. As he ate alone, he remembered the letters that had been handed to him by the reception clerk.

On finishing his breakfast, Scott returned to his room, found the letters and opened them. Two were false business letters, inviting him to visit factories during his stay in Buenos Aries. The third letter, was from AI, it read:

Dear Tony,

Pleased you are able to visit during your stop over in Argentina. I will send a car to collect you in the morning. You can leave the hotel, as we will be able to provide accommodation. We are all looking forward to seeing you again. Love,

Al and Ingrid.

Scott re-packed his suitcase. The letter had made it quite clear he would be leaving. He lay on his bed and waited.

At about ten-thirty the bedside phone began to ring. Scott picked up the receiver.

"Yeah."

"A car has been sent to collect you Sir, the driver is waiting at reception."

"Right, thank you, can you tell the driver I will be down in a few minutes?"

"Certainly Sir."

He replaced the receiver, then completed a final check around the room. Happy that he had packed everything, he left and headed for the elevator.

The doors slid silently open as the elevator reached the ground floor. Juan spotted Scott's case and came over to carry it for him.

"Are you leaving Mister Tony?"

"Yes Juan, I'm afraid so."

"Will you come back?"

"I certainly hope so."

"I will take your case to the car."

"Thank you."

Scott went to reception and settled his account, asking that all the staff be praised for making his short stay so welcome, especially the restaurant staff. With that he went outside to the car.

"Thank you Juan, your English is excellent, I can't speak your language at all." He gave him a generous tip.

"Thank you Mr Tony, thank you, please come again."

"See you Juan, and be good."

Scott climbed into the rear seat of the taxi.

"Hi Tony."

It was George.

"George, great to see you." She was dressed in her taxi driving clothes again, but he could see through the disguise now.

"Did you sleep well?" she asked.

"Like a doornail."

"I do not understand."

"Sorry, in England it means I slept very well thank you. How are you this morning?"

"I am happy."

"Good, bye the way, where exactly are you taking me?"

"I am to take you for briefing."

"I wish you were going to debr. . ." Scott stopped in mid-sentence, realising that he may have miss read the sign of the previous evening. "OK, it's about time I knew what was going on."

George drove through the morning traffic, making her way to the Buenos Aries municipal airport. At the airport she drove across the tarmac to a large hanger, bearing the name of International Exports Ltd. As she approached the hanger, the two huge doors opened enough to allow her to drive straight in. She stopped the car in front of a very tall, imposing man, dressed in a dark suit, white shirt and black tie.

They got out of the car.

"Scott McLenan?" the tall man asked in a quite yet powerful voice.

"Who's asking?"

"Micheal Llewelyn."

"Who is?"

"Your case manager."

"Oh. Since when have I been a case?"

"You had better come into the office."

Scott followed the giant up a flight of stairs, hoping he was friend, not foe. The giant ducked as he negotiated the office door, ushering Scott in after him. The office was basic, one filing cabinet, one desk, and two tubular metal chairs. Scott turned to offer George a chair, but found himself alone with Llewelyn.

"Have a seat."

"Thanks."

"Have you any idea what you are up against Scott?"

"I had a briefing on the way, but I get the impression that nobody knows a great deal."

"That's about right, we are hoping you will fill in a lot of the gaps for us, we know of your military exploits, we think you may succeed where others have failed."

"Why?"

"You have the know-how of the SAS, and you have the motivation, and we think you have the right attitude for a mission such as this."

"You mean you think I'm a prick, and it won't matter a toss if I get killed."

"No. We think you have been a prick, but you are a prick that survives, you can't be trained for that."

"So what do you think I'm getting into?"

"I honestly don't know, I can only tell you, that no one has ever made it back, we aren't withholding anything, we simply and honestly don't know."

"Made it back from where?"

"Barilcoche."

"What's Bariloche?"

"Bariloche is a famous ski resort close to the Andes,

other agents have made it that far, but no further, your brother's wife worked down there, at a local mining company, the trail always ends there."

"I like skiing, and I definitely need a holiday."

"I don't think holiday is the right way to describe your mission."

"So what do you want me to do?"

"We want you to go to Bariloche, break into the mining company, and take a look around." he said. He removed some photographs from an envelope on the desk, and passed them to Scott. They were aerial shots of the mining complex. There appeared to be high fences, guards and dogs.

"Just like that?"

"Just like that."

"And how do I get to this Bariloche?"

"George will drive you."

"Who's paying the fare?"

"You won't be going in the taxi."

"Thank Christ for that, when do we leave?"

"In about two minutes."

"What?"

"In about two minutes, I'm sorry we can't be more helpful, you will virtually have to play it by ear."

"Has anyone told George?"

"Yes, she's waiting for you now, so let's go."

Scott followed him out of the office and back down the stairs. A nice shining white BMW waited for him, engine purring, George at the controls.

"Well Scott, I sincerely hope we meet again, all the best." Llewelyn said, offering his hand.

"Thanks." he said as they shook hands.

Scott walked to the passenger side of the car and got in.

"Let's go skiing George."

She smiled, selected drive, released the handbrake and eased her foot down on the throttle. The car moved forward effortlessly. The hanger doors opened, and they emerged into the bright morning sunlight. The hanger doors closed, it was just the two of them from here.

"You're quiet George, what's the matter?"

"I have waited for a long time to be given the chance to find my brother, now I am frightened."

"Frightened of what?"

"I do not want you to get hurt looking for my brother."

"Don't worry about me, I'm a big lad now, I can look after myself."

They drove on in silence, the bustle of Buenos Aires engulfing them, their thoughts lost in the traffic and noise, their fears causing their stomachs to flutter. Neither of them had ever felt so isolated. Neither of them noticed the Mercedes following at a discreet distance.

They drove all morning, stopping at a roadside tavern for lunch. After lunch, Scott drove throughout the afternoon. As evening approached they began to search for a motel. Eventually they came across a motel that appeared quite modern. They were a few miles out from Santa Rosa. Scott pulled off the road and into the motel car park. They both got out of the car and stretched, it had been a long day.

"We'd better see if there are any vacancies George."

They headed off to the office. George spoke to an unshaven, sweaty man behind the desk. To Scott it sounded as if they were arguing, raised voices, and plenty of arm waving. Perhaps that's how they talk to each other he thought.

Eventually the sweaty man handed over a set of keys. George paid in advance for the rooms, which pleased Scott. They left the office and walked back to the car for the cases.

"What were you arguing about George?"

"There is only one room, we will have to share."

"Oh, do you want to try somewhere else?"

"Why?"

"Well, I hardly know you, you might try and take advantage of me."

"I might," she laughed, "If you are lucky."

"I'll tell me mum." he said coyly.

After collecting their cases, they set off to find the room. George opened the door and entered, followed by Scott. The first thing they both noticed was the double bed.

"I do not believe it." said George angrily. "That idiot at the desk said there were two single beds."

"Well, if you want to sleep on the floor, I don't mind."

"No way."

"You don't snore, do you?" Asked Scott.

"No I do not."

"Well, it's not all that bad then, is it?"

"Do you Tony, or should I say Scott."

"I don't know, I'm always asleep."

"You English are so crazy, are all Englishmen the same?"

Scott laughed. He was unaware that George had asked for a room with a double bed. She had fallen for him during their first evening together. She also didn't want to be left on her own in the middle of nowhere in particular. Scott dropped the cases onto the floor, and slumped down onto the bed. George collapsed onto the bed beside him.

"It's been a long drive George." he said mopping his forehead.

"There is still a long way to go."

"Yeah I know, do you think we will make it all the way?" His question like a double edged sword.

"I'm sure we will." she said, as she drifted off to sleep.

Scott followed the cracks in the ceiling, seeing faces and places. Shannon had only died recently, and yet here he was laying next to a stunningly beautiful young lady, hoping their relationship would go further. He knew it would take a very special woman to help him to get over the death of Shannon, and George was very, very special. His thoughts were of Shannon as he fell asleep.

The singing from the shower room woke Scott. It was George singing an old song called 'Johnny remember me'. He looked at his wristwatch, it was eight in the evening.

The shower and the singing stopped simultaneously. George came into the room wearing just a towel around her waist. Tiny droplets of water glistened on her exposed breasts, as if they were bedecked in diamonds.

"Sorry." Scott said, quickly looking the other way.

"It is ok Scott, please do not be embarrassed, there are no larger towels."

He turned back towards her. She had a fantastic figure, a figure that any top model would have been proud of, sun tanned and perfect.

"You're absolutely beautiful." he said lowering his head.

"Thank you Scott, we have to live and work together, there are bound to times like this."

"Ok, but I hardly know you."

"You English, so stuffy." she said, turning her back to him, and sitting on the bed, drying her hair.

"Right, I'll have a shower, then I think it will be time to eat."

"Hurry Scott, I am starving."

Scott showered quickly, his thoughts locked onto George. In a matter of weeks he had fallen for two women, both perfect, yet in their own individual way, the past years of loneliness, now forgotten, the time span of his future, now his only uncertainty.

He felt fresh and alive as he stepped from the shower. He opened the cupboard door and reached in for a towel. It was a full size bath towel. He wrapped it around himself and walked into the bedroom.

"Who's been telling porkies then?"

George looked at him with a knowing smile growing across her face.

"What is porkies?"

"Pork pies, lies." Scott said.

"Oh, just a little white one." she said sheepishly, suddenly making a lunge for his towel.

"Control you emotions madam." he said, side stepping her, as he did his towel slipped, but he caught it just in time. George laughed loudly as he struggled to control the towel. Eventually he sat beside her on the bed.

"George."

"Yes."

"I'm glad we met, you've lifted a curtain that had come down on my life, now I know I want to live again, I thank you for that."

"Scott." she paused momentarily, "Will you hold me please."

They lay back on the bed locked in each others arms, not speaking, not moving, their heart beats the only motion, the power of the moment lifting their lives out of their respective shadows. They lay together, lost in their own thoughts and memories, each believing they had found their future, each hoping the feelings were reciprocal.

Sometime later George stirred.

"Come on Scott, we must eat."

They dressed quickly, then left the motel in search of

food.

It was nearly midnight when they returned to the motel room. They had found a small tavern, the food had been basic, but nicely prepared.

"Thank you for a lovely evening Scott."

"No, thank you, you're great to be with, I didn't want the evening to end."

She came to him, and kissed him, a long, loving kiss, that needed no further explanation. He began to unbutton her blouse, as she unbuttoned his shirt, still joined in their first embrace. With all their clothing removed, they lay on the bed, hands exploring bodies, kissing as if this would be their last night together, not their first. There was no need for words, their bodies spoke for them. They made love, slowly, carefully, as if each was trying not to hurt the other, wanting their first nexus to last for an eternity.

They slept through the remainder of the night, still entangled in their final, spent, caress.

When Scott woke next morning, he felt the warmth from George's body, as she slept in his arms. He felt he had betrayed Shannon's memory. He felt so guilty. George had come between them, and he hadn't had the strength to resist her. He knew he couldn't, even if he had wanted to.

George began to wake. She smiled as she looked into his eyes. She kissed him, long and hard, and they began to make love again, more intensely, more recklessly than the previous night, their final release, severing them from the past, leaving only their futures, together.

After showering together, they re-packed the cases, had breakfast, and then resumed their marathon journey.

George felt a great sense of release. She had become totally enmeshed in the search for her brother, now she could share the search.

They drove through Santa Rosa heading toward Neuquen and Zapala. The journey was long enough for them to seek out each other's secrets, their hopes and fears. They shared the driving, the BMW taking the mileage in it's stride.

They located a motel close to Zapala, the routine of the evening, much the same as the one previous, only both of them feeling a little more apprehensive, as they knew Bariloche lay ahead.

The following morning they made an early start, the final leg of their journey, being shorter than the previous two. They reached Bariloche in the middle of the afternoon. They drove through the town in search of a hotel, eventually finding the Hotel Panamericano. George parked the car in front of the main hotel entrance. They left the BMW and headed for the reception desk.

"Hi, my name is Tony Hewitt", he said to the receptionist, "I would like a room for my wife and I, I'm not sure how long for at the moment, is that a problem?"

"No Sir, I can book your room for a week, then if you feel you would like to alter the booking, we can do." He said in perfect English.

"Excellent," Scott said, "Where did you learn to speak such good English?"

"I was born in England Sir."

"Where abouts?"

"London Sir."

"There's no trace of a cockney accent now, I'm from Preston in Lancashire, please, don't keep calling me Sir, my name's Tony, and this lovely lady with me, is George."

"Great, well it's very nice to meet you both," he said, shaking their hands. "I hope your stay in Bariloche will be a long and pleasant one, your room number is 204, I'll get the boy to show you the way, have you any luggage?"

"Yes, it's still in the car." Scott informed him.

The receptionist summoned the boy, who then accompanied them out to the BMW. Carrying their cases, he escorted them to their room, which was on the second floor.

"What is your name?" George asked the youngster.

"Pele, I was named after the Brazilian footballer."

"Do you play football?"

"All the time, I will play for Argentina one day."

"I am sure you will, thank you for carrying the cases Pele." Here. She handed him a small tip.

"Thank you, I will be your boy all the time you are here." With that he left the room.

"Look at this view George." Scott called.

George joined him at the window. It overlooked Lake Nahuel Huapi.

"It is beautiful Scott."

"Like you George, perfect."

"Scott, do you love me?"

"You know I do George."

"Then come with me." She led him to the large double bed. They undressed each other and lay down. They held each other tightly, as their bodies united as one. They looked into each other's eyes, then kissed.

Both of them slipped into a deep sleep, the marathon journey, finally taking it's toll.

Scott was the first to wake, quickly realising that it was morning, and that they had slept all through the night. He felt tired and groggy, as if he had slept for too long. He got out of bed and headed straight for the shower, hoping to wash away the musty feeling.

The noise of the shower roused George. She lay in bed thinking of her brother. It had been years since they had seen each other. She wondered if his personality had changed. She wondered if they would still be each other's best friend, as well as being brother and sister.

George got out of bed and joined Scott in the shower. The cascading water brought them both to life. They soaped each other's bodies, arousing their sexuality. They made love in the shower, as the water caressed their passion, their fears for the future, lost in a crescendo of unbridled love.

They realised they had fallen deeply in love, and both gained strength from it.

They left the hotel after breakfast, exploring Bariloche, making tentative enquiries about the mining company. They discovered that the mining company, and tourism, were the two mainstays of the local economy. The mine was situated ten miles south of the town, in an area known as the Argentine Lake District, and was bored straight into the Andes Mountains.

"We have to go and get a look at this mining company George." Scott said, "We won't bother today, we'll set off early tomorrow morning, let's hope we can find your brother."

"I hope so Scott, I miss him so much."

"He's lucky to have somebody like you on his side, somebody that won't give up on him."

"Thank you Scott, we are very close, I know he would do

the same for me."

"So would I."

"I know you would, do you really love me Scott?"

"Of course I do George, why do you ask?"

"Sometimes you seem so distant, as though you want to be somewhere else."

"George. I love you with all my heart, and hope you feel the same for me. But I've been through a lot recently, and I do keep thinking it over, accusing myself of not doing the right things at the right time, causing people near to me, to be hurt."

"I am sorry Scott."

"Don't apologise George, I should be more attentive, especially to someone so beautiful, only an idiot like me could be day dreaming in your company. Anyway, I should be asking you, do you love me?"

"You know I do, forever."

They walked beside Lake Nahuel Huapi, as they talked over their plans for the morning.

That night they ate in the hotel's restaurant. It was named La Rondine, and specialised in Italian cuisine.

They retired early, both of them struggled to find sleep, as they both knew that the dangers that had been distant, were now within reach.

At eight the next morning they left the Panamericano, George driving. Neither of them spoke as their private tensions and anxieties grew. George concentrated on the road, Scott took in the breath taking scenery. They were so encompassed in their own worlds, that neither of them noticed that a shabby, rusting van, had joined them on their journey.

"There it is George." Scott called out excitedly. "Keep driving, don't look.

"Ok."

"Did you see it?"

"How could I, you told me not to look."

"Oh yeah, there were armed guards everywhere, a bit much for a mine."

"Perhaps it's a gold mine."

"Could be, I never thought to ask anyone.

About one hour later, they drove past again in the opposite direction, George wanting to look, in the faint hope she could catch a sight of her brother. Again they drove by without stopping, and headed straight back to Bariloche.

"Why would they need so many guards George?" Scott asked her, as she drove.

"To keep people like you, out."

"Or keep people in."

"How do you think we will be able to get in Scott?"

"We, are not going in, I am."

"No Scott, you must let me come, I want to find my brother, and I want to be with you."

"It'll be too dangerous."

"I do not care."

"Then you should, these people are killers."

They drove the remainder of the way in silence.

Once back in the hotel room, Scott drew a map of the mine outbuildings, to the best of his memory.

"What do you think of the map George?"

"I think you would need the British Army to get in there, too many guards, it is hopeless." She said pushing the map back at him.

"We must get in George, I haven't come this far to give up."

"I am sorry Scott, I am not giving up."

"Good, now then, how do we get in."

"Perhaps you could knock on the door."

"Of course, then they will invite me in, and tell me everything." Scott said becoming annoyed.

"I mean, pretend to be a salesman. What about tours?"

"What do you mean George?"

"Tours for tourists."

"Brilliant, in the hotel lobby there is a rack full of pamphlets, I'll go down and see what there is."

Scott took the elevator to the ground floor. The rack was stacked with advertising pamphlets. He worked his way through them carefully, and found it. It was titled, The Future Mining Company. Scott read with interest. The tours were daily events during the week, including a tour, and lunch in the mine.

Scott went to the reception desk, and booked a tour for

the two of them, for the following day.

He rode the elevator back to their floor. He almost ran along the corridor to their room.

"We're in George, tomorrow." He said excitedly, passing her the leaflet.

She read it. "I hope I will see my brother."

"So do I. On the other hand I'm a little puzzled."

"Why?"

"Guards to keep people out, tours taking people in."

"Perhaps we will see very little?"

"Yes, but we will be able to take a closer look at the outbuildings, to compare them with my map."

That evening they wined and dined, followed by a romantic walk in the moonlight, beneath a cloudless sky. They returned to the hotel and went straight to bed. Neither of them wishing to make love, they simply held each other until sleep came between them.

ELEVEN

MORNING came too quickly for them. They had both slept restlessly. At breakfast they talked over the day ahead, with ever rising trepidation.

At 10.00am, the mining company coach arrived in front of the hotel foyer. Four other guests joined them, along with a number of other tourists, from other hotels in and around Bariloche.

The tour guide, seated at the front of the coach, told them a brief history of the mine, as they drove.

Digging had begun in the early 1930's, by a man the locals named the Mad German. Over time, more miners arrived to help with the expansion of the mine. Rumours spread that he had struck gold. The mad German always had money. Whenever he came in to Bariloche, he would always purchase the best equipment and supplies. The money earned by the mine, and spent by the miners, had boosted the economy of Bariloche. In time, fewer and fewer miners bothered coming into town, as facilities at the mine had become far superior. As more gold was found, the mine owners had to increase security, installing guards and fencing.

The guide waffled on, but Scott had stopped listening, he was taking in the countryside, trying to memorise landmarks, for future reference.

After a drive of about thirty minutes, the coach pulled up at the main gate of the mine. The tourists were invited to leave the coach.

"Here we go George, keep your eyes peeled."

"What do you mean?"

"Keep a sharp lookout for anything that might be important."

"Ok."

They alighted from the coach, and were escorted toward the main entrance of the mine, which was a huge metal door. Inside the door, they could see two mine shaft openings, marked A and B. The tour guides ushered them to shaft B.

They were shown various aspects of mining, even being allowed to talk to the miners. There was also an underground museum, filled with photographs and antique equipment, dating right back to the beginnings of the mine. There was even a photograph of the mad German, but his face meant nothing to Scott.

At the end of the tour, Scott realised he had seen nothing of importance, and certainly nothing mysterious. He asked the guide if they could see shaft A, but was politely refused, on safety grounds.

After their long day, the coach dropped them back at the hotel. They went straight to their room.

"What did you think George?" "I thought it was an odd place."

"Why?"

"I am not sure, perhaps it was too quiet."

"Yes, my own thoughts centred on how few people there were, working or walking about, I believe that shaft B is no more than a dummy,it was all too clinical, when I've seen pictures of mines, they are always dirty places, shaft A has to be our target. We must get in as soon as possible."

"How?"

"We'll break in, cut through the fence."

"While the guards all look the other way?"

Scott thought for a moment. "Yes, exactly, you will divert their attention, while I, cut my way in."

"When?"

"Tomorrow night. We'll spend the day resting and planning. We need to discover as much as possible, then get back out and alert the authorities."

"What about my brother?"

"George, I hate to say this, but I'm afraid your brother must come second to the main operation. If I happen to find him, I will bring him out, but this part of the operation is reconnaissance, I must get in and out quickly, I won't have time to go searching, but I promise you, I will go back for him one day."

"Do you have a plan?"

"A sketchy one. How does this grab you? You drive up to the main gate in the beamer and stop. You get out and have a look round. You then shout to the gate guards, asking them if they could have a look at the car for you. Tell them that it's making a noise. They won't be able to find anything, but you must keep them occupied, for at least two minutes while I cut through the fence. Then get back into the car and drive off, simple."

"Too simple."

"I think the best plans are simple, this way, we both know exactly what we have to do, and when to do it."

"Scott, what is a beamer?"

"The BMW. Also, at night there will be fewer people in the mine."

"That might be a disadvantage." She cut in.

"Yes, on the inside, but not on the outside. Once I'm through the fence, I can use the cover of the outbuildings almost right up to the mine entrance."

"What if it's shut?"

"Then I will have to wait for it to open."

"What do I do?"

"Once you have distracted them, you must go. If I don't make it in, I will meet you here." He said, pointing to a position on his map. If I do make it in, wait there for one hour, no more. If I don't make it back to the car in time, return to the hotel and wait. If I haven't returned by mid-day, assume the worst and contact AI, ok?"

"Scott I am frightened." She said embracing him.

"Good, so am I, fear can be an asset, you are at your most alert when self preservation kicks in.

They spent the next few hours going over the plan, adding details, getting the timing right. Scott knew that nobody had ever made it back. He knew he faced killers who intended to keep their secret just that, secret.

The next day was spent relaxing by the hotel pool. Their conversations were short and irritable, as they were both lost to their own thoughts and fears of the events that lay ahead.

Evening came too soon. Scott dressed in a black sweater and black trousers. George dressed in the shortest of mini skirts. The silence in their room was heavy. At 22.00 hours they left the hotel and it's comparative safety.

At the rendezvous point George stopped the car. Using George's make-up, Scott blacked his face and hands.

"Right George, action stations."

"Scott, please be careful." She pleaded with him.

"You too George, and remember, I will always love you, so don't do anything silly, please."

"I love you too Scott, come back safely to me, please."

"I will, now, at precisely midnight, stop at the gates, keep the guards occupied, I will only need a minute or two, then make an excuse and leave, returning here, ok."

"Ok."

Scott took her in his arms and kissed her. He looked deeply into her eyes, as if looking for a reason to stay with her. He kissed her again and was gone.

Scott moved silently through the night. The sky was cloudless again, he would have preferred it to be overcast. As he neared the mine, he crawled on his stomach, presenting the smallest possible target, gruelling but necessary. One hundred yards from the perimeter fence, he found that the vegetation had been totally cleared. He could only move in between sweeps of the searchlights, as they searched the area in the immediate vicinity of the perimeter fence. He reached the fence with one minute to spare, and immediately began cutting a hole through it.

Near the main gates, George arrived right on time. She got out of the car and kicked a tyre. She bounced each corner of the BMW, as if checking the shock absorbers. A shabby rusting van came to a halt behind her. The driver got out and asked George in Spanish if he could help. She answered in English that the car was making a strange noise.

"Aah, I speak the little English." Said the van driver.

"Could you have a look at my car please?" She asked him in her little girl lost voice.

"One moment."

The van driver walked towards the main gate and spoke to the guards. George felt more confident now that the plan was apparently working. The driver came back with the two guards, while the guard in the tower shone the searchlight on the BMW.

George emptied some gravel from her shoe as they approached, raising her left leg high enough to be sure they would catch a glimpse of her knickers, ensuring their full attention. The guards came right either side of George and grabbed her roughly by the arms, forcing them behind her, and handcuffing her. Next, they took great delight in searching her for weapons, dwelling on her breasts and crotch for an unnecessarily long time. George spat into the face of one of the guards, as he stood in front of her, and kicked him hard between the legs. He howled in pain, much to the great delight of the remaining guards. Regaining his composure, he slapped her hard across her face and mouth, splitting her lip, causing it to bleed. For George, her resistance was over. The laughing guards led her away toward the mine entrance.

From his cover in the shadows, Scott had seen everything. He promised himself that the guards would pay later. He held his position for two hours, waiting for the commotion to die down, waiting for the guards to feel drowsy as the night wore on.

When he felt the time was right, he moved swiftly toward the main gate, where he found one of the guards was missing.

The gate guard didn't see Scott as he came out of the shadow, he only felt the cold, sharp, Sheffield steel of a British Army bayonet, as it pierced his skin, and searched for his heart. He slumped to the ground, dead on arrival. Scott pulled the body into the darkness. Within a moment the second guard appeared, pulling up the zip on his trousers. From out of the darkness, a powerful hand reached out and clamped his mouth shut. Once again, the Sheffield steel eagerly found it's target. As he died, the guard heard Scott whisper.

"Tell your friends I'm here."

He pulled the lifeless body into the darkness, and piled it on top of the other. As a final gesture, he kicked them both. He stood for a few minutes to compose himself, and regain his breath, then silently made his way to the mine entrance, the huge door was slightly ajar.

He quickly made an entry, and headed for shaft A. There was an eerie silence throughout the place. The shaft was illuminated by a reddish orange light, which added to the foreboding atmosphere. Slowly he made his way deeper into the shaft, utilising anything that afforded cover, every muscle in his body, primed and ready for action. About one hundred yards into the shaft, he came to an intersection, the shaft split into two again. The shafts were numbered A1 and A2. The walls of these shafts were as smooth as glass, almost as though the rock had been melted, not hewn. He opted for shaft A1. This shaft was darker than A2, as if closed for the night, the only illumination being provided by tiny blue lights. Scott waited until he was satisfied that his eyes had adjusted to the darker conditions. He inched his way along the shaft, until he came to a door. He tried to open it, but it was locked. He knew he could go no further. He turned to retrace his steps. As he did, large overhead arc lights were switched on, temporarily blinding him, forcing him to shield his eyes.

A few moments passed before Scott could open his eyes. As his eyes opened, he could see a number of automatic weapons aimed at him, he raised his hands in surrender.

"Drop your weapons or die here, the choice is yours." The voice came from nowhere, yet somewhere.

Scott dropped his weapons, he couldn't die yet, he had a job to do. A guard approached him carrying handcuffs. Scott proffered his hands in front. The guard handcuffed him, and then punched him full in the face, as hard as he could. Scott slumped to his knees, hoping to avoid further punishment. A boot caught him on the chin, sending him reeling backwards, already unconscious.

It was some time before Scott regained consciousness. His head ached with a vengeance, and his ribs were also very sore, as if someone had been using them as a football, while he had been laying unconscious. He slowly opened his eyes, but there was nothing to see, as the room was in total, pitch darkness. Reaching outward, he felt the smooth rock of a wall to his left, and moved to lean against it, causing much discomfort to an already aching body. The cold of the rock felt good.

He began to take stock of his situation. He had no idea if George was dead or alive, he only knew that these people killed as and when required. For some reason they had kept him alive, perhaps they intended torturing him, perhaps he was to die when they were ready, and not before. He quickly realised that he could only wait. Eventually, the mercy of sleep returned.

Several hours had passed before Scott woke again.The pounding in his head had dissipated, but his rib cage felt as though it would ache forever. Getting slowly to his feet, he began to feel his way around the cell, it was tiny. He located the door, and felt for handles. There were none. He tapped on the door, hoping for a response. None came. He tapped again, a little harder. This time he heard movement, followed by the sound of bolts being carefully drawn back. Slowly the door opened. The light blinded Scott as it flooded into the room.

"Water. Please, water." He pleaded.

The door closed again, wrapping Scott in a cloak of darkness. He heard the bolts being repositioned. Alone in the black hole, Scott gained strength from his memories of Shannon, and vowing to avenge her death, even from this seemingly impossible position.

An eternity passed before he heard movement again. Once more the bolts were withdrawn. The door opened. Shielding his eyes, Scott could see the mug being offered. He took it, drinking small sips, even before the door had closed.

"Thank you, thank you." He shouted toward the door, there was no response.

The ice cold water was nectar to his throat, yet he resisted the temptation to drink it all, not knowing when he would be allowed another mug. It was also reassuring. If they intended to kill him, why bother with the water. He counted it as a small victory, one step in the long, difficult, fight back, a fight he intended winning. One problem presented itself. Why had they tried to kill him in the UK, but not here? To pass time in his solitude, he began devising his escape plan. He listened at the door. There were no so sounds of people working or talking, just a deathly silence. Perhaps he thought, there was only one guard. He thought back to the two occasions the door had been opened. The guard hadn't talked to him or anybody else, if the fight was to be one to one, he knew he would win. For now, Scott decided to rest and compose himself. He lay on the cell floor, soon drifting of into a tormented sleep, thinking of Shannon. Thinking of George, and the mess he had dragged her into.

He had no idea of how long he had slept, when the sounds of the cell door opening, roused him with a start. Something metallic crashed to the floor, and the door closed quickly. From somewhere above him, a dim red light glowed, illuminating the cell. On the floor he saw the tin plate with food on it. He ate a mouthful using his fingers. Whatever it was, it was disgusting, but he ate it anyway. After about a minute the red light was switched off once more. Again the darkness left him disorientated.

In his dark tomb, Scott began to exercise, press-ups, sit ups, walking on the spot, the aches beginning to ease, his spirits beginning to rise. Eventually he heard the sound he had been waiting for.

The cell door opened. Scott's boot caught the guard squarely in the crotch, sending him whimpering backwards across the passage. With eyes squinting, Scott was onto him in a flash, quickly breaking his neck, relieving him of his pain. He grabbed the guard's automatic pistol from it's holster, checking it for ammunition, it was fully loaded. It was time. Time to let these people know exactly what they were up against.

The successful escape from the cell lifted Scott's spirits to new highs. He looked about. The passage appeared to be endless in both directions. He began to move in the direction he was facing, breaking into a run, putting distance between him and the guard's body.

Scott stopped abruptly. Ahead of him was a metal door. He proceeded almost on tip-toe. At the door he listened, nothing. He attempted to open the door. It was locked.

"Mr McLenan, drop the weapon." A voice said from nowhere.

Scott looked for a speaker or a camera, but could see neither. He tucked the gun into his trousers. He was puzzled. The voice had used his correct name.

"Mr McLenan, I am growing impatient, now drop the gun."

Scott knew they could see him, and reluctantly dropped the gun, kicking it away.

"Thank you. Let me put you in the picture. At present you are one-and-a-half miles inside the Andes, in one of hundreds of passages, with countless locked doors, and many guards. You cannot escape. Make life easier for us all, just obey orders."

Scott realised the situation was hopeless. He answered, "OK." The door opened. Four guards faced him, dressed in black overalls and berets, all with automatic weapons aimed at his heart. Scott decided not to resist. He raised his arms. A guard motioned him to come through the door, which he did. He was sure the guards seemed to be more frightened of him, than he was of them. He was pointed in the correct direction, and pushed forward, along what appeared to be another endless passage. He walked deliberately slowly, until the barrel of a weapon, gave him a sharp prod in the back, suggesting that he move a little faster, which he did. The party marched along five similar passages, until they arrived at yet another locked door. Scott stood still, facing the door. Nobody spoke. Scott began to fear the worst. After an unnecessarily long wait, the door opened with an electronic whirr.

Through the door, Scott could see people, ordinary people, no uniforms, no guns, he knew they had to be the work force.

The gun prodded him forward. He passed through the door, looking left and right. He found himself, in what appeared to be a giant engineering factory. Machines formed neat lines as far as he could see, in both directions, he was staggered by the size of the place. He was prodded forward again. As he walked he passed countless machines, he realised that thousands of people must work here, yet the place was secret. He could only imagine one way to stop people from talking, the thought bothered him.

"Halt." The guard shouted.

Scott took an extra couple of paces to annoy him, he succeeded, the prod in his back confirming it.

The guard removed what looked like a television remote control from his trouser pocket. Pressing a button, a door to the left of Scott opened. Another prod sent Scott stumbling through the door, which closed behind him. He found himself, in a luxuriously appointed office. Classical music played quietly in the background.

Scott sat thankfully into a leather armchair that was one of a five piece suite. He surveyed his surroundings. There were many gold ornaments and figurines tastefully displayed around the office. They looked like Inca or Aztec to him, but he wasn't sure. The walls were adorned with paintings, large and small, illuminated by their own individual lighting, but they held no fascination for him.

The voice from nowhere spoke again.

"You will find a bar in the adjacent room, Mr McLenan, please help yourself."

Scott had died and woken in heaven, or so he thought.

He looked but couldn't see a door. Suddenly a hidden panel slid open. Scott walked through.

He had entered what appeared to be a games room, with a well stocked bar, snooker table and television. On a table in one corner was a computer. Behind the bar, he found a small refrigerator, and helped himself to a bottle of ice cold pils. He played on the snooker table as he began to relax. After three or four more bottles of pils, he lay on the couch, taking time to reassess his situation, but very quickly fell into a fitful sleep.

He had no idea of how many hours had passed when he woke, but overall, he felt well rested, and ready for action. As he rose from the couch, he noticed that another panel had opened. Looking through the panel, he could see the most beautiful bathroom he had ever seen. Hastily removing his clothes, he headed straight for the shower. The cascading water cleared his body and mind as if by magic. He turned the control to cold, then wished he hadn't. He now felt alive.

His thoughts turned to George. How could he rescue her, if he didn't know where she was. He didn't even know where he was. He knew he could never forgive himself if they had harmed her. The thought of losing two loves to these people angered him.

He turned the water off and stepped out of the shower. His clothes had gone, replaced with fresh underwear and a pair of overalls. He had no option but to wear them.

Coming out of the bathroom, he was surprised to see that the guards had reappeared, one of them motioning towards the office. Scott walked into the office, where he found himself surrounded by even more guards, dressed completely in black, the meanest and biggest he had met yet. They also looked far fitter than the ordinary guards, they were obviously some elite force. The outer office door opened. All the guards stood to attention as the man entered.

He was five feet ten tall, Scott guessed, lean in stature, and evil in looks. For a fleeting moment, Scott thought he recognised the face. The man came and stood in front of him, staring at him, unblinking, expressionless. Scott stared back, unblinking, expressionless, trying not to laugh.

"We meet at last McLenan."

"Mr."

The gloved hand slapped Scott hard across the face, his nose began to bleed.

"Still defiant, I like that. You have caused me much trouble Mr, McLenan, and cost me a lot of money, not to mention the people you have killed."

"Well I would like to mention the people you have killed." Scott interupted. "In fact, that's why I'm here."

"Yes I know, but unfortunately there will always be killings attached to a project the size of ours, thanks to you, that number is on the increase."

"I don't know who you are, but if you're the action, I'm the equal and opposite reaction, and I'm ready to react."

"Big words, but futile Mr McLenan, I control your destiny, your life or death is for me to decide, you should try being nice for a while."

"Ok, but not for long."

"Good, you see, I want to tell you a story."

"Why, is it bedtime?" Scott interrupted again.

"I admire your spirit Mr McLenan, please sit down."

They sat facing one another, the leather of Scott's chair squeaking as he sat, it took all his will power not to laugh. The guards were dismissed.

"My story goes back longer than you could guess Mr McLenan."

"Then I won't bother guessing."

"Lighten up McLenan."

"Mr to you. Where's George?"

"That doesn't matter, I want you to save your judgement of me until later, let's start with a clean sheet shall we?"

"Ok, let's hear it."

"The story I am about to tell you, you will find totally unbelievable, please listen with an open mind, because I want you to understand why you are still alive. I want you to take time to think about what I have said, because later, you will be given a choice, you will be able to take your destiny back under your own control, do you understand?"

"I think so, when you kill me, it will be my own choice."

"If you like."

"Well let's hear it then."

"Would you like a drink or something to eat?"

"No." Scott paused. There was a tense silence. "No thank you."

"That's better. Most of my captives are simply killed Mr McLenan, I have no use for them, luckily for you, I think you may be different."

"I was born different, are you going to get on with the story or what?"

"Ok, my story begins, somewhere in the region, of thirty thousand years ago.

Twelve

"THIRTY thousand years, you're right, I don't believe you." Scott was quick to inform his captor.

"Wait, let me tell my story, then judge the whole of it.

"Ok, I'm sorry, please carry on." Scott said, realising that the longer he listened, the longer he lived.

"My story begins at least thirty thousand years ago, during the Paleolithic period, in what is now known as the Neander valley, in West Germanys, Rhineland.

"The Neander valley, isn't that where some old bones were found?"

"Yes, that is correct. The year was 1856. A school teacher named Johann Fuhlrott, discovered the bones, and quickly realised that they belonged to an upright walking, bipedal creature, but not a bear or gorilla. Archaeologists were sent to the region to search for more remains. In one cave, they found what was obviously a grave. Within the grave they made more discoveries. With the skeleton, they found flowers and food, they presumed, to help the deceased on his journey to the after-life, or perhaps a precursor to a form of ancient religion."

"Who was it, your great great-grandad." Scott interrupted.

"Let us not be childish McLenan," Scott's captor said angrily, "why not try listening for once in your life, who knows, even you may learn something."

"Ok, I'm not planning on going anywhere for a while."

"Also in the grave was an artefact, that in 1857, nobody could identify. The archaeologists numbered and boxed everything from the find, and had them transferred to the German Historical Museum, Berlin."

"So what was it." Scott impatiently interrupted.

"I'm coming to that Mr McLenan, I really want you to get hold of the time scale involved."

"Should I take notes."

"I'm beginning to lose my patience McLenan, do you really want to live?"

"Oh, you mean I have choice?"

"Yes, for the time being."

"Then I choose to live." He paused. "For now."

"Good. The boxes lay undisturbed for almost eighty years, until 1935, then something happened, that would change the course of history. An amateur archaeologist was rummaging about in the basement of the museum, when he came across the boxes from the Neander expeditions. Casually, he went from box to box, barely glancing into them, but then he opened box number NV125\1857. In the box was something he recognised instantly, but could not fathom why it should be there. His first thoughts were that it had been placed in the wrong box. After checking with the curator, and the museum records, he realised that the artefact had been placed in the box at the time of discovery, and had remained there ever since."

"Well what was it?" Scott asked impatiently.

"According to the museum records, what had been found, was a ceremonial head dress, possibly used for religious ceremonies. He searched the boxes once again, but there was only this one piece, that was of interest to him."

"What was it?"

"You will not believe me when I tell you."

"Tell me." Scott implored.

"It was a headphone."

"Of course it was, why didn't I think of that." Scott said with more than a hint of sarcasm.

"Do not mock me Mr McLenan, I did warn you, and this is only the start, there is much more that you will find difficult to comprehend."

"You're right, I am finding it difficult, but tell me this, what was it that made him think it was a headphone?"

"Just a hunch, the general shape and appearance of the artefact, he actually tried it on his head, and to his surprise, it fitted perfectly."

"So what did he do next?"

"Well, he still could not believe the find, so he re-checked the records, and spoke to the curator again. Eventually he gained permission to take the artefact away for testing."

"And?"

"He took the artefact to a friend, who was a radio engineer. His friend informed him that the first real breakthrough in radio, didn't occur until 1894, thirty-seven years after the Neander graves were found. His friend agreed. He too, thought the artefact was indeed a headphone."

"What happened next?" Scott asked.

"The archaeologist took the headphone to a Luftwaffe airfield near Augsburg, about thirty-five miles from Munich, and went straight to the radio room. There he explained his theory to the engineers. Thcy quickly wired the headphone into the system, and guess what Mr McLenan?"

"What?"

"It worked perfectly. Not only did it work, but it was superior to anything the Luftwaffe possessed."

"After thirty thousand years, this has to be a joke?"

"No joke."

"You don't honestly expect me to believe this crap, do you?" Scott asked incredulously.

"No, not yet Of course, everybody in the room was stunned, and like you, could not believe it."

"It's hardly surprising is it?"

"No."

"You haven't told me the name of the archaeologist, let me guess, Hitler?"

"No, his name was Hess."

"Rudolph Hess?"

"No, his father. He had worked in Egypt as a businessman, and had become interested in archaeology, mainly through his visits to the Pyramids. Young Hess had served in the Flying Corps during the First World War, and was regularly seen at Augsburg on training flights. It had been at Augsburg, where Hess senior had noticed headphones being used, hence, he was able to make the connection. He informed his son immediately. On seeing the evidence with his own eyes, Hess quickly informed Adolph Hitler, who ordered that the discovery must remain secret. Hitler also ordered, that a new expedition should be funded, to return to the Neander valley in search of further relics.

"And what did they find?"

"Nothing, not at first anyway. Hess senior had gone with the expedition, as an amateur, as reward for his achievement. For months, nothing was found. Hess had wanted to excavate an area previously untouched by the archaeologists, but as a minor member of the team, he had been overruled. So, and much to the annoyance of the team leader, Hess began to excavate the area in his own time. The area he was interested in, was a small hill, he said later, that it was the shape of the hill that had caught his eye, it looked artificial, more man made than natural, he assumed it would be the burial mound of some Neanderthal chieftain."

"And was it?" Scott asked impatiently.

"No. He adopted a new approach. Instead of removing soil from the top of the hill, he tunnelled into it, expecting to find a chamber."

"Did he?"

"No, he did not find anything. The tunnel was prone to collapse, and much of his time was wasted clearing away the loose soil. The work was back breaking, none of the other team members willing help. The expedition was called off after six months of fruitless searching. On the final evening, while the other members of the expedition held a leaving party, Hess went to his tunnel as usual. He believed in his heart, that there was little point in digging, but he did anyway. As darkness approached, Hess finally had to admit defeat. In anger, he raised his pick and slammed it into the Neander soil. He turned to walk away, then stopped. He wondered if he had been hearing things, or had he heard a metallic clang from the pick. He stood, not knowing what to do. He took a few more paces forward, then changed his mind, turned, and went back to the tunnel and lifted the pick. He struck into the soil again, and once again heard a metallic clang. He now dug quickly, scraping the loose soil away with his bare hands, until he had a square foot of metal revealed. He ran excitedly, calling out to the others. They all came rushing to his tunnel. One by one, they touched the metal. By now it was dark, so they rigged up lamps to work by. As they worked, they realised that they were actually on top of the object, and that the hill would have to be removed, as they still had not found an edge. For the next few days they dug, until all of the soil had all been moved. Hess in the meantime had found the edge, and had been following it, trying to ascertain the size of the object. This was to be their next staggering discovery. The object was circular, and looked to be made of aluminium. It had a diameter of sixty feet. Hitler was informed of the discovery, and immediately sanctioned further funding for the expedition. Hess junior left Berlin and headed for the Neander Valley."

"And now you have had your fun, you're going to kill me?"

"Not at all, my story is still in it's infancy."

"Fancy sounds about right."

"Let me continue."

"Keep talking."

"The archaeologists found themselves standing on a sixty foot diameter, metal plate."

"With a ten foot knife and fork beside it?"

"McLenan, do you have any idea, how immature, your inane little remarks make you appear?"

"Sorry." Scott said, and meant it.

"Thank you. Now that it's circumference had been found, they had to dig down. By now Hess junior had arrived, and joined the excited archaeologists in the dig. They had split into two teams, the anti-clockwise team, and the clockwise, digging around and down, both teams competing to expose most of the find. As they dug, they realised that the object was tapered, the top being the lesser diameter. Their excitement grew, along with the growing amount of the object unearthed. After three days of digging, there was an almighty shout from the clockwise crew, they had found what appeared to be an entrance, and it was partially open. The anti-clockwise crew left their side to help, and very soon, all of the entrance was cleared."

"What happened next?"

"Hess senior, was invited to enter the object first, and he agreed, as long as his son, Rudolph, entered with him. He had no hesitation, he was already beginning to sense the enormity of the find. They took torches and entered. What they had found, was some sort of craft."

"What sort of craft, a boat?"

"They didn't know what it was. Their first steps were slow and nervous. Inside the craft, the torchlight showed the interior, to be very well preserved. They were also stunned to see four seats."

"Seats?" Scott interrupted.

"Yes, two of the seats had what appeared to be consoles

in front of them."

"Come on, if you're going to kill me, kill me, but don't patronise me."

"I told you at the outset, the story would be unbelievable."

"Yes, but you didn't say it would be ridiculous."

"Please let me continue, listen with an open mind, I'm not insisting that you believe, I'm only asking that you listen."

"Ok."

"Hess and his father stood dumbfounded, what they were seeing was impossible. Behind the front two seats, were two others, surrounded by banks of knobs and switches. They looked at each other, but neither could speak. They shone their torches around the interior. Hess senior reached out and flicked some of the switches, you'll never guess what happened."

"What." Scott asked excitedly.

"Nothing. Just getting my own back." Said Scott's captor.

"Brilliant."

"Plucking up their courage, they ventured further into the craft, where they discovered, what they could only describe as, sleeping quarters."

"Sleeping quarters, for who?"

"They didn't know who, but there were, what we would call, bunk beds, twenty of them."

"I don't believe this."

"The beds were approximately six feet long, giving them some indication of the size of the crew. Their next discovery had them convinced that they had gone completely mad. Beside each bed was what looked like a locker. Hess junior opened one. His jaw dropped in utter amazement. His father, seeing his son's face, came and looked. They couldn't believe what they were seeing. In the locker was a flying suit, more modern than anything either of them had ever seen."

"Wait a minute, wait a minute." Scott interrupted again. "Are you telling me they had found an aeroplane, thirty thousand years old?"

"No, I'm telling you, but they didn't know it then, what they had found, was a space craft, thirty thousand years old."

"Of course they had, what else could it have been?" Scott said incredulously.

"You're doing it again McLenan."

"I'm sorry, but I think you would need more than an open mind to believe this lot."

"I know, it is fantastic, but let me continue. As I said, they didn't know that it was a spacecraft, but Hess junior, was beginning to think along the lines of, some sort of flying machine. He went to fetch the rest of the archaeologists. As they entered the craft, they were as amazed as the Hess's had been. They stood with their mouths open, like goldfish in a bowl. They were astounded by what the find implicated."

"And what was the implication?"

"Don't you know?"

"No, you tell me."

"The craft was obviously from another world, and it had failed to return. That implies a crew of advanced beings, stranded here, on earth, thirty thousand years ago. Nature being what it is, we can probably guess what happened next."

"Can we, what?"

"We believe they alien beings cross bred with the Neanderthal, to perpetuate their species, or they bred amongst themselves."

"So?"

"So, Mr McLenan, we can only draw one conclusion."

"Can we?"

"Yes, we can. If the North American Indians can be used as an example, we must assume that the alien species were dominant, and the remnants of the Neanderthal tribes, were absorbed into the new society. We believe the graves we found, could have been the remains of the last, true Neanderthals."

"Is that it?" Scott asked, almost annoyed.

"No, the fact that these beings settled in the Neander valley, can only mean one thing, the German people must be direct descendants of them, in other words, they truly are, the Master Race. Until this discovery, the Jews believed they were the chosen people."

"So, are you saying, that Hitler was right?"

"Yes. Hitler had always believed the Germans to be superior, and the find was the proof he craved. Anyway, I'm getting ahead of myself."

"I think I know what's coming next." Scott said. "This is the weapon, that Hitler thought would win the war for him, isn't it?"

"Let me tell the story chronologically. A message was sent requesting Hitler to visit the site. In the meantime, the archaeologists worked harder than ever to dis-entomb the craft. After three days, Rudolph Hess noticed that he could see dim lights on the consoles and control panels."

"Don't tell me, the battery was flat?" Scott said sarcastically.

"Almost, on the fourth day, Rudolph was sat at the controls again, when he realised the control panel lights were brightening, then suddenly, concealed lighting, illuminated the craft. Just as suddenly, all the lights extinguished. Rudolph ran for his life. Outside, he realised the sun had set. His mind raced over the implication, yet he knew it was impossible."

"What was impossible?"

"That the craft drew it's power from the sun."

"Solar power, thirty thousand years ago, no way."

"The next morning, Mr McLenan, before sun up, Rudolph positioned himself in what he believed was the pilots seat, as the sun appeared over the horizon, his father called from outside. Rudolph sat and watched as the panels slowly came to life, followed later by the concealed lighting."

"That's totally unbelievable."

"Exactly. The very same day, Hitler arrived. He inspected the craft, inside and out. The full impact wasn't lost on him. He ordered total secrecy. His excitement was obvious. He gave orders for the craft to be removed to a secret location within Berlin. To Hitler, the craft was the final proof of his destiny. Proof that he had been chosen to rule the world. Proof that the German people had been chosen. He had long planned to rid the world of the Jews, and other unwanteds, in his mind, the craft was his licence."

"Yes, and we all know what happened next."

"No, I don't think you do. The craft was taken to Berlin in the utmost secrecy, and hidden in a secure location. Here, the most senior scientists were assembled to assess it. They assured Hitler that the task of back engineering the craft would be quite simple, and very soon, the production of the machines could begin in earnest. Hitler was elated. It was probably this moment in history, when the tides of the future began to flow against him. It was 1935. The scientists constantly reassured Hitler that they were making significant progress, the truth was, they were making almost none. The technology was far to advanced, they were faced at every turn, by a machine that defied understanding. By 1936 they still hadn't been able to open or close the door. They were well aware of the Fuhrer's temper, and so an elaborate labyrinth of lies and misinformation, began to surround the craft. By 1939, Hitler was assured the craft was about to enter the production phase. Impatient for expansion, Hitler ordered the invasion of Poland. As you well know, this led Great Britain into the Second World War. Would you like anything to drink Mr McLenan?"

"No thanks, I'm finding this history lesson absorbing, please carry on."

"As the Allied bombing of German factories increased, it became obvious that the craft had to be moved. The one safe haven at the time, was Argentina. Quickly and efficiently, the whole operation migrated to Argentina, including families."

"Here?"

"Yes, the mine workings were only moderate at the time, but sufficient for the scientists to work in peace. Rudolph Hess was one of the few men that Hitler could trust, in fact he was his Deputy Fuhrer. He came to Argentina to take command."

"No he didn't, he flew to England." Scott said indignantly, as if discovering a flaw in the story.

"Actually, he flew to Scotland."

"I don't understand."

"Do you understand the word 'Dopple-ganger'?"

"Yes I do." Scott replied.

"On the 10 May 1941, Rudolph Hess took a Messerschmitt 110D, and flew to Scotland, hoping to land at his friend, the Duke of Hamilton's, estate. On the same day, Rudolph Hess boarded a U boat, and sailed for Argentina. One Hess parachuted from his plane, landing near the village of Eaglesham, south of Glasgow. The other Hess, was never seen again."

"What was the purpose?"

"Hitler needed a strong leader in Argentina. However, if it had been discovered that Hess had come to Argentina, the Allies would have known something significant was in the air, and would have sent agents to search for him. Simple solution, let the Allies capture him, the deputy Fuhrer, what a prize, a real ego booster."

"So who did the Allies have in Spandau?"

"That's irrelevant, but I can say, he was the most loyal servant one could wish for."

"So you are saying Rudolph Hess lived out the remainder of his life in Argentina?"

"Yes, with his wife Ilse, their son Wolf-Rudiger, and also his father, coincidentally, both Rudolphs died during the same year, 1987, both aged 93.

"Why his father?"

"I will come to that later, suffice it to say, that Hess planned years, rather than days ahead."

"So, you must be Wolf-Rudiger?"

"No. Let me continue. As more Germans were secretly brought to Argentina, the mining complex grew, allowing experts in each field to design their own departments. Once here, there was quite literally nothing else to do but work on the craft. From this time, exciting progress was visible to all. They quickly mastered the techniques, of solar acquisition, what today you call, solar energy, converting sunlight into electricity by means of photoelectric cells."

"Yes, I know what solar power is." Scott said impatiently. "What next?"

"The next major breakthrough was lasers."

"Lasers?"

"Yes, remember, we are years ahead of the so called 'super powers'. During the war, the technology became so advanced, that if parts manufactured in Germany had been captured, nobody would have known what they were."

"And I assume all this research was being funded by the Nazi treasure?"

"That depends on what you mean by Nazi treasure."

"Stolen gold, and art collections, why, is there something else?"

"Let me come back to that later. To get some idea of the scope of their success, answer this question. How many of the worlds leading electronics companies are German?"

"Plenty."

"That's right, each one is living testament to the discoveries made here. Even so, progress was still hindered by the war, as parts and materials failed to arrive, or arrived months late. Hitler became more dispirited, he had been promised craft that would win the war and present him the world, yet the reality was, that the craft were years away from flight."

"Did Hitler ever visit Argentina?"

"No, he trusted Hess totally, and it would have been far too risky. No, Hitler controlled research in Germany."

"What research?"

"The craft would be solar powered, but the scientists knew that weight limitation was vital, and they required crew members, small in stature, miniature adults if you like."

"And where did they find them?" Scott interupted.

"We made them."

"Of course." Scott said sarcastically. "What did you use, one of Adams ribs?"

"No Mr McLenan, we used Auschwitz. Experiments in miniaturisation failed completely. Next, experiments on children took place under the guidance of Dr Mengele. The idea was to implant an adult brain into a child's skull, needless to say, the results were horrific, and all experiments failed. Dr Mengele is a name still despised throughout the world, yet he made a discovery that today, creates great joy and happiness, among people the world over."

"What was that?"

"In Vitro conception."

"Test tube babies?"

"Yes, the worlds first test tube baby was born in a laboratory at Auschwitz, not only that Mr McLenan, it had been genetically engineered to fit the requirements of the craft, the year was 1940."

"This is all very hard to believe."

"I know, but it's true. The first babies were grotesquely deformed, the head to body ratio was way out, but they survived, long enough for further experimentation. The Jews were less than nothing in the eyes of Mengele, he was unconcerned with how many died, to him it was no different from modern day animal experiments. As he became more successful, Hitler decided to move him and his team to Argentina. Eventually they created the perfect miniature human. From the day of birth, their whole life was programmed toward piloting the craft."

"And did they?"

"Oh yes."

"I don't believe you."

"You will. It was becoming obvious to Hitler's advisers, that the tide of the war was beginning to turn against them, and it was suggested that Hitler seek refuge in Argentina. Hitler to his credit refused, saying he would stay, and fight out the war with his people. It was at this time, that Dr Mengele suggested a new idea to Hitler."

"What was that?"

"You wont believe it, but I'm going to tell you anyway. Mengele's idea was simple. Hitler and Eva von Brown would donate sperm and eggs, to be taken to Argentina, where Mengele could produce children, who could one day lead their country again, in the name of Hitler."

"You're joking?"

"I'm not, Hitler named the donations, the Nazi Treasure."

"I thought the Nazi treasure, was gold and art collections?"

"So did the Allies, to this day, special agents still search for the stolen gold and art, but the real treasure is here. We still hold many of the sperm and eggs that they donated, hardly any have been used."

"Are you telling me, that you're scientists have tried to create a new Hitler?"

"Yes."

"Successfully?"

"Not the first five, the sperm was found to be very weak, the scientists believed that Hitler was a drug addict, which was affecting his sperm, however, after these initial failures, a new technique was tried, that compensated for these weaknesses. The new technique was a complete success."

"Are you telling me, that out there somewhere, there is another Hitler running loose."

"No."

"Well what are you telling me?"

"I'm telling you, that you are talking to him."

Scott's mouth dropped open, it tried to utter something, but failed. Before him stood the son of Adolph Hitler. His mind tried to evaluate the consequences of what he had been told, but struggled to come to terms with the enormity of it.

"Impossible." Was all he could manage to say.

Thirteen

SCOTT looked at Hitler. He found everything that he had been told, extremely difficult to believe. Hitler sensed his suspicion.

"I want you to keep an open mind for the time being, if you are not convinced by my story, then so be it, but I think you will be."

"What you have told me, raises many questions."

"Ask them, if I can answer them, I will."

"Why did Eva commit suicide?"

"Hitler had confided in her, she was well aware of what was happening here, she could not be allowed to live, as it was, she decided she could not live without my father, so the choice was hers. They committed suicide at half-past three on the afternoon, of Monday, April 30th."

"Did the Russians really find their bodies?"

"No. The Russians found two bodies in the Chancellery gardens, and for their own propaganda purposes, they declared them to be, Hitler, and Eva."

"So what happened to the bodies?"

"Have you heard of Odessa?"

"Yes."

"The network was created to help top Nazis escape the purges, that would surely follow the end of the war. Their most important assignment was to remove the bodies of Adolph and Eva, to a safe haven. This they did."

"Are their bodies here?"

"No, I can tell you no more about them."

"Have you seen the bodies?"

"No, honestly." He replied to Scott's suspicious look.

"But you know where they are?"

"Yes."

"Why didn't Hitler and Eva come to Argentina, it seems everybody else did?"

"My father knew that the war would never end if he lived on, he knew that the work here was more important than one man, his death ended the war and the Nazis, in the eyes of the world."

"Why did so many Nazis come to Argentina after the war?"

"They had heard the rumours, but of course did not believe them, but when everything else crashed around them, they came here in the hope of finding some way of resurrecting the Nazi party. As it was, their coming here left a trail anyone could follow, but this place was so secret, not even our own could find it."

"How did you keep it secret, somebody had to build it?"

"The various parts were manufactured all over Germany, no factory knew what the parts it manufactured would be used for. As the mine workings grew here, more and more of the manufacturing processes were moved here. We did have a minor success before the war was lost."

"What was that?"

"The Americans named them, the Foo fighters."

"Oh yeah, little balls of light that trailed the bombers?" Scott said, knowing something at last.

"They were not balls of light, they were metallic discs, remotely controlled. They appeared to glow at night because of the action of the photoelectric cells, which, curiously enough, made them invisible in daylight."

"What was their purpose?"

"In truth, they were actually too small to do anything but fly, they were purely experimental, but my father secretly hoped they would have some sort of psychological effect on the air crews, but the idea failed."

"A lot of Hitler's ideas failed."

"True Mr McLenan, but if men did not try, and did not have failures, perhaps we would still be living in the Neanderthal caves."

"You are." Scott said, pleased with his little victory.

"Very droll Mr McLenan, progress is built on a foundation of past failures, but the Foo fighters were our first LPC's."

"What's LPC?"

"Light powered craft, they were in essence, a miniature version of the Neanderthal craft. Through them, our scientists knowledge of light amplification accelerated."

"So now you were able to make the craft, and the crews to fly them?"

"Exactly, the 'in vitro' project was a huge success. We could manufacture humans that only knew the mines, they had no desire to go outside, they were totally unaware of an outside world. We gradually built our own workforce. In fact Mr McLenan, you have killed some of our best products."

"Which ones?"

"All of them."

"They were all home made, I don't believe you."

"It is true, the beauty of it is, that when they die, nobody misses them, nobody comes looking for them, it is perfect."

"It's gruesome." Scott said, as his face grimaced.

"But necessary. Our miniatures were ready to fly, but we did not achieve flight in a full-sized craft, until 1946. So near Mr McLenan, so near. If my father had managed to hold off the Allies for one more year, the world would have been very, very different, today."

"So you had the perfect flying machine, flown by a perfect crew?"

"No, in fact, far from it. The photoelectric cells, were, if you will forgive the pun, light years ahead, your scientists had actually dismissed light as a power source, but ours still had one major problem."

"What was that?"

"We could achieve daylight flights, but not night. Our cells were incapable of attracting sufficient night light to power the craft."

"So what happened next?"

"Can you not guess?"

"No."

"1947 happened."

"Well it would after 46."

"Mr McLenan, try and take this seriously, does the name Kenneth Arnold mean anything to you?"

"Yes, he was the first person to report seeing space ships, somewhere near Washington I think." Scott felt quietly pleased with himself, for at least knowing one minor detail. Everything that Hitler had told him so far, although ridiculous, did add up.

"Correct. Mount Rainier to be exact, except they were not space ships."

"I suppose you are going to tell me they were yours?"

"Exactly, our first squadron, and our first big mistake, or so we thought at the time."

"Why?"

"The LPC's were supposed to be above top secret. Unfortunately, on that first full squadron flight, all of the navigational computers were rendered useless by the effects of a huge solar flare. Our wonderful new craft were totally lost, they were forced to fly below the cloud ceiling, to regain their bearings, that is when Arnold saw them. That is when our luck changed. Arnold radioed the airfield telling them what he had seen, by the time he landed, the press were waiting for him. It was a member of the press who coined the phrase, Flying Saucer. Now, there is only one direction that spacecraft can come from, so the world looked towards the skies, and our secret was safe again."

"Were they manned?"

"Oh yes, using our specially manufactured crews."

"You mean the dwarfs?"

"No, I mean miniature adults, they were just like you or me Mr McLenan, except for the skull to body ratio. Their skulls were out of proportion, due to the adult size of the brain."

"I suppose all this emanated from Auschwitz?"

"That's right. At about this time, our scientists began to make major strides in the solar power field. As the solar panels increased in efficiency, so the conversion and amplification increased, causing a special effect that nobody could have imagined."

"What was that then?"

"As the craft powered up, they became invisible, we still do not know why, we literally had to switch them off to find them, now we realised we could really cause some confusion."

"How?"

"Just imagine the scenario Mr McLenan. You see from your bedroom window, what you believe to be a UFO, in other words, spaceship. You rush to find a camera, then as you are about to take the world's finest UFO photograph, it disappears before your eyes. To all witnesses it can mean only one thing, fantastic speed, yet in reality, it is still there. This gave us control, we could decide when and where the craft would be seen, the UFO buffs call the effect, a UFO flap."

"So you are behind all the UFO stories?"

"Not necessarily all of them, but the majority."

"Why did you abduct people?"

"We did not perform any abductions, these stories are the invention of sad, lonely people, craving a moment of notoriety. Some of the early 'abductees', thought they would be able to make money out of their ludicrous stories, but most of them became the laughing stocks of their communities. Later 'abductees', tried to lend authenticity to their stories, by announcing that they did not want payment, they just wanted to know the truth. The truth is Mr McLenan, there are no 'abductees'."

"I'd always hoped there would be aliens, coming to save the planet from mankind, never mind, what happened next?"

"Our next exciting breakthrough also came in 1947, that was the NLP's."

"Excuse my ignorance, what's an NLP?"

"Come on Mr McLenan, think."

Scott thought.

"Give up? Night light panels. These latest panels could accumulate enough light from a night sky, to give us night flight. These fantastic panels also brought with them a new problem, or so we thought. As the panels gathered light, from whatever source they could, they gave off a reflected coloured light, which was clearly visible in a night sky. The colours ranged from blue to red and white. Once again we can thank the ordinary man for diverting attention away from us. To anyone who witnessed them, they were still alien craft, it was a simple deception that we did not even have to manipulate."

Scott interrupted. "I've seen coloured lights over the UK, and I knew they couldn't be ordinary craft."

"Definitely not ordinary. We flew hundreds of test flights at night, up until the accident, then the test programme had to be severely cut back, at least until the dust had settled."

"Dust had settled on what, exactly?"

"The Americans called it The Roswell Incident."

"Yes, I've heard of the Roswell Incident, the Yanks made a right pigs ear of it."

"What is a right pigs ear of it?"

"It means, they made a complete mess of it."

"Yes. Ok." Hitler said, still certain that the British were a law unto themselves.

"The Yanks denied it all didn't they?"

"They had to. It was July 5 1947, slightly more than a week since the Arnold sighting. During that day, people resident in Roswell, reported seeing a large disc- shaped craft fly over the town. Some even reported that the craft had appeared to have stability problems. That night, a local rancher reported hearing a large explosion, but had dismissed it, as being caused by a thunderstorm that was taking place at the time. The rancher's name was William (Mac) Brazel. Later the next day, Brazel came across a large debris field on his property. He collected a pickup full of a strange metal, and took it back to the ranch. On hearing stories of the flying discs, he contacted the authorities. The Americans got into a tangle by releasing two different versions of what they had recovered. Within a few days, the Americans began receiving reports of another crash site, causing absolute panic among the top echelons. The area was quickly sealed off, and guarded by armed soldiers. At this latest site, the Americans found two crashed, saucer-shaped craft, and a number of bodies. The appearance of the bodies elevated the panic level. One of the beings lived for forty-eight hours after the crash, but did not regain consciousness."

Scott interrupted. "How do you know it lived for forty-eight hours?"

"All the miniatures had transmitters placed within their bodies, the transmissions from these were picked up by our receivers and stored in data banks, everything from heartbeat, blood pressure, brain activity, it was all stored for research, we knew the exact moment the last pilot died. The best part of it all, is that the Americans were now totally convinced that aliens had landed. What they actually had was another of our failures. The two craft had indeed been caught in the thunderstorm, and had actually collided. The debris field that Brazel discovered, was in reality, debris from both of the craft, that is why it was so widespread."

"So what happened to the bodies and the craft?"

"They are now stored at a location known as Area 51. Of course, the Americans deny the whole incident. We know they recovered the transmitters from the bodies, what they did not know, is that the senders worked perfectly for years, until some boffin took them to pieces. They were so accurate, we even knew which hangar of Area 51 the bodies were stored in. At Area 51, the Americans have started on the same long road that we set off on, all those years ago, they are back engineering, in fact, a lot of today's little trinkets have their origins in our two craft."

"I don't understand." Scott said, puzzled by the statement.

"The Americans being their usual arrogant selves, have claimed certain discoveries as their own, for instance, micro chips, CD ROM, even pocket calculators and electronic diaries. Even PC's have their origins here, the miniature versions used onboard the craft, had the Americans baffled for years, until they realised the potential of the micro chip."

"Are you saying all these gadgetry things were invented here?"

"No, we copied them from the craft."

"So that leaves the Yanks forty to fifty years behind in the race?"

"More now, their egos got in the way for many years, they considered it more important to land on the moon before the Russians, than to spend large quantities of dollars, back engineering the two craft, now they are more motivated. One mistake the Americans made, was to believe that Wernher von Braun was one of our top people."

"I think I know the name, but I can't think why, who is he?"

"Von Braun was the director of the German rocket research centre, based at Peenemunde during the Second World War, his rockets were powered by liquid fuel, they relied on brute force to punch their way through the atmosphere. The very nature of their fuel made the rockets very dangerous, and their range finite. The truth about von Braun, is that he was not considered competent enough to become involved with a project of this magnitude."

"Did von Braun know of the craft?"

"Not from us, or, I suspect, from the Americans. To the Americans, he was still a German, I doubt they would have confided in him over something as sensational as the two craft. Actually von Braun unwittingly helped us, by pointing the Americans in the direction of the moon, this project used up valuable resources, leaving very little, by comparison, to be spent on the craft."

"So what happened next?" Scott asked.

"After the loss of the two craft, we totally changed our programme. We had to make use of the fact the Americans thought they had captured spacecraft and aliens. Also, it was decided to make the majority of test flights over sea, if we lost a craft, at least we could be reasonably certain no more would fall into the wrong hands."

"How many craft have you lost altogether?" Scott asked, beginning to admire the achievements of the Germans.

"Eight. We know the Americans have two, one crashed in the UK, and five are unaccounted for, one of which started a war, but I will come to that later."

"One in the UK, that's been covered up well."

"Yes, we do not believe the British have managed to recover it, in fact, they may not even believe that it is there."

"Where?"

"Loch Ness." Replied Hitler

"I don't believe you."

"It is true. Thankfully, the loch is very long and very deep. The chances of it being located are slim, the British could not mount a search without causing a lot of interest, so we believe they have decided to leave it, let it rest in peace, it would cause more problems if they recovered it."

"Why don't the British want a craft of their own?"

"Like I said, they may not even know they have it."

"So where are the others?"

"At the bottom of the sea."

"Any particular sea?"

"Most have been lost in an area you might know as the Bermuda Triangle, we test fly here, because the area has attracted the attentions of all the crazies, one more UFO sighting among all the other unbelievable stories, is soon forgotten."

"Are you responsible for any of the disappearances?"

"Yes, not boats in the area, but quite a few of the aircraft that go missing can be attributed to us."

"Do you shoot them down?"

"No, of course not. Our LPC's can reach tremendous speeds, any plane passing close enough, is hit by a shock wave that disintegrates them, we try to avoid contact because of this, and of course, security."

"So you have never deliberately downed a plane?"

"No, but we did sink a number of ships."

"How and why?"

"Certain people betrayed my father, the profits of their betrayal allowed them to become shipping tycoons. The ships they own, regularly passed through the Bermuda Triangle. Once we had the technology to destroy them without trace, we did."

"What technology."

"It is complicated, but put simply, every motor produces waste, or exhaust, our motors are no different. Our motors produce what the scientists have termed, Black Light. This light is harnessed and accumulated, then fired as a beam, it destroys totally.

"It's bloody evil."

"Name a weapon that is not evil, is your bayonet any less evil, it may be more personal, but the result is the same, death."

"I take your point, but why would you want a weapon of such power?"

"Think about it, Mr McLenan."

Scott thought for a few minutes, what was in his mind, he didn't like.

"Like father, like son, you want to carry on in your father's footsteps don't you?"

"Absolutely. And I am going to succeed, I have the craft that my father should have received, we may be half a century late Mr McLenan, but his dream will come true."

"I get it now, the father, the son, and the unholy ghost of the Third Reich."

"Not the Third Reich, the Fourth Reich, and I will rule the world Mr McLenan, I will rule the world."His voice had risen to a crescendo. "It is the destiny of the German people. We are the master race. We will rise from the ashes, and the rubble and blood of Berlin. We will remember those who humiliated our nation, they will bow their heads to the new power, they will hear the voice of Adolph Hitler as he speaks again from the dead. I will rule the world McLenan, have no doubts, I will rule the world." He slammed his fist into his desk, as if to denote that his pronouncement was over.

Scott felt the hair rise on the back of his neck. He had seen films of Hitler at Nuremberg, he had used his voice to stir a nation from it's complacency. Now Scott could hear that voice again.

"And the Argentine government have stood by and allowed you to use their country as a base?" Scott said calmly.

"Yes, of course, they are unaware of the real nature of the project. They offered a safe haven to the fleeing Germans, during and after the war, for as long as it was required. Peron distanced himself from the war itself, but he could see the commercial value of permanent lodgers. We pay a fortune to lease this land, and in taxes, like any other business.

"So the Argentine government don't interfere in anyway?"

"No, that is not strictly true."

"What do you mean?"

"They helped us during the Falklands crisis."

"I don't understand." Scott said.

"Yet another of our craft crashed over the Falkland Islands, we believed it had actually crash landed onto West Falkland, the date was 25th March 1982. We were panic stricken, if news of this craft had leaked out, it would have meant the end for us. I contacted the Argentine government, and asked them to invade the islands and seal them off, due to the top secret nature of our craft, promising to finance the operation."

"Wait a minute, you have enough money to finance an army, to finance a war?"

"Yes, of course." Hitler replied without hesitation. "On 2nd April 1982, the Argentine forces invaded, there was a small amount of resistance from a company of Marines, but that was quickly overcome. We then sent in our special recovery team, to locate the craft and remove it as soon as possible, unfortunately, they found nothing, they quickly realised that the craft must have crashed into the sea, the rest, as they say, is history."

"Let me get this straight, because you thought a craft had crashed onto the Falkland Islands, hundreds of Argentine and British servicemen lost their lives?"

"Yes, I am afraid so."

"Did you pay for the war with the Nazi treasure?"

"Yes."

"So you know where the treasure is?"

"Yes, but I can say no more on this."

"So the Argentine government are going to help you rule the world, is that it?"

"No, we won't need them when the time comes, hopefully there will be no bloodshed either."

"When is the time?"

"Soon, we are almost ready Mr McLenan, you may even be part of our brave new world."

"What have you done with George?"

"Nothing."

"I don't believe you."

"Well you can, she is fine, do not worry about her."

"Earlier, you said you could prove this story of yours, so why don't you?"

"I can prove it, come with me."

Scott followed Hitler into the adjoining room. Hitler went over and faced a large wall that was covered with a beautiful mural.

"What do you think Mr McLenan?"

"I'm not really into pictures."

"This is not called a picture, it is a mural, watch."

Hitler took what to Scott looked like a TV remote control from his pocket. He clicked a button. Scott could hear the faint noise of a motor start up. The mural quietly slid upwards, revealing a huge panoramic window. Scott wanted to say something, his mouth moved involuntarily, miming words, but no sound came out.

Beyond the window he could see the spacecraft. It's beauty captivated him. He felt as though he had forgotten to breathe in. Concealed floor lights illuminated the craft perfectly. It appeared to be made of aluminium. He stepped nearer the window. The craft was round, and huge, standing on four legs, at the base of which, were round, padded plates. Scott could not see any windows, or a door. He was awe struck.

"Oh my God it's true." He said at last.

"She is beautiful. Just as I told you."

"When did you build it?"

"We did not build it Mr McLenan."

"I don't understand."

"This is the craft that Hess discovered."

"Thirty thousand years old, no way." To Scott the craft appeared to have been manufactured only recently, it's metal so bright and shiny, it's design so ultra modern.

"At least thirty thousand years old, we do not know for sure, it could be more."

"It looks like new to me, it's unbelievable, it's beautiful, tell me it's not real."

"It is real Mr McLenan, believe me, it is real."

"Can I touch it?"

"Of course, but let us have lunch together first."

For the first time since his capture, Scott knew what time of day it was, although now, it seemed irrelevant.

"I couldn't eat now." Was all Scott could say.

Hitler pressed another button on his remote control. A hidden door opened beside the panoramic window.

"Come on then Mr McLenan, we can eat later." He said, offering Scott the chance to walk through first, with a wave of his arm.

Scott hurried through, eager to touch.

"Conditions are controlled in here at all times, we are unsure as to what erosion may occur if the craft was left in normal atmospheric conditions."

"It's bloody beautiful," Scott said walking towards the craft, "I've always believed in UFO's, but I never thought I would see one, I can understand how you Germans arrived at all your conclusions."

They approached the craft. Scott looked up in awe at the machine. It's massive structure, certainly did have the appearance of being built recently. He had never seen anything so unbelievable. He could fully sympathise with the Germans for being completely captivated by their find. Realising that it was at least thirty thousand years of age, made the craft even more enigmatic. If Scott had been asked to describe the craft, he realised that the most fitting description would have been, 'flying saucer'. He began to look for more detail on the body of the machine, but there was none. He walked up to the machine and touched it, as if to confirm that it was a solid structure. He stood back.

"This is one story my grandchildren will never believe." He said, shaking his head in disbelief. "Does it fly?"

"Oh yes, but we do not fly it, for obvious reasons."

"How do you get in it?"

"Entry is quite simple, or I should say, it is simple now."

He pressed another button on his remote control. Directly in front of Scott, an otherwise invisible door opened, followed by the unfolding of a stepladder. Scott stood shaking his head from side to side, convinced that he was watching a sc-fi film.

"I'm going to wake up in a minute." He said. "Can I have a look inside?"

"Of course Mr McLenan, be my guest."

Scott began to tentatively climb the ladder, suspecting a trap. Hitler laughed at his obvious suspicion.

"Go on, it is alright."

"I'm sorry." He said. "I've seen too many Bond films, where the floor opens up, and the victim falls to his death, sorry."

He continued his ascent, then entered through the door. Hitler followed. The interior of the craft was exactly how Hitler had described it. The four seats, the consoles, the banks of controls. Scott felt like a child with a new toy. He walked round the cabin with a big, silly, uncontrollable grin on his face. He sat in what he believed to be the pilot's seat. Hitler sat in the co-pilot's seat.

"Impressed?" Hitler asked.

"I'm much more than impressed, this is stupendous Mr Hitler, I'm beginning to realise how your father came to the decisions and conclusions that he did, it's magnificent."

"You can call me Adolph if you like."

"I'm Scott."

"Yes I know."

They shook hands as if meeting for the first time.

Fourteen

I REALLY can't believe this." Scott said.

"Well it is time to start believing Scott, this is the proof of my story." Adolph replied.

"It's very hard to believe the time scale, thirty thousand years, and still looks as good as new."

"Yes, what is even more unbelievable, is the small amount of work we had to do, to bring it back to this condition."

Scott didn't answer, he sat playing with the controls and switches, like a child on Christmas morning, twisting knobs, using the joystick as if the craft was in flight, all the time looking about for something new to admire.

"Adolph, this is the coolest, can I take it home with me?"

"I am afraid not Scott, when the rest of the world's people are shown the craft, we hope their reaction to it will mirror yours, we hope they will believe in it enough to accept one leader. We can prove that millions of people have been lied to, this is only one proof."

"What if the people think you borrowed it from Hollywood?"

"They might, it will be our task to convince them that it is authentic. We have film of the discovery, and we hope to take it on a world tour."

"Did your father ever sit here?"

"Yes, his reaction was identical with yours, but even sat inside the craft, I am sure he still doubted it at first."

"I can understand that, I've always believed in UFO's, but sitting here inside one, that is something else."

"Would you care to look at the rest of the craft Scott?"

"Does the Pope pray?"

"Pardon?"

"Sorry, I mean try stopping me."

They both left their seats. Adolph pointed Scott in the right direction and followed him.

Scott's thoughts turned to the beings who came to earth,

and presumably, never left. Thirty thousand years ago, these spacemen would have appeared as gods to the Neanderthals, he wondered if they had bred amongst themselves, or had been forced to interbreed with the Neanderthals in order to survive on earth. He turned and entered the first door he came to. He found the bunk beds just as they had all those years ago, and just how Adolph had described them. He opened one of the lockers, and there, just as Adolph had said, hung a spacesuit. He shook his head in disbelief. The suit appeared thoroughly modern, and would not have looked out of place, if it had been worn by the Space Shuttle pilots.

Adolph tapped him on the shoulder causing him to catch his breath.

"What are you thinking?"

"I'm thinking it's beautiful, I'm thinking about the crew, if they were stranded here on earth, what does it feel like when you realise that you are not going home." Scott added the last part of the sentence to gauge Adolph's reaction. There was no reaction.

"I do not think we can ever know exactly what happened Scott, but the discovery of the craft certainly convinced my father that the German people were the chosen people, not the Jews. To him, this was the overwhelming proof that the German people were superior in every way, and had been for thousands of years, I do not think there can be any doubt that these advanced beings were our forefathers, perhaps soon we will be able to prove it beyond doubt. Perhaps Germany, is the true 'promised land'."

"How?"

"DNA testing Scott, we have bones from the Neander valley, we have the German people, if we can find a match, who could argue against it?"

"DNA, that's way above my head."

"And mine to be honest, but my scientists say there will be no problem."

Scott looked around the sleeping quarters, utterly amazed.

"It's a good job the craft wasn't found in the UK, the aristocracy would have arrived at the same conclusion as your father, they are already convinced that they are somehow unique, way above your average earthling."

"Are you impressed with the suits?"

"Most definitely, I can imagine how Hess' father felt when he first saw them, as well as the craft."

Scott wanted to explore further, with Adolph's permission he left the sleeping quarters, with their bunk beds as described, and moved deeper into the craft. Following Adolph's directions he came to what appeared to be a dead end, immediately his suspicion was aroused.

"What's this?" he asked Adolph, pointing at the blank metal wall.

"Watch." He said, as he clicked a button on his remote control. Another apparently invisible door slid open, as with the outer door, the fit had been so perfect, Scott had been unable to see it. Adolph led the way. He descended a metal stairway, with Scott following. Scott couldn't see very clearly, as the concealed lighting was very dim, but with another click of his remote control, Adolph made the lights brighten.

"Fanbloodytastic." Scott exclaimed slowly.

"This is the power plant Scott, please do not embarrass me by asking how it works, but believe me, it does."

Scott surveyed the apparatus, it was awesome, he had never seen anything like it before in his life, and never would again. There were pipes and tubes everywhere, dials and gauges proliferated, the closest example he could think of, was the intestines of a submarine.

"Fanbloodytastic." Scott repeated.

"You like it then?"

"Wake me up, I must be dreaming?"

"It is not a dream Scott, touch it." Adolph invited. "In laymen's language, the outer panels gather light from any and every available source, the light is accumulated and converted into energy by this little baby." He said, affectionately patting the huge machine that Scott was caressing as he talked. "And that is it, easy when you know how."

"Where did they come from, are they coming back?"

"We are uncertain of their origins. However, Alpha Centauri is a triple star system in the constellation Centaurus, Alpha Centauri C, otherwise known as Proxima Centaura, is the closest star to our solar system, only 4.3 light years away, perhaps there is a hidden planet, much like ours, I believe we will never know."

"Maybe their planet had been as badly abused as ours, and they had to leave, perhaps the crew were the last remnants of a dying civilisation."

"Very possible, perhaps every advancing technology abuses their home planet, in the name of that advancement, which can only ultimately lead to space travel, the space travel becoming absolutely essential as the home planet dies from abuse, they find a new planet, and then the vicious circle process begins again. I would imagine that, if my theory is correct, we could be the latest in a procession of planetary exchanges, after all, the Americans are already planning their escape from earth, probably to Mars."

"Who gets to go, it won't be ordinary people like me?"

"Exactly, that's where we enter the equation. Our scientists and engineers, have already solved that problem. We have manufactured giant craft, capable of carrying many people to the new home planet. There will be people left behind, we will only want good citizens, we will even take animals, in DNA form, our craft will be nothing less than a modern version of Noah's Ark. Our problem is convincing the masses, that we really are the only hope they have.

"How will you do that?"

"That is not for me to tell you at this stage, but we are sure we have the answer."

"Are you implying there is more to this than just an ancient spacecraft?"

"I can say no more Scott, when I feel that I can, I will."

"Is it bigger than this?"

"Much bigger, please do not ask any further questions, unless they are to do with the craft."

"Sorry, but I'm beginning to believe you, and I want know more."

"Have you seen enough of the craft?" Hitler asked Scott, trying to steer him away from his secret. "Would you like something to eat?"

"Not really, I'm fascinated, there is one small question that is puzzling me though."

"Then ask it."

"In England you tried your utmost to have me killed, now I'm your captive, I'm receiving this history lesson, why am I still alive?" Scot asked in a puzzled tone.

"I believe I am good judge of character Scott. You have killed some of my top men, that makes you special, I need special people for me, not against. I am showing you all this in the hope that you will join us in our mission. I believe that if you can come to terms with our history, you can become part of our future. Ultimately the choice will be yours."

"And what if I don't like your future?"

"The project must remain secret, you are alive because I have chosen it, staying alive will be your choice."

"That seems to have narrowed my options?"

"Listen to me Scott, I want you to feel overwhelmed by this craft and all that goes with it, you have always been a rebel, you have always been a survivor, you know the world has to change."

"For better or for worse?" Scott interrupted.

"Come with me." Hitler ordered, leading Scott back up the stair and out of the craft. He led him back to his office.

"Sit." He ordered, pointing to the chair he wanted Scott to occupy.

Hitler sat behind his desk. For what seemed like an age, he stared at Scott. Neither man looked away. Hitler pressed a button ion his intercom.

Hitler pressed a button on his intercom.

"Send Albert in please."

"Sir." Came the sharp reply.

The office door opened. Scott turned to see who the newcomer was. It was an absolute giant of a man. Scott steeled himself for a beating or a fight, though he couldn't think what he had said wrong. The giant approached Scott.

"What would Sir like for lunch?" the giant asked with a slight growl in his voice.

Scott relaxed. "What can I have?"

"Anything." Hitler replied.

"Well, fillet steak and chips would fill a corner."

The giant turned and left the room without further comment.

"I get the impression he doesn't like me?"

"He hates you, you killed his brother."

"I hope he takes it as a warning. How can he have a brother if they are all home made"

“They were brothers made from the eggs of the same donors. Would you like to know which one was his brother?”

“Would it matter?”

“No.”

“Then I don’t need to know.”

Hitler stared at Scott again.

“I am sure you would fit in perfectly here.”

“We’ll see.”

They began a long conversation taking in the craft, the Second World War, the third, if there was one. Scott listened intently, and found himself in total agreement with a lot of Hitler’s ideas. They had talked for about twenty minutes, when their conversation was interupted by the re-emergence of the giant, carrying their lunches on trays. As Scott watched him enter, his eyes lit up. Closely following the giant was the beautiful George. Scott leapt from his chair.

“George, are you alright?” he asked taking her in his arms.

“Of course, why should I not be?”

“I saw the guards hit you.”

“They had to.” She said matter of factually.

“What do you mean, had to?”

“Try a guess Scott?” Hitler said, smirking.

“No, just tell me.” He said, addressing George.

“It was my task to bring you here. I had to make certain that you entered the complex, once I had been hit, your macho ego took control, you just had to come and rescue me.” she said mockingly.

“You shit.” Scott said shaking his head.

“Calm down Scott, it is the oldest trick in the book.” Said Hitler laughing.

“You bitch, so all that whimpering about your brother was a load of bullshit?”

“No, he did come here, and has never been seen since, but only because he works here. He had been with AI for long enough as a double agent, so he came up with the plan to disappear, then along came his loving sister desperate to find him, and AI were happy to take me on board.”

“Very clever.”

“Yes, we think so. When events in the UK began to go wrong, we realised that someone like you would surely make it to Argentina, sooner or later, I was the obvious choice by both sides, the rest you know."

"So it was just a job to you?"

"At first."

"What's that supposed to mean?"

"It means I began to fall in love with you, but I know it cannot be." She said with her head bowed, unable to look him in the eye.

This statement worried Scott. He knew now that they were going to kill him, it was just a matter of time.

"I have another little surprise for you." interrupted Hitler. He leaned towards his desk and pressed a button on the intercom. "Send in the dis-information officer please."

A moment passed in silence, then the office door slid noiselessly to one side. The elegant lady almost marched into Hitler's office, she turned and faced them. She was quite tall for a woman. She had a short, almost manly, blond hairstyle. She wore no make-up. Her two-piece suit was immaculately pressed. The white blouse beneath her jacket was unbuttoned just enough to expose a small percentage of her cleavage. She turned and faced them.

Scott's heart missed several beats, then began pounding in his chest. His left arm raised involuntarily as he pointed at the newcomer.

"I don't believe this," he said shaking his head, "I just don't believe this."

"It is true." Hitler said, obviously delighted at Scott's reaction.

"Hi Scott." Said the lady.

Scott didn't reply at first, he was totally lost for words. He took a step towards the lady, as if for a closer look.

"Lynn?" He said in disbelief.

"Of course."

"But, you're. . ."

"Dead. No, not yet." She interupted him.

"Well who is then?"

"My double of course."

"My double of course." Scott mimicked. "Well that makes everything Ok then doesn't it?"

"Now now, let us not quarrel," Hitler intervened, "eat your lunch Scott, it will give you time to think it all through."

“I’ve lost my appetite, your surprises are too much for me.”

“Come ladies, I think we should leave Scott to his own thoughts for the time being.” He ushered them out of the office. Turning to Scott he said.

“Take time to come to terms with your situation, you can meet the ladies later if you wish.” With that he left the office, the door sliding closed after him.

Scott sank back into one of the chairs holding his head between his hands. Thoughts became entangled in his mind as he tried to unravel the events so far. He realised he had been so skilfully used that he had failed to notice. To be fair, he thought, he hadn’t been looking. He was angry with George, he was angry with Lynn, they would pay later, especially George, she had tarnished his love for Shannon, he could never forgive her or himself for that.

Scott remembered the meal, looking at it, he suddenly remembered his hunger. He lifted the tray onto his lap and ate voraciously, the meal had cooled, but he didn’t care. He wondered if it was to be a ‘Last Supper’.

Scott’s mind turned over and over, the flood of information inundating every corner of his brain. The choices were obvious now, go along for the ride and live a little longer, resist and die, he quickly reached a decision.

The meal finished, he poured himself another drink, downed it in one, then poured another. He had a feeling that he was being watched, probably by hidden camera, so he sat down looking toward the spacecraft.

After a few minutes the office door re-opened. Lynn marched into the office almost soldier-like.

“What do you really think of it all Scott?”

“To be honest, I think you are the biggest shit on earth, and if I get the chance to kill you, let me assure you that I will, but the craft is awesome.”

“I know you can never forgive me, but please try and understand why.”

“Oh, I understand lady, you allowed my brother to be killed in the name of progress, did you get promoted for your loyalty?”

“No. You don’t understand. I believe the world needs to re-assess itself. The people deserve to know the truth.”

"Whose truth, Hitler's or yours?" Scott cut in.

"Scott, listen to me please, your life depends on the next few hours, try to understand what is really happening."

"Well why don't you tell me?"

"Everything you have been told is true. Hitler does want to rule the world, but not in the way his father would have. He believes that one ruler can unite the world, we must leave this planet eventually, but it will need all the people of earth working together to achieve it."

"Why?" Scott asked.

"Fossil fuels are finite, when the reserves begin to dwindle, there will be world- wide wars for control of those reserves, the human race could easily destroy itself in the fight, but if the people are united in a quest for survival, that won't happen."

"So Mr Hitler is our saviour?" he said mockingly. "Not only does he think he can rule the world, he thinks he is God Almighty as well."

"No Scott, that's not it."

"Well what is, it, then?"

"We believe our destiny is to proceed with the journey."

"What journey?" Scott cut in again.

"The journey began by the builders of the craft."

"Where to?"

"We are going to Mars via the moon."

"Of course, where else?"

"Don't. For all we know we may be going back. Nobody knows where the craft came from."

"The Moon and Mars are both dead planets surely?"

"At the moment."

"What is that supposed to mean?"

"The Americans found signs of life on the Moon."

"Bollocks." Scott interrupted, becoming convinced he was hearing a bedtime story.

"No Scott, it's true, on the dark side of the Moon, there were signs of life."

"Like what?"

"Buildings."

"Yeah yeah, made of cheese?"

"Don't be ridiculous."

"You started it."

"Do you want to hear this or not? I'm losing my patience, you can die now if you like, I really don't care."

The tone of her voice caught Scott's reply in his throat. He realised now, without a doubt, that his life meant nothing to her.

"Go on."

"We believe the buildings must be connected to our craft, perhaps an outpost, we just don't know at the moment, and obviously we can't approach the Americans. We also believe they detected something dangerous, whatever, they have not been back to the Moon since."

"Like what?"

"Your guess is as good as mine."

"Or you're not telling me?"

"We don't know. Honestly." She added seeing the look in his eyes.

"So why do you want to go there?"

"If there is life, we hope they will recognise the craft, they will know then who we are."

"After all this time, I don't think so, does he think he can rule space as well?"

"No, he believes that by revealing the Moon's secrets, the people of the Earth will unite as one people, with a common goal, that is, to escape mother Earth."

"So where does Mars come into it?"

"We believe Mars will be favourable to the creation of an atmosphere, Mars has polar caps, we also believe there to be vast oceans of frozen water beneath the Martian surface."

"But nobody has made it to Mars yet?"

"Only the unmanned craft, but we are talking about the future Scott, and I might add, the not too distant future."

"You're crazy, you really believe the world will unite under the banner of this clap-trap?"

"Not just the craft."

"Well what?"

"I'm not at liberty to say anymore."

"Great, God only knows what you people are up to, and let me guess who will be making all the profit, A H in person?"

"You still remain unconvinced Scott?"

"I've seen your tin-pot craft, I've no doubt Hollywood could make one that would fool me."

"But what about this place, you know something must be going on here, people have died to keep it secret?"

"Yes I know, so convince me."

"Wait here, I will be back shortly." With that she left the office.

Scott felt very lonely and vulnerable all of a sudden. He had no weapons except his hands. His gut feeling was that he had said too much. He made a silent promise to Shannon to at least try and take one or two more of the enemy with him. He wondered if anyone would ever miss him. Probably not he thought, that's why they had used him.

The office door slid open. He could hear muffled voices in the passage outside. He steeled himself for the final showdown.

"Scott." Lynn called out. "Come on."

"Where?"

"Come on, and see for yourself."

"See what?"

"For heavens sake Scott, do you want me to hold your hand?"

"Ok, but stand away from the door."

He moved to the wall furthest from the door and inched his way along, never taking his eyes off the opening.

"What are you playing at?" She asked.

"Just checking."

"Come on before I change my mind and shoot you myself."

"You really know how to reassure a guy don't you?"

He walked to the doorway, suspiciously looking either way down the passage. Lynn watched him shaking her head.

"Follow me, and don't be silly, there's nowhere to go, ok?"

"Ok."

He followed her obediently, the passages seemed to go on forever. At each door she used an electronic gadget to open them. He knew he had to have one, if he was to have even a remote chance of escape.

"Is it much further?"

"No, almost there, come on."

They walked for a few more minutes before encountering yet another door.

"Are you ready for this?"

"For what?" He said feeling apprehensive once more.

"For this." She pressed a button on the gadget and the door opened. "After you."

"Ladies first."

Lynn went through, closely followed by Scott.

"Oh my God." He said in a stunned whisper.

Before him was a massive complex. Row after row of LPC's stretched as far as he could see. Hundreds of people milled about, obviously maintaining the craft. He noticed that they did not wear uniforms. There were no guards. He could hear people laughing, talking, whistling, the atmosphere was almost surreal.

"Impressed?"

"Am I already on the Moon?"

"No."

"It's just what I imagined a Moon base would look like. Yes, I am more than impressed."

"Good, we hoped you would be, do you find yourself beginning to believe the rest of the story now?"

"Oh yes, I might be a bit slow on the up-take, but even I have to believe this."

"Come on." She led him down a flight of metal steps to ground level.

"If you want to ask questions or board the craft you can do, I will leave you for now, George will be here shortly to look after you." She turned and walked away.

Scott watched her go, trying to imagine her goose stepping back to the Fuhrer's office to report. He stood glued to the spot as he surveyed the scene. It was almost too incredible to believe. The craft were real. They were attached to hoses and wires and computers, to him it looked like they were being jump-started. He found himself beginning to admire the achievements of Hitler and all these people. He involuntarily reached out and touched the nearest craft, pulling his hand away as if he had been burned.

"Would you like to look inside Sir?"

Scott swung around startled.

"Would you care to look inside Sir?"

"Sorry, I was miles away, yes please."

"My name is Hienz Grubber, I am the pilot of this craft, LPC 159."

"My name is Scott McLenan, pleased to meet you."

"Come, if you have any questions, please ask."

Scott followed him up a flight of stairs, a smaller version of the sort used to board planes.

"Would you like to sit in the pilot's seat?" Hienz asked.

"Try stopping me, will you teach me how to fly it?"

"It's not that difficult actually, everything is controlled by computer, all the pilot does is point it in the right direction using a fairly conventional joy-stick."

"Can I take it for a spin, excuse the pun?"

"I think we would both be in trouble if you did."

"How many LPC's are there?"

"At the moment we have two-hundred-and-seventy-three complete and working, I believe the target is three hundred minimum."

"What do you mean, target?"

"There must be enough craft to show to the world, like you English say 'first impressions'."

"Are you really free to leave?"

"Yes, but I have not met anybody that wants to yet, what is there to go back to?"

"You say 'go back', so I take it that you weren't born here, so where are you from?"

"A small town in West Germany called Detmold, where are you from?"

"Preston, England."

"I know Preston."

"You're joking, how?"

"I studied at Oxford University for four years, while I was in England I travelled extensively, Preston was a good place to stop on the journey to Scotland."

"And now you are a flying saucer pilot?"

"Yes, although we do not call them flying saucers."

"What's this?" Scott asked pointing at a large red control.

"It is the E and E control."

"What's E and E?"

"Entry and exit."

"What, through the earth's atmosphere?"

"No, through the front door." Hienz said.

"I don't understand."

"There is only one way in or out of the complex for the

LPC's, the opening is barely large enough for the craft to pass through, this control enables the craft to be guided externally, much like the robotic assembly lines of a modern car factory."

"Oh yeah, I've seen them on the telly, I suppose that invention originated here?"

"It certainly did, it's simple but very effective, we sell our robotic systems all over the world, but unfortunately we are unable to claim the glory."

"Do you really believe this one ruler theory?"

"Well, think about it for a minute Scott. Under one ruler there would be no wars. First, we would ban all religions, as they are mostly hypocritical and certainly not built on truth. There would be no need for military forces, every country would benefit financially by not having to waste so much expenditure on arms. There would be no ruling classes. There would be no borders, are all these such bad dreams?"

"No, I don't think so."

"Tell me Scott, how many people die every year in the name of religion?"

"Too many."

"That is right, and do their various Gods really want that, I do not think so?"

"It's a valid point, I just can't believe all the tin-pot leaders will just let you walk into their countries and ruin their lifestyles."

"What are you saying?"

"I'm saying there is bound to be bloodshed, and if you don't believe that, then you really are kidding yourself."

"When the people of the world see the LPC's, they will want to be part of the Fourth Reich."

"During the last war, you couldn't even convert all the German people to your way of thinking, never mind a whole world."

"I think it was Hitler's methods that people disagreed with, not the idea."

"What are your plans for overcoming resistance?"

"We honestly believe the craft will win the people over, they will realise at once that their own governments have lied for years, they have deliberately covered the problem up in the hope that they could eradicate it before it developed, there won't be any bloodshed."

"It all sounds to good to be true Hienz."

"It will be ok Scott, you will see."

"If I live long enough."

"You will Mr McLenan." The voice from behind startled him. It was Hitler.

"I have just been discussing the bloodless take over with Heinz, did you forget to tell him how many people have died in the UK recently?"

"The people in England died for the greater cause."

"And I'm sure they're all very happy about it, the fact is you killed my brother for what you thought he knew, when he actually knew nothing, all the others died as a direct result of that."

"McLenan, I do not like people to question my motives."

"Exactly my point, that makes you a dictator, just like your father."

"I think it is time you made a choice McLenan, you are either for us or against us, life or death."

"I will need a few days to think about it."

"You have very little time." He turned and called." Lynn, take McLenan to his room."

From outside the craft he heard her reply.

"Yes mein Fuhrer."

Scott descended the steps behind Hitler, and watched him march off surrounded by scientists and bodyguards.

"Fuhrer, I thought those days were over?" He asked her.

"It was never over Scott, just put on hold."

Fifteen

THERE'S one thing puzzling me." Scott said as they walked away from the craft.

"And what might that be?" Lynn replied.

"How did my beautiful English rose become rooted in all this horse sh', I mean manure?"

"It's a long story, but I'll try and keep it short," she sighed. "It all began with my grandfather, he disappeared during the Second World War, missing presumed, you know the sort of thing, anyway, at the time, my grandmother was pregnant carrying my father. She woke one morning to find a wounded British soldier, unconscious and bleeding heavily, in what was left of her back garden. She nursed him for almost two weeks, keeping his presence secret from the Gestapo, until she managed to locate other British soldiers who took him back to their lines. One day, while working in the back garden she found a wallet, looking at the pictures inside, she realised that the wallet obviously belonged to the British soldier. At the end of the war she was able to post the wallet to England, sending a photo of herself and a letter explaining how she had come into possession of the wallet. A few months later there was a knock at her door, and guess who it was, yes, the soldier, he had been posted back to Germany and had come to find her and thank her, especially for her bravery during the war. One thing led to another and they married, eventually moving back to England, by this time my father was a few months old. When he was old enough, my grandmother explained to my father that the man he regarded as his father, was actually his stepfather. From this moment on my father was haunted by the desire to trace his real father, and to learn as much as he could concerning the Third Reich, and in particular he tried to find out if his real father had survived the war. When I was old enough, I helped my father with his research, and without boring you to death, that is just about it really."

"So are you related to this lot?"

"Yes, my grandfather didn't die during the war, he came here, he died sometime during 1946, saving my mum from becoming a bigamist. You see, he had been a coal mine manager before enlisting, his expertise helped to design and develop this place."

"How did you find out, if this place was so secret?"

"I can't say too much, suffice it to say that the Third Reich still has many supporters in Germany."

"I see, the old Kraut network?"

"If you like."

"Some things never change."

"What do you mean?"

"You Germans are still killing people, nothing has changed."

"I know, and it saddens me, honest." She added noticing Scott's look of utter disbelief.

"How many murders have you Germans decided on, as your limit for your bloodless take over?"

"Scott, you don't understand."

"I understand perfectly, history is about to repeat itself."

"No Scott, I don't think so."

"Then think again lady, these craft are weapons not toys, they are designed for no other reason than to kill off the resistance. Wake up Lynn, you're staring World War Three in the face."

"No Scott you're wrong, when the nations of the world realise just how advanced we have become, they will want to join and share our knowledge, the poor strive to be rich, not the reverse."

"So you see yourselves as benefactors not murderers, well try spreading your goodwill amongst my brother and all the other innocent people that now lay dead in England thanks to your peace-loving Fuhrer."

"What people?"

"Ask Hitler, he knows, he gave the orders, England is littered with his victims, I'm sure he didn't bother asking any of them to join him in his new-world."

"I don't believe you." She said indignantly.

"Then what am I here for, my bloody holidays?"

Lynn couldn't answer, after all the years she had spent

wrapped in the beliefs of her father, she found it impossible to believe, any negative information regarding the Fuhrer, whom she regarded as a symbol of peace, ready to lead the new world forward, in the name of peace.

"Why am I here?" Scott cut into her thoughts.

"Vengeance."

"For what reason?"

"The death of your brother."

"Wrong. For the death of my brother, and my lover, and God knows how many others. Remember the concentration camps Lynn, how many Germans knew about them, yet how many people died in them, stop pretending for once in your life, this place means death on a wide scale and you dam well know it."

"But it's different this time Scott, believe me."

"Is it?" Scott said angrily. "Megalomaniacs never change their spots, nothing will be allowed to get in his way, for Christ's sake, can't you even see that?"

"What lover," she said changing the subject, "the reports I read said you were a drunken drop-out?"

"Was."

"And what are you now?" she said sarcastically.

"Captive in the new free world, you tell me what I am, do I have a future?"

"You've had a look around the complex, do you see slaves or people working freely for a brighter future?"

"Lynn, to me you are all slaves, slaves to one man's ideology, locked away in a mountain for years, that's not my idea of freedom."

"I know what you are saying Scott, but believe me, once we have sufficient craft, we will throw off the shackles of secrecy and show the world our achievements."

"That sounds like a borrowed speech, why so many craft?"

"We want to show the craft to as many countries as possible, simultaneously. We want the ordinary people to see them, to realise how advanced we are, we want the ordinary people to want to be with us, then following the Fuhrer's unification speech, the people of the world will unite under him."

"Or else," Scott interupted, "the North American Indians

were overpowered by a superior race, but I don't recall any stories of them begging to join it."

"It's right here, not far now." She said, directing him to his room.

They walked on in silence, both busy with their own thoughts. As they approached yet another door Lynn stopped him.

"Now Scott, I want you to close your eyes."

"Don't I get a bag over my head, like normal?"

"Just close your eyes Scott, it's a surprise."

"Not nasty?"

"For heaven's sake, if the Fuhrer wanted you dead, by now you would be, close your eyes." She said, losing her patience.

Scott reluctantly closed his eyes. She took him by the hand and led him through the door as it opened.

"Now," she said, "you can open them."

"Oh my God, I don't believe it." Scott said shaking his head.

"This is hangar 2, these for want of a better name are our the mother ships."

Before them stood five gigantic LPC's, as far as Scott could ascertain they were about twice the size of a jumbo jet. They appeared to have been constructed of aluminium, replicas of the craft that Hitler had shown him, only on a huge scale.

"Unbelievable." He said. "It looks like a scene from a science fiction movie."

"Yes, we are rather proud of them," Lynn smiled, "would you like to look inside?"

"Try stopping me! You know, I've heard stories of giant craft, but didn't believe a word of it, have people seen these on test flights?"

"Yes, we knew the disbelief caused by the small LPC's, once people began reporting these, we knew they would be classed as loonies, and they were, come on, let's take a look."

They boarded the nearest craft, if Scott had been amazed earlier there were even more shocks in store for him.

"This is the cargo deck." Lynn said with the wave of an arm.

"God!" was Scott's only reply.

"Come on," she said, "follow me, these escalators lead to the passenger decks."

Scott followed saying nothing, he began to wonder if the beating had sent him insane, or perhaps he was unconscious and merely dreaming it all.

"You're quiet?"

"I know, the magnitude of everything I've seen is too much for a humble sqauddie to take in, am I dreaming or what?"

"No Scott, the dream belongs to the Fuhrer, these are the reality that will make his dream come true, on this craft there is seating for five-hundred passengers, it can accommodate five-hundred tonnes of cargo, impressed?"

"Oh yes, are these light powered as well, and what is their purpose?"

"Yes, they are light powered, their purpose is simple. In our world the people will be able to live wherever they wish, these craft will transport them and their belongings, the energy is free, so there is virtually no cost, save the pilot's wages."

"Fanbloodytastic, I don't believe it." He said in awe.

"It's all true, remember, we've had fifty years of uninterrupted research, plus a model to work from, we were well ahead by the end of the war, eventually the Americans would have achieved this technology."

"What do you mean 'would have'?"

"When we unite the world, all our technology will be shared."

"Sounds almost too good to be true."

"I know Scott, but do you agree that the people of the world have wasted far too long fighting each other?"

"Yes I do agree, but you must see that most wars erupt when one man tries to impose his will on others."

"That's true, but the Fuhrer is a thoroughly modern man, he believes in people and their freedoms, but there will always be a need for, if you like, a hierarchy, to control daily life."

"And let me guess, the hierarchy will be German?"

"Well, yes, I suppose so, to begin with." She stuttered.

"Exactly, and that's where the trouble will kindle, until it bursts into flames, the flames of World War Three."

"You're just an old pessimist."

"I think realist may be a more accurate description. Don't misunderstand me. I am totally impressed by what you have achieved here. It is nothing short of miraculous, there is so much to be admired, but I still believe your plans fall well short of a united, peaceful world. Every person on earth has a dream, if your world doesn't fit that dream, there can only be conflict."

"I see what you are getting at, but we believe the people will see what the future can and will be through us, we are trying to create a heaven on earth, is that such a bad idea Scott?"

"No, but lives have already been lost in the name of your heaven, how many more must die before conditions are perfect?"

"We sincerely hope that now you are here, the killing is over."

"I don't understand."

"The timing of the unification is everything, what we don't need are false rumours, information leaks that could easily cause great misunderstanding. We want to announce our intentions to the whole world simultaneously, you were the only thorn in our side, now you are here, we hope you will be convinced of our sincerity."

"What if I'm not?"

"Then you will have to remain here until the unification is complete."

"Brilliant, your free world will have it's first political prisoner, before the end of day one. Can't you see, it's beginning to go arse over head all ready. I'm not even your first mistake, the bombings caused an outrage in the UK, is that your idea of Utopia? I witnessed both of the UK explosions, it's time you stopped kidding yourself about Mein Fuhrer, nothing will stop him, except death."

"You're wrong Scott, honestly."

"Am I, how many other deaths does he have on his score card?"

"None, we knew Danny was working for the secret service, so we fed him with misinformation, but never anything of worth, so when he suddenly disappeared, we knew he had found out something big."

"So you killed him?" Scott interupted.

"Yes, it was unfortunate."

"Unfortunate?" Scott said raising his voice.

"Yes, back in England we realised that Danny had discovered the identity of the head of UK operations."

"Surely not that useless lard arse Bell?"

"I don't know Bell, he must have been a minor agent."

"Who is it then?"

"I'm sorry, I can't tell you that."

"Why not, I'm not going anywhere?"

"No, I mean I can't tell you, I only know her code name."

"Her!" Scott said.

"Yes."

"Well what's her code name then?"

"Marigold."

Scott couldn't help but laugh. "Now I know you're lying."

"Look Scott, I've said too much already, come on, I'm supposed to be showing you to your room."

"I don't want to go to my room just yet, is there nothing else to see?"

"There is something you may enjoy."

"Then please show me." He implored her, hoping to buy himself a little more time.

"Ok."

She led him down a series of passages until they arrived at another metal door, using her remote control she opened it, Scott passed through.

"Jesus H Christ," he mumbled as he surveyed the latest revelation, "an underground village!"

"No, not exactly."

"Then what exactly?"

"It, is a city

"It can't be." He said incredulously.

"Yes it is, it's not actually that difficult to construct, many ancient civilisations have done much the same."

Scott recalled seeing television programmes investigating underground cities. He felt a need to impress her by using their names, but could only remember one, Petra. He could see that there were streets with names and street lamps, pavements with people milling about, shops with window shoppers and customers, in fact, it looked like a scene from any normal, above-ground city.

"I'm finding this all very difficult to take in, it's incredible to say the least. There is one thing puzzling me at the moment, why are there street lamps when the place is so perfectly illuminated anyway?"

"Simple really, at night the day lighting is switched off and the street lights come on, it's to make it feel more natural."

"You appear to have thought of everything?"

"Yes, we like to think so, one of the major problems was keeping people here, so it was decided to build a city better than anywhere else on earth, so that hopefully, nobody would want to leave."

"And what is the name of this beautiful conurbation?"

"Berlin of course, this has been the true capital of Germany since the end of the war."

"Are you telling me that nobody ever leaves?"

"No, but before they leave, the Fuhrer makes them swear an oath of allegiance and silence, remember that almost all of them have relatives here."

"Of course, Hitler would put all this at risk on a promise, come on, get real Lynn, tell me, how many have ever returned?"

"I don't know." She said peevishly.

"Yes you do," Scott said angrily, "it's none, isn't it?"

There was no reply.

"It's none and you bloody well know it." He shouted.

She ignored him. They walked on in an angry, threatening silence. Scott fearing he had said too much, Lynn fuming at the fact that this unimportant nobody could raise a doubt about her beloved Fuhrer. She had curtailed his tour of the city and was heading him straight to his room. As they passed through the LPC hangars, the intercom system burst into life, it requested them both to return to the Fuhrer's office. Scott's fears began to heighten as he sought a means of escape. They entered the Fuhrer's office.

"Ah Mr McLenan, I do hope you have enjoyed your guided tour, how would you rate our achievement?"

"One, I most certainly have, and two, if I hadn't seen this with my own eyes I would never have believed it, it's fantastic, and you deserve any credits coming your way."

"Well thank you, I had hoped, quite sincerely, that you

would be impressed, I know you are not entirely convinced about my ruling the world, but can you disagree with the idea of a perfect world?"

"Nobody would disagree with your motive, but I firmly believe you will have great difficulty with your method, why do people like you always build weapons for peace, it's like having sex for virginity?"

"I believe the sight of the LPC's cruising the airways of the world, will convince the masses of their particular governments hypocrisy and ineptitude, these craft are the future, a future that no other leader on earth can offer, a future where all are equal."

"In my book people aren't equal, they don't want to be equal, people are individualistic, eclectic, how dare you insist that people should consider themselves as equals, it will never happen, it never has in the past, and it wont in the future."

"You have a very cynical outlook Mr McLenan."

"I don't think so. In my country, do you really think that the Queen believes that I am her equal, because I have no illusions of being her equal?"

"But that's exactly my point Mr McLenan, in my world there won't be a Queen."

"And how equal will you be Mr Hitler?"

"There must be a leader."

"Exactly, but what if I want to be the leader, after all, we are all going to be equal?"

Hitler ignored the question, he didn't much like being interrogated by his captive.

"The people of your country have already accepted a united Europe, surely what we are striving for is the next logical step?"

"We voted for the Common Market, it was the politicians that forgot to mention a united, political Europe. My belief now, is that the German people realised that they could never invade Great Britain with an army. So you quite intelligently decided, to fool our easily led, gullible politicians, into believing that we are all friends, and we should all work and live together, happily ever after, am I right?"

"Well done Mr McLenan, now you are beginning to think like a German. Of course, I have not personally been involved from the beginning. It was Rudolph Hess, he was the original mastermind. It was Rudolph Hess who originally devised the plan for a united Europe and a single currency, controlled from Germany, of course. He correctly surmised that the Allies would win the war, and began to plan the Fourth Reich, a united Europe was the cornerstone of that plan, and as I have said, a united world is the next logical step."

"So what we actually have, is a non-aggressive, commercial and political invasion of all those countries in the union, the remainder eventually and inevitably being sucked in. I must admit it, that, it is an absolutely brilliant idea."

"Mr McLenan, we are within a very short time of realising our dream, the Fourth Riech is ready to unite the world, you can help us in our mission, or you can stand aside, the choice really is yours alone, have a think about it." Turning to Lynn he said. "Take Mr McLenan to his room please, then return to my office."

They both turned and left the office without a word. Lynn led the way along a series of passages, Scott had no idea where he was within the complex, he knew that if he was to escape he would need a guide, or a hostage. Eventually Lynn stopped at a door.

"Well, this is your room, you will find everything you need in there, for attention, just press the wall bell." She opened the door and Scott entered. The room was sparse, but at least there was a bed.

"Thank you," he said politely, "will I see you later?"

"Probably." She closed the door and left.

Scott tried the door handle, but found it to be locked, realising there was nothing he could do for the present, he lay down on the bed and shortly fell asleep. He had a troubled sleep in which he dreamt of being lined up against a wall and shot by firing squad. When he woke he lay on his bed going over the recent events of his life. He thought about his flat in Preston. it was no more than a slum, but it was his slum, and at least he had been anonymous there. He remembered his short time with Shannon, how his love at first sight had been reciprocated. He remembered George, the most beautiful snare that he had ever been trapped by. He thought of escape, but knew it was impossible.

He raised himself from his bed and went over to the door. Turning the handle, he was pleased to feel the door open. He peered through the small gap, almost expecting to be reprimanded, or worse. He leaned forward, looking out into the passage. It was clear. Going back into the room, he showered, and, finding a change of clothes in a cupboard, he dressed quickly. As he made his way back toward the door it opened. It was Lynn.

"Hi Lynn, I'm starving, can I get a bite to eat round here?"

"Of course, would you prefer to eat alone?"

"No, I would appreciate some company."

"Come on then, follow me."

Scott did as instructed. He followed her, watching her body glide along the passages. She had certainly looked after herself over the years. He knew he must be on the road to recovery, until now his main concern had been self-preservation. She opened yet another door using her remote control. Through it, Scott could see the street lamps of the city, he realised it must be evening on the outside. She beckoned him to walk on, which he did. He was totally amazed at the scene, if he hadn't known that he was subterranean, he would never have guessed. The city was perfect. The streets were clean, no dog dirt, no rubbish, no cars. People smiled at them as they passed. He saw no hint of the forced labour the first Adolph Hitler had used and abused, perhaps, he thought, things could be different this time.

"Come on slow coach, we're nearly there."

"Nearly where?"

"Here." She said pointing toward the next building.

Scott caught up to her, and looked up at the sign above the front window, he read it out aloud. "Italian restaurant."

Lynn took him by the hand and led him through the front door.

"Table 22 please." She said to the headwaiter as he approached.

"Don't tell me you have real Italians?"

"No, better, they are Germans that cook Italian."

"Would Sir like to order drinks?" the headwaiter enquired.

"Yes please, what would you like Lynn?"

"Half a lager please."

"Half a lager for the lady, and a vodka and orange for me please."

The headwaiter thanked them and left.

"Since when did you drink lager?" Scott asked Lynn.

"Since I stopped smoking, when are you going to stop drinking vodka?"

"When I start smoking, in other words, never."

"Have a look at the menu, order what you like, it's all free."

"Are you kidding?"

"No."

"Let me guess, the Nazi treasure?"

"I suppose so, there is a lot of it. From what Hitler has told me, we have barely scratched the surface of it. The Jews had such vast wealth. It was the main reason that his father hated them so much. He came from such a poor background, he despised the imbalance, although his logic was possibly over simplified. The Jews had what he wanted, so he killed them and took it, in his mind he was solving two problems at once. We are a very wealthy organisation."

"An organisation built on the blood of World War Two."

"Tell me Mr moral campaigner, if you inherited a fortune, how concerned would you be where it came from?"

"But we all know where this came from."

"Then who should we give it back to?"

"I don't know, I think I will have the rump steak, what about you?"

"We can't give it back, we are investing it in the world's future, not just the Jews, everybody will benefit, I think I will have the chicken."

The headwaiter returned with their drinks, took their orders and left them to their debate.

"We believe," she continued, "the treasure will build the new-world, a world for all, not just the privileged."

"With your gang in charge?"

"We are not a gang Scott, you have seen our achievements, why don't you join us, help us to make it happen?"

Scott drank his vodka in one, to the annoyance of Lynn. His drink problem had begun before she left him. What she didn't realise, was that it was his suspicion of her affair with his brother that had turned him to drink. He ignored her disdainful look. They talked at length of the ten years they had been apart. Scott was hurt to realise that she hadn't missed him at all.

The waiter re-appeared with their meals. He served Lynn first, then came around to Scott's side of the table with his steak and a steak knife.

"That looks perfect, thank you." Scott said to him, as he turned and left. "You know Lynn. I believe, that what you have achieved here should be considered as the eighth wonder of the world. But don't you think you are all wearing blinkers, you all refuse to see the other side of the argument, which is quite simply, what if the rest of the world is happy enough as it is?"

"We have worried about that, that is why we believe secrecy is so vital. If our plan leaks out in dribs and drabs, the world's leaders would have time to build a resistance, using dis-information. If we can make it happen simultaneously, we believe the people will seize the opportunity for themselves, the only people to stand against our plan, would be the world's leaders, for obvious reasons."

"Yes, I can agree with that."

"Then join us on our journey Scott, be there to make sure that it's as we promise, be part of our new-world, you've earned it, what do you say?"

Sixteen

SCOTT didn't answer Lynn's question immediately. He ate his steak and looked her in the eye. He thought her to be genuine in wanting him to be part of the Fourth Reich. He had been overwhelmed by what he had seen. The massive structures, the LPC's, the subterranean city. He believed it possible that he could make a difference. It was obvious, even to him, that the technology involved was so far advanced that they must surely triumph in their quest, he realised that any form of resistance from him would prove to be futile, he also recalled an old saying, 'If you can't beat them, join them'.

"Yes," Scott said, breaking the silence, "I believe I would like to be part of your adventure, but I'm still bloody angry about the bombings in the UK."

"That is the right decision Scott, I promise you. Try and think of it in another way. How many British soldiers were killed and tortured by the Germans and Japanese during the Second World War? Nobody knows, and what for? Nothing! Absolutely nothing. All three nations trade together, the past, pushed to one side in the name of business. How many of today's young people really care about the war. It's history. It's not their problem, they are only interested in the future."

"So you're saying, forget the recent past for the sake of a wonderful future?"

"Yes, well no, you cannot forget the past, but remember, it is past, it can't be altered."

"But the future can?"

"Exactly, come with us and shape it."

"I would like to make a difference."

They finished their meals, during which they recalled their stormy past together. Scott told her of how his life had fallen to pieces when she had left, and how the last ten years had been particularly awful. Lynn explained that she had never loved Danny. That everything she had done had been in the name of the Fuhrer. They knew Danny was trying to investigate, so she had to get close to him to control him. The 'dopple-ganger' had been sent in so that she could spend all her time at Berlin, as the unification day was drawing ever closer,

"When will that be?" Scott asked.

"Tomorrow."

Scott was stunned. "What can I do?" he asked.

"I'm sure there will be plenty for you to do Scott. All the LPC's will take off during the morning, and head for their predetermined positions. At noon, the Fuhrer will take up his position above the White House, from where he will announce our intentions. The broadcast will interrupt television stations the world over, allowing the maximum number of people to see it as possible, the internet will be used to answer the people's questions."

"What about resistance?"

"As in your country, we have infiltrated the armed forces and the police forces in every country of any importance, these people will be responsible for arresting the trouble makers, and keeping them under control until the unification is complete."

"How will you control them?"

"I believe they are to be held in camps."

"Oh I see," Scott replied, "what about the people here?"

"They will be free to leave, or they will be allowed to stay and carry on their research, above ground of course, I would imagine this place will eventually become a museum or something."

"Sounds great, when do I start?"

"We'll start now by going to see the Fuhrer, and asking him what he would like you to do, come on."

They finished their meals then left the restaurant. Lynn leading the way, she failed to notice that Scott had taken the steak knife, stealthily pocketing it as he talked.

"Ah Mr McLenan, did you enjoy your meal?" The Fuhrer asked

"Perfect."

"Scott would like to play his part during the unification process." Lynn said almost excitedly.

"Would he now, and what part would you like to play?" He asked Scott.

"I would like to pilot an LPC, in particular the one heading for the UK."

"Why?"

"I would like to be the second Guy Fawkes."

"Who is Guy Fawkes?"

"He tried to blow up the English government, but unfortunately he didn't have an LPC."

"So why would you like to blow up the government?"

"Because my brother worked for them, under their orders he stole my wife, ruined my career and my life, they stole ten years that can never be replaced, now I believe it's pay back time."

"But you came here to kill me."

"That's right, and if I had had a gun, I would have shot you on sight."

"And now?"

"Now I see the bigger picture, I can understand the need for total secrecy, a few lives now, could save millions over the next few days."

"Exactly, good, I am not to sure about you piloting an LPC, but we may put you on one." Hitler promised.

"Excellent, I can't wait."

"For now I would like you to wait outside." He said looking toward the door.

Scott left Hitler's office, almost bowing as he went, he wondered if he had convinced them, or were they planning his execution as he waited.

"Do you believe him Lynn?" the Fuhrer asked.

"Yes I do Fuhrer, he always was a loner, but now I believe he is frightened. He is homeless and friendless, there is nothing for him in England, I think he is looking for someone to blame, and that makes him dangerous, I believe that anger will be saved for the British government."

"I am not so sure, instruct George to spend some time with him, tell her to keep him talking, he may open up to her."

"Yes Fuhrer." Lynn turned and left the office. She found Scott dutifully waiting.

"Come with me." She ordered.

Scott did as he was told, wondering why her attitude had changed, alarm bells began ringing in his head. He knew that he hadn't fully convinced them. He was led to yet another door. Lynn knocked. The door opened. To his relief, it was George that answered.

"Hi Scott, what is it?" She said ignoring Lynn.

"The Fuhrer would like you to entertain Scott for the remainder of the evening." Lynn replied.

"Ok, come on in Scott."

He did as instructed, Lynn turned and walked away. George closed the door. As she turned to Scott, he slapped her hard, leaving a frenzy of red finger marks across her face,

"I loved you bitch."

George began to cry, softly at first, tears streaking her mascara, then she began to sob violently. Despite everything, Scott couldn't help but feel sorry for her. He took her in his arms and apologised. Her beauty shone through the tears. He used both hands to lift her face, and kissed her fully on the lips.Her head slipped onto his shoulder as they stood embracing. After a while her crying ebbed away. She looked at Scott, her eyes so blue and melting, he knew he could never hit her again.

"I deserved that." She said.

"Yes, you did, but I'm sorry."

She began to unbutton her blouse as she kissed him passionately. Within moments they had both undressed and were making love on her bed. They made love as if it would be for the last time, their bodies writhing rhythmically until they reached their crescendo together. They lay in each others arms, looking into each others eyes, as if searching for an explanation.

"I'm so sorry." George whispered.

"It doesn't matter." Scott kissed her passionately on the lips. Their bodies began to respond. Once again they made frantic love, the world around them shut out, or so they thought. The concealed camera, activated by the micro-chip hidden in the collar of Scott's overalls, relayed the pictures back to the Fuhrer's office. There, Lynn monitored the proceedings with an ever-growing annoyance.

Their love making complete, Scott and George fell asleep, locked in their final passionate embrace.

They woke with a start as the intercom system suddenly burst into life.

"This is your Fuhrer speaking, unification has been

postponed by twenty-four hours, due to abnormal weather conditions over most of Europe, the new countdown will begin at 05.30 hours tomorrow, in the mean time all personnel will carry out their normal daily duties."

"Well George, it looks like we may have some more time together, what shall we do?" Scott asked.

George pulled him on top of her and began kissing him and touching his body, after a good night's sleep, Scott was refreshed, and responded instantly. Their love-making was now slower than the night before, as if they had been reprieved, and now they had the time to renew their relationship.

Later, they showered together, once more taking the opportunity to re-explore each other.

As he dressed, Scott noticed a small lump in the collar of his overalls, using his knife, he made a small incision into the fabric. As he peered into it, he realised instantly what it was. He now knew for certain that they did not trust him, and that George was probably being used to get him to talk.

As George came out of the bathroom, she noticed Scott's expression.

"What is it darling?"

"Don't darling me, you trapped me once, you won't do it again."

"I do not know what you are talking about."

"Don't you, we'll see, get dressed, I want to find out what I am supposed to be doing today." He looked about the room trying to spot the camera, but it was too well concealed. "Come on, hurry up."

"Why are you being like this?"

"Just hurry, your time's up."

When she had dressed he ordered her to take him to the Fuhrer's office. They walked in silence, George unaware as to why Scott's attitude had changed so suddenly. As they approached the Fuhrer's office the door slid open, confirming Scott's worst fears, he was now in no doubt that he could be tracked anywhere in the complex.

"Good morning Mr McLenan, I trust you slept well?" said Hitler, as he stood before him, resplendent in full Nazi uniform, identical to the one worn by his father. At his side stood Lynn, also in uniform, only hers was the uniform of the Gestapo.

"I see we're all showing our true colours this morning." Said Scott.

"Are we?" asked Hitler. "And what colour are you Mr McLenan?"

"I'm the colour of money Mr Hilter, you know what I can do, how much are you going to pay me to do it?"

"I like your style Mr McLenan, if you help us through this transitional period, you will be very well rewarded, that I can promise, we need people like you to act like, like disciples, to spread the word, explain the new order, win people over to our way of thinking."

"You make it sound like a new religion."

"People need to believe, they need faith, we need to teach them to believe in us, after all, the craft alone will convert most people."

"Agreed, they've got my vote, what do you want me to do?"

"Well, nothing for the moment, take time to look around the craft and the complex if you like, George will escort you, tomorrow is the dawning of the new age Mr McLenan, I am rather pleased that you have chosen to be part of it."

"Thank you, come on George, show me round." He said grabbing George's hand and leading her out of the office.

"Keep monitoring the situation Lynn, I am not yet convinced."

"Yes Mien Fuhrer." She replied sharply.

Scott stopped George once they were well away from the Fuhrer's office.

"Why are they still watching me?" he asked.

"They watch everybody, not just you, look around, there are cameras everywhere, they can probably listen as well, it is not a problem, is it?"

"No, I don't suppose so."

"When did you decide you wanted to join us?"

"Last night, to be honest, I don't think I could live without you George."

"Thank you, after what I have done, I thought you would hate me."

"You are too beautiful to hate, if being with you means being here, then this is where I want to be, I have nothing and nobody in the UK, you are all I need George, I hope the feeling is mutual?"

"Oh Scott, you know I love you, at first it was just another job for me, but as soon as I met you, I fell in love with you, I just want to be with you, forever."

"Come on then George, show me round our new home."

They entered the giant LPC hangar. It was alive with the noise of preparation.People were hurrying and scurrying everywhere. Technicians carried out last minute alterations, cleaners constantly cleaned the light panels, checks were being carried out, over and over again, an air of expectancy filled the cavern, each LPC had it's own ground crew, their efforts so vital to the successful completion of the unification.

"Can I have another look inside an LPC?" Scott asked George.

"Of course, come on, let us have a look in this one."

They climbed the stairway to the entrance, and went inside.

"Karl, Joseph, I have a friend who wants to be an LPC pilot, can we have a look round?"

"Hi, my name is Karl, I am the captain, this is my co-pilot Joseph, we are pleased to meet you."

"Pleased to meet you too, my name is Scott." He said as he shook hands with them both. To Scott, they were both typical of his picture of a German, blond hair, blue eyes, muscular, first to the seats by the pool.

"So you want to be a pilot Scott?" Karl asked him.

"Yes, but I've only ever driven a car in my life, and not very well at that."

"Come, we will give you your first lesson." Joseph said, as he led him to what was obviously the cockpit area. "Please, sit here." He said pointing toward the right hand seat. "Right, the first lesson is, how to start it, it is simple, just depress this large red control, that exposes the primary light panels, which provide enough power to move the craft within the hangar."

"But how do you see?" Scott enquired.

"The craft has three VS's."

"What?" Scott interupted.

"Vision systems."

“Of course, sorry, I’m a bit slow, British.”

“It’s ok, one system is basically closed-circuit television, only enhanced for far greater vision, the second is radar, and the other is this.” He depressed a blue button beside him on the console. A large visor receded, exposing a panoramic windscreen.

“Superb!”

“Not really,” Karl replied, “we tried for years to perfect glass that could withstand high speed flight, but failed, then you British invented the Concorde with it’s simple solution, the visor, our problem was solved. Our latest craft are equipped with glass so strong as to make the visor obsolete, but we still use it, especially during re-entry of the Earth’s atmosphere.”

“Have you ever approached the Apollo or Shuttle flights?”

“Yes, what the astronauts saw were German craft and nothing else, we believe our ancestors were from the only other planet whose people achieved space flight, perhaps they crashed here, perhaps they never intended going back, we just don’t know.”

“What about ET’s?”

“We haven’t seen any, but that doesn’t rule them out, I personally think distance is the greatest hurdle against planet hopping, also, what have we on earth that is worth coming here for, nothing.”

“We have water.”

“Good point, but only assuming other species need water.”

“Do you believe there are ET’s?”

“I do, Joseph doesn’t.”

“Where are all the gauges?” Scott asked, changing the subject.

“When we said we are at least fifty years ahead, we meant it, there are no gauges for us to worry about, everything is controlled by the on-board computers, we virtually only have to steer the thing, and even that can be done via the computer. We use the joystick for direction and power. By pressing the green button on the left of the stick, we increase the amount of panelling exposed to light, thereby increasing power. By pressing the red button on the right, the panels are re-covered, by pressing the amber button, the night-light panels are exposed, our scientists strive for simplicity, I think they did rather well don't you?"

"So what are the black buttons for?"

"Nothing really, they are the DLF's, we never use them."

"What's a DLF?"

"I'm not allowed to say, orders, sorry."

"That's ok, I shouldn't ask so many questions, I think it's time George and me left you to get on with your work, thanks for showing me the controls, I think I'm going to have to buy one of these to play with."

"There not toys," Joseph interupted, "they're. . . "

"That is enough Joseph," said Karl, cutting him short, "perhaps we can get together for a drink sometime Scott?"

"Yes, I would like that," turning to George he said, "Come on then, see you later chaps."

Scott and George descended the stairway, back into the bustle of the hangar. For the first time he noticed a very thin silver line inlaid into the floor, he assumed this would be the guidance system for the entry and exit mode of the LPC's, if it was, it had to lead to the exit. Together they roamed the complex for the remainder of the day. Eventually they arrived back at what Scott recognised as the door to his room.

"Would you like to come with me for a meal this evening Scott?" George asked.

"You know I would, so long as it isn't my last supper, so to speak, I have no decent clothes to wear though, I will have to come in my scruff."

"I do not think so, your clothes should have arrived from the hotel by now."

"Ok then, about eight thirty?"

"I cannot wait." She kissed him and walked off down the long corridor.

Scott closed the door, then instinctively tried to open it again. It was locked. He showered, then lay down on the bed to think over what he had seen. To him the complex was like the set of a Hollywood sci-fi film. There was no doubt in his mind that the Germans were light years ahead of the Americans, when the masses were offered the chance to share in this technology, this new order, he knew they would probably take it.

At eight he began to prepare for the evening. As he

dressed, he found that another microchip had been installed in the collar of his shirt. At eight-thirty he heard a little click emit from the door, trying the handle, he found the door was unlocked. Opening it, he was surprised to find George just about to knock, and realised that Hitler must have her tagged as well.

"Good evening George, I've missed you."

"And I have missed you to Scott." She said, just before planting a kiss on his lips. She wore a strapless evening dress, of the purest white, worn simply as a second skin for her body, Scott was captivated. Her figure would guarantee attention in a monastery. She had the kind of body that would look good in mechanic's overalls

"You look more beautiful each time I see you." Scott said drooling.

"Thank you, you look better in your own clothes."

"I look even better out of them."

"Who said." She slapped him playfully on the shoulder.

"You did, last night."

"Come Scott, let us go and eat, would you like to go to the restaurant again?"

"How do you know I've been before?"

"That would be telling, come on."

They followed the same route as he had the previous evening with Lynn, only he was much happier to be with George, he slowed the pace of the walk so that he could hold her for longer. Despite everything, he couldn't resist her beauty, he knew that, even if he lost his life because of her betrayal, he would forgive her. They arrived at the Italian restaurant and entered.

"Table 22 please if it's available?" he said to the headwaiter.

"Certainly, would Sir and Madam care to follow me, thank you?"

He led them to the table, Scott had enjoyed sitting here, the position of the table afforded him a good view of the restaurant. He could see most of the other diners, he had spent a lot of time studying their faces, looking for a dissatisfied expression, a nod or a wink, anything that might have indicated a possible ally, there were none.

"Would Sir care to order drinks?"

"Would you like to share a bottle of wine George?"

"Yes please."

"What would you recommend my friend?" he said addressing the headwaiter, "anything from the Mosel valley would be suitable."

"I have just the wine for you Sir." He half bowed, then turned and left them.

"Where is the Mosel valley?" George asked Scott.

"It is one of the main wine growing regions in west Germany, if he knows his wines, he will bring a 1969, that was a great year for wine production in the valley."

"How do you know all this?"

"I've drunk most of it all ready."

The headwaiter returned carrying a bottle of white wine and an ice bucket. He removed the cork with consummate skill, Scott knew there would be no bits of cork floating in the wine this evening.

"It's 1969 vintage Sir."

"Thank you very much, that will be perfect, would you pour?"

The headwaiter poured out the two glasses of wine. He produced two menus and left them to select the meals.

"Do you think we are being monitored George?"

"Monitored, no, I do not think so, I do not know for certain, why, are we?"

"No, I don't think so, it's just a feeling I have of being watched wherever I go."

"It will be the CCTV, the cameras are everywhere for security reasons." She reassured him.

"Are you ready to order George?"

"Yes, are you?"

Scott nodded, he beckoned the waiter, who took their orders and left.

"This place is bloody marvellous."

"It is just an ordinary restaurant."

"No, I mean the entire underground workings, they're fabulous, I wish I could have come here years ago."

"I believe Hess is the man mostly responsible for what we have here today. He wanted to do things differently from Hitler, he believed the only ambition of a captive slave, is to escape, but the ambition of a free man is to leave his mark on the world, this place has been built by free men."

"Did it cost many lives?"

"Yes, an undertaking of this size will always cost lives. We have built a hall of remembrance. Not just for the dead, but for the living as well. Each person has recorded a message on CD, in years to come, their relatives will be able to visit the site, and by playing the CD, they will see exactly what part their relation played within the complex, plus they all record a personal message. Every CD is like a little history book, giving every different view point."

The waiters arrived with their meals.

"George, why didn't you trust me enough to tell me about all this?"

"Because you were SAS through and through, how could I invite you to come and visit the embryo of the Fourth Reich?"

"Good point, but you must know that I've always been open to new ideas."

"Yes, but it is quite an idea."

"It's a hell of an idea, the outside world certainly has a shock coming it's way."

"A pleasant one though."

"Maybe, but you still haven't convinced me that everybody is going to accept the one-ruler system with open arms."

"If the masses are with us, who can stand against us?"

The question went unanswered as they ate their meals. Scott had never tasted food as well prepared as the two meals he had eaten at this establishment. When they finished their meals, they left the restaurant, and went for a walk around the underground city. It was palatial on a massive scale. He had always regarded the Germans as hard-working people, the complex stood as a credit to them all as a nation.

"Well Scott, I think it is time we returned to our rooms," she said as she stopped walking, "I have an early start in the morning, so do you."

"What do you mean?"

"I believe the Fuhrer has a task for you."

"Like what?"

"I do not know, you will find out in the morning."

George escorted Scott back to his room, he realised that he still could not find his own way around the labyrinthine complex, he wondered how everyone else managed.

"Here we are Scott, I hope you have enjoyed our evening together?"

"Of course I have, I've been with you, haven't I."

"Thank you, you are very sweet."

"I would invite you in for a coffee but there isn't any."

"I can stay for a little while if you would like me to."

"Then please come in." Scott opened the door and motioned with a wave of his arm, for her to enter first.

The room, or cell as Scott had called it during the evening, was sparsely furnished, so they sat together on the bed. Neither of them knew what to say, both of them knew what they wanted, but were afraid to admit it. Scott broke the silence.

"George, I want you to know, that you are the most stunningly beautiful woman I have ever met," he said taking her hands in his, " I could have loved you deeply, I still can't believe that you betrayed me."

"I'm so sorry Scott. At first, as I have said, it was just another job for me. But then I realised what a wonderful person you were. You were the man that I wanted to be with, even spend the rest of my life with, but it was too late, I had to complete my task, if I had not, my brother would have been in grave danger."

"Yes I realise that now, ok, I forgive you this time, but if it happens again, I will be seriously annoyed." Scott realised that she could betray him as often as she liked, her beauty fascinated him, to him, she was irresistible.

"Can you really forgive me?" she said, as she moved closer to him.

"Yes." He took her in his arms and kissed her passionately.

They lay together on his bed, not talking, just kissing and exploring each others bodies, as if rediscovering each other once again. They removed each others clothing, slowly, sensuously, all the time touching, kissing, caressing. Their bodies reacted to the dual stimulation of sight and touch. Once again their bodies united and became as one, any thoughts of the betrayal, quickly forgotten. They made love with an unrestricted freedom, a freedom that knew no bounds. When they had made love, they lay in each others arms, oblivious to the world, their happiness complete. As in the past, they made love several times before yielding to their tiredness, eventually falling asleep, locked forever, in their final orgasmic embrace.

Above them, a hidden camera recorded every movement, every sound. In her office, Lynn angrily punched the stop record button.

Seventeen

SCOTT woke with a start. He realised that he was in bed alone, George had completed her task well. She had entertained him for as long as required, now she had gone. Once again he realised she had betrayed him. He admonished himself for being so easily led. It was now the day of unification, and he was helpless. Perhaps, he thought, the SAS had been right to throw him out.

The intercom system gave out a constant stream of commands. He climbed out of bed and went to the door, trying the handle, he found himself to be still a prisoner of the Fourth Reich.

He washed and dressed quickly. Before putting his overalls on, he used the steak knife to cut the miniature transmitter from the collar, and placed it in his pocket, he knew they could still track him, but only for as long as he let them. He tried the door again, and this time, to his surprise, it opened. Stepping out into the passage, he joined the swarm of people, who all appeared to be heading in one direction. Over the intercom, Scott heard his name.

"Mr McLenan to the Fuhrer's office please, Mr McLenan, Fuhrer's office immediately please."

Scott had no idea how to get to the Fuhrer's office, and so asked one of the many people flooding the passage, for directions.

"Simple, just follow the colour code above the doors. You want to follow the red squares," The young German said, pointing to the coloured pattern above the door where they stood, "if your colour isn't above a door, keep going to the next one, and so on until you find it."

"Thank you." Scott said as he looked up at the door where the German indicated. Sure enough, above the door, a row of different coloured squares that he had never noticed before, on this one, there was no red square, so Scott proceeded along the passage. At the next door, there was red square, so Scott passed through. A few doors later, he found himself stood at the door to the Fuhrer's office. It silently slid open and he entered.

"Come in, come in, Good morning Mr McLenan."

"Morning, so today's your big day?"

"Yes, at last, our long wait is now over Mr McLenan, more than fifty years have passed since my father's death, but today his dream will be realised. The Fourth Reich stands at the threshold of the new world, with our new world order, it is our second chance, we must get it right this time." He emphasised.

"You must be very proud of your achievements?"

"Not just me Mr McLenan, all the people you have seen and met here, I owe it all to them, I'm no more than a figure head, a catalyst for the new tomorrow."

"Some say 'tomorrow never comes'." Scott replied cleverly.

"It is here now, today Mr McLenan, today."

"Well I hope everything goes as peacefully as you have planned."

"It will, you cannot beat our machines, you may as well join them, as you so rightly said."

"Did you have a task in mind for me?"

"I am afraid not, all tasks are assigned, but I want you to stay here and watch as events unfold, we may need your assistance later in the day." Hitler pressed a button on the large control panel in front of him. Two large covers moved to the sides to reveal a large panoramic window, which overlooked the gigantic hangar where most of the craft were docked. Through the window Scott watched as hundreds of ground crew carried out their final preparations and adjustments. The hustle and bustle looked like the rush hour of any normal town.

"Could I go down onto the hangar floor for a last look around?" Scott asked Hitler.

"Certainly, but try not to get in the way, they are all very busy."

"Thank you, I wont interfere, what colour do I follow?"

"Yellow."

"See you later." Scott left the office and followed the colour codes, until he found himself in the main hangar. He knew he had been watched all the way. He walked over to the nearest

LPC, which was easily visible from Hitler's office, and busied himself studying the undercarriage and fuselage. He knew he stood looking at, and touching, the answer to all of the UFO stories, the achievement could only be admired.

The intercom spat out it's staccato messages incessantly. As take off time for the first wave of craft drew nearer, the tension could be felt to rise. Crews began to board their craft, after much hand-shaking and saying their goodbyes.

"Good morning Scott," a voice called out, "are you ready to rumble?" It was Karl.

"And good morning to you, no, it's looks as though I will be staying here."

"It is a big day Scott, the world will never be the same again, whatever happens."

The note of doubt struck Scott.

"What do you mean?"

"Nothing."

"Come on, you said 'whatever happens', what did you mean?"

"Nothing, forget it, I'm just a bit nervous." He looked away.

"Nothing can beat these machines, surely?" Scott persisted.

"Please, let it go Scott."

"You know something, there is a weakness, isn't there?"

"No," he said in a loud, aggravated manner, "listen Scott, I have accepted you as a friend, but don't push it, there is only one thing that can beat an LPC, but forget it, ok?"

"You can't tell me that much."

"Forget it." Karl walked away. Scott went after him.

"I'm sorry Karl, listen, I'm a bit short of friends at the moment, I'll drop it."

"Ok Scott, come on, there's plenty of work to do."

As they walked, Scott wondered what it was that could beat an LPC. Then the answer came to him. Another LPC. He knew that his only chance was to capture one of the craft, simple he thought. After a few minutes they reached Karl's craft, it was almost smothered in technicians.

"Why do I get the impression, that there are more people working on your craft, than on the others?"

"Mine is the most complex, it is the command craft, from

it, I will oversee the day's events as they unfold."

"And what is about to unfold?"

"The plan is simple, we will station a LPC over as many capital cities as possible, so that the masses can see them, as well as the authorities, while this is occurring, we will use satellite technology to broadcast our friendly intentions to the world. We want people to assume that we are from outer space, and that resistance will be futile. However, we are expecting resistance from the USA and the Russians, so we may have to give a demonstration of our craft's abilities."

"You mean kill someone?" Scott cut in.

"As a last resort. We have chosen daylight hours so that people can see the craft clearly, obviously there will be countries in darkness, we just hope that they have their televisions switched on, we will also be using the internet to answer people's questions."

"Well I think you will find there will be more resistance than you care to admit to, and with that, more bloodshed."

"Why would you say that?"

"Because the 'one ruler' idea has never succeeded, there have been many empires, but no one ever got to rule the world."

"Ah, my friend, nobody has ever had the LPC's before."

"The LPC's seem to be the key to the whole operation."

"Yes, I suppose they are, but there is something else, only Hitler and the Inner Circle know about." Karl added.

"What Inner Circle, what else?" Scott felt uneasy.

"Hitler has intimated that the craft are only part of the unification process, that he has something even more astounding lying in reserve, to convince the masses of their various governments deceit, if and when required, he will reveal this secret."

"And you have no idea what that secret is?"

"No, I'm not a member of the Inner Circle."

"Come of it, you must have some idea?"

"My grandfather knew, but I have never been close to the hierarchy."

"Who was your grandfather?"

"Rudolph Hess."

This answer staggered Scott. Even after seeing the craft, he had still regarded the whole story as too fantastic, but to have the descendant of a top Nazi as a friend, rendered him speechless.

Karl added. “Perhaps we will all find out today.”

Regaining his composure Scott replied. “I wouldn’t have thought anything could be bigger than the LPC’s.”

“All we have been told is that the revelation should remove any lingering doubts the people may harbour, thereby ending all resistance.”

“Is the secret here?” Scott asked.

“Only Hitler knows.”

“Is it something to do with the last war?”

“I honestly don’t know, and I don’t think Lynn does either.”

“Are you saying that she is a member of the Inner Circle?”

“Yes, anyway, it’s time for me to board, wish me luck.”

“Good luck.” Scott said as he turned away, and he meant it, he had come to like Karl, he believed he had given him as much information as he could.

Scott hadn’t liked what Karl had told him. An inner circle meant that there was already a hierarchy to this one ruler system, this new, open system of rule, that was already keeping secrets from it’s people. He knew that after the dust had settled, nothing would have changed for the ordinary people of the world, he also knew he must try to prevent it happening. He wandered freely through the hangar, the craft were too numerous for him to bother counting them. He followed what he presumed to be the magnetic track, for guiding the craft to the exit, that was inlaid into the floor. When the track terminated, he looked for the exit, but couldn’t see it. The work force were obviously under no pressure, there were no signs anywhere of the slave labour that Hitler’s father had so cruelly used. The intercom crackled into life.

“Mr McLenan to the Fuhrer’s office please, Mr McLenan.”

Scott realised he must have been very close to the exit, even if he hadn’t seen it. He headed back towards the Fuhrer’s office. As he walked, he noticed George coming towards him. She waved and Scott returned the gesture.

“Hi Scott, I have come to be your escort.”

“Why, is it execution time,” he said scornfully, “am I to be the next victim of this bloodless enterprise?”

Her expression didn't alter. "That depends entirely upon you Scott, so if I were you, I would be a little more careful with my choice of words."

"Well you're not me," he argued, "so stuff your advice." He was angry that she had left him during the night, without telling him where she was going, or why.

"Now now Scott, you keep this up, and you will be dead sooner than you think, do not be a hero, it cannot get you anywhere, you could not even find the exit." She said mockingly.

"You know George, there's nothing I detest more than a smart arsed bitch, don't forget lady, I owe you one, you are the one who should be considering life and death, you've pissed me off, and that ain't healthy."

"Big talk Scott, but that is all, how many of us do you think you could kill, one, two, twenty?"

"I've already sorted some of your finest, the rest don't bother me."

"They should," she said pointing, "left here." She guided him out of the cavern and into one of the long passages that crossed the complex. They argued all the way to the Fuhrer's office, the door opened as they approached.

"After you." George said.

"No, after you." Insisted Scott. He followed her into the office.

"Good to see you two getting along so well, come in Scott. I am afraid I have some rather bad news for you old chap." He said in his best English accent.

Scott froze and didn't reply.

"Do not look so worried, I have decided that you can live a little longer, to give you chance to prove that you really are with us."

"I'm ever so grateful." Scott replied sarcastically

"Lynn believes you are ready to assist us, but I'm not so sure. How can you prove to me that you really are with us?"

"Well, you could send me on holiday to the UK, and see if I come back."

"I do not think so Mr McLenan, would you kill Lynn if I asked you to?"

"I'm going to kill her whether you ask me to or not, she betrayed me, so did George, I want to really hurt them both."

“Um,” the Fuhrer said as he paced the room, “we do seem to have a problem, go back to your room, I will send for you when I have made a decision, George, take him away.”

She led Scott out of the office. Scott knew that time was running out, he had failed to convince the Fuhrer of his allegiance, if he was going to make an escape, it would have to be very soon.

Scott followed George through the passages, his mind in overdrive. He realised he had wasted his time marvelling at the wonders of the complex, when he should have been attempting to formulate his plan of escape. Now his only option was to play it by ear, the worst possible option. His only weapon, the small steak knife stolen from the restaurant.

“What colour leads to the entrance George?” He asked in hope.

“Green, it will lead you to where you saw the guards hit me.”

“Are you sure?”

“Of course.”

Scott was puzzled by her answer, he hadn’t expected one, now he had to decide if she had told him the truth. He had thought of taking her hostage, but he knew Hitler would kill both of them without hesitation.

They passed through a door, which finally led to the hangar where the giant transporters were docked. It was like rush hour in London, he thought. George grabbed him and pulled him to one side, so suddenly, he almost lost his balance.

“Kiss my neck.”

“Kiss my arse.”

“Kiss my neck.” She said angrily.

“Get stuffed.”

“Kiss my neck for Christ’s sake, and stop bloody arguing.”

Scott had never heard George speak like this, the Latin American accent had all but disappeared, replaced by the Queen’s English. He leaned forward and began to kiss her neck.

“Do you want me to show these Germans how a real man makes love?”

“Do not kid yourself, now shut up and listen,” she said with some authority,

“Scott, we must stop the craft before they exit the complex.”

He looked up, and was about to argue, but the look in her eyes told him it was time to listen. He began to kiss her neck once more.

"We have guns, we have explosives, and we have you. You may not know it, but you are being monitored, there will be a device sewn into your clothing, you must find it and remove it."

"I have found it, but I'm keeping hold of it for the time being, I don't want them to know I know. Who are you talking about when you say 'we'?"

"I cannot tell you that yet, in case our plan goes wrong, or you are forced to talk."

"Well, I think you had better listen for just one moment, in the not too distant future, I am going to start killing people, and fighting my way out of here, now it might help if I know who not to kill, you are going to have to trust me."

"It is my brother." She whispered.

"That's great, I've no idea who he is, you had better just tell him to keep out of my way, it will be safer."

"Listen Scott, we have very little time, the first craft exits at ten precisely, you must not do anything until we start, do you understand?"

"Yes, but if Hitler decides to have me killed before the start time, I may have to begin without you."

Their whispered conversation was interupted by the intercom.

"Mr McLenan please return to the Fuhrer's office immediately." The message repeated.

"I don't think I like the sound of that George, it hasn't taken him long to come to a decision about me."

"You must go alone, I have so much to do, if you have to start early, then so be it, but try to give us as much time as possible, now go, and Scott," she paused, looking deeply into his eyes, as if searching for an answer, "remember, I will love you always." With that, she kissed him and walked away.

Scott wanted to go after her to tell her that he loved her too. In his heart he had forgiven the betrayals. He realised now that he really had been a very small and insignificant part, in a much larger plan. It was now apparent that he had become a crucial element to the success of that plan, and that he must not fail. Failure would be an insult to all the dead, especially Shannon. He set off in the direction of the Fuhrer's office, breathing deeply, trying to calm his knotted stomach. Following the red colour code he arrived sooner than he had wanted to. As expected, the door slid silently open as he approached.

"Come in Mr McLenan," Hitler called, "come and watch as the future and history unite."

"What is your schedule Mr Hitler?"

"At exactly 10.00hrs, the exit will become exposed, the craft will vacate the hangar in single file, the command LPC leading, when all are in position, we will interrupt all television channels, and I will inform the world of the new order, simple, what do you say?"

Looking at the clock on the office wall, Scott realised that there were only fifteen minutes to launch, and he still had no idea what he could do. In his days with the SAS, every action was planned down to the last detail, and even then things went wrong, he didn't like his position at all.

"I hope you haven't over simplified."

"What do you mean?"

"Well, perhaps people will not react as you hope, perhaps you have taken their reactions for granted."

"I do not think so Mr McLenan, but I do take your point," he said, rubbing his chin in thought, "some people always want to complicate matters, I do not think we will need them, do you?"

"No." Scott believed he had just answered the very question Hitler was pondering over concerning him, and of course, he had given the wrong answer.

"Well Mr McLenan, the time has come for me to leave you. I have a date with destiny. You may stay here and watch events unfold on the television, after the unification, I will return, then we will have to do something with you, I am sorry you cannot come along for the ride, until I return, treat the office as your own."

Scott felt the handle of the steak knife in his pocket, it was nine-fifty-one, nine minutes short. As Hitler turned to leave the office, Scott pounced, the steak-knifecut into Hitler's neck, but not very deeply. He called out for the guards as he struggled with Scott. Scott stabbed with the knife again, this time cutting into Hitlers ear lobe, causing him to cry out in pain.

The first punch knocked Scott away from Hitler, causing him to drop his knife, he hadn't seen the guard come into the office, but he had certainly felt him.

"Kill him," Hitler ordered, "and make sure the little shit suffers."

"The little shit will be waiting when you come back Hitler, and that, is a promise."

Hitler didn't acknowledge. He left the office. There were now two guards facing Scott. He glanced at the wall clock, nine-fifty-three. He hoped his attack on Hitler had been sufficient to distract him, hopefully he hadn't missed George.

The first guard came into range, Scott tried to look his most menacing, but the guard came right at him. The first kick made the guard stop and take a very deep breath, before mouthing a loud scream of pain. As he doubled over, the second kick removed most of his upper front teeth. In an instant, the second guard pounced on Scott, punching and kicking for his life, one punch caught Scott on the eye and sent him reeling to the floor, the skin above the eye opening up and bleeding profusely. The guard tried to dive on top of him, but Scott rolled to one side, but felt the pain of metal tearing into the skin of his shoulder. He noticed his steak knife close beside him and picked it up. As he stood, he was knocked over again by the onrush of the guard. He slashed out madly with his knife as he fell. They both landed in an angry cursing heap on the floor. Scott slashed out again, and this time was pleased to hear a scream as the knife tasted flesh once more. Getting to his feet, he noticed that the guard had dropped his knife. They both went for it at the same instant. The guard reached it first, but Scott quickly stood on his fingers, bringing another shrill scream of pain. Scott picked up the knife and stabbed it urgently into it's owner. The guard rolled over, trying to avoid Scott, but it was to no avail, his own knife sought his heart and found it, his fight was over. As Scott removed the knife from the now lifeless body, a kick in the ribs sent him reeling, crashing hard into Hitler's desk, but this time he kept a firm grip on the knife. Another kick caused Scott to grimace in agony, he knew that he must have suffered broken ribs. He rolled across the floor, trying to avoid further punishment. The next kick landed on the side Scott's head, splitting the skin just below his right eye, his face immediately began to swell, causing the eye to close, making it difficult for him to see where the attacker was. He knew he had to get to his feet or he would be finished. He slashed out with the knife again, causing the guard to step back, giving Scott the second he needed. They faced each other. The guard began to laugh, a toothless, raucous, fearless laugh.

"What's so funny Goofy." Scott asked.

"I have been watching a video of you in bed with your woman," he said, "you cannot fight either."

Scott knew he was stalling while he got his breath back, but he didn't mind, he was trying to recover as well.

"I would rather be bad in bed with a woman, than be an ugly shirt-lifter like you Fritz, did you kiss your boyfriend's arse goodbye before I wasted him."

The enraged German lost control and lunged at Scott. Scott side stepped him and plunged the knife into the nearest part of his anatomy. It was a good hit, but it didn't stop the German, who turned and came at Scott again. Scott stabbed him again, but the power of the man sent Scott crashing to the floor, the guard landing on top of him. He had both hands wrapped around Scott's throat, both thumbs pressing hard on either side of Scott's Adam's apple. The pain was excruciating, much worse than anything Scott had ever had to endure before. His will to live kicked in, as he began to drift into unconsciousness. Using every last vestige of strength, he stabbed violently into his assailant. Again and again he stabbed, until he lost his battle to remain conscious. The two men lay on the floor, motionless, locked in their final fight, like the bodies discovered at Pompeii. They both contributed to the pool of blood as it grew on the floor beneath them.

As Scott began to recover consciousness, he became aware of the guard's heavy body weight pinning him to the floor, his hands still firmly clamped about his neck. Scott felt the comfort of the knife still within his grasp. He lay motionless as he regained his composure, then, without warning, rammed the knife into the guard's neck, only stopping when it reached the hilt. Scott was unaware that the guard was already lifeless. He pushed the body off himself, then slowly rose to his feet. He wiped the blood from his eye, improving his vision. He noticed a remote control device near to the body of the guard and picked it up, knowing that he would need it later. He glanced at the clock on the office wall, it indicated nine-fifty-nine and fifteen seconds. He stumbled to the window. It was too late, the command LPC, was leading the craft towards the exit point. As the command craft approached the rock face, the clock registered ten. He watched helplessly, knowing Hitler would be on the lead craft. A tremor reverberated across the floor, and in the background Scott heard the quiet hum as a huge electric motor sprang into life. He watched in awe as the rock face divided and moved to the sides, revealing an aperture in the shape of the craft. The command craft entered the tunnel. There was no explosion.

Scott was angry with himself for believing George once again. Her plan must have been so simple. Tell the English fool that she would blow up the complex, and sure enough, he would sit back and let her do the work. Scott couldn't believe that he had been so naïve. He cursed himself for being such a failure. He swore to kill her, if another opportunity ever presented itself.

As he watched, a young man appeared from nowhere, running as fast as he could towards the command craft, passing the long line of slowly moving craft. A guard stepped out to stop him, but the running man felled him with one blow to the side of his neck, and without pausing, ran on toward the lead craft, which by now had entered the tunnel. Scott watched in disbelief, as the running man appeared to be pointing at the command craft, which was now completely into the exit tunnel. Then Scott realised what was happening. The man had to be George's brother. In his hand he held the remote detonation device, which for some reason, must have failed. Scott began to cheer for him as he ran, willing the explosive to detonate. As the running man neared the craft, Scott watched in horror, as a guard stepped out behind him, aiming his machine gun. The gun clattered into life. The running man stumbled forward three or four more paces. The gun clattered once again, The man crashed onto the hangar floor. Scott's heart sank with him. The last hope of stopping Hitler, lay dead or dying, only yards from the craft. It was over. It was yet another failure for Scott McLenan to add to his long list of failures.

Scott blamed himself. He knew what the problem was.

AI had bestowed their trust in a known failure. True to form, he had failed. This latest failure would accompany him, for the rest of his failed life

His thoughts returned to Shannon. In his mind he apologised to her. It was his fault that she was dead. She also had placed her trust in him. So many people lay dead because of him, he didn't know if he could live with the guilt.

On the hangar floor, the body of George's brother lay crumpled and broken, but not quite dead. Unseen, and with the last ounce of life in his bleeding body, he continued to press the detonate button.

Eighteen

THE explosion ripped the heart out of the command craft. It was instantly engulfed in a huge orange, blue and yellow fireball, which quickly spread forward and rearwards, overwhelming the second craft, and starting a chain reaction. The fire spread with amazing rapidity from craft to craft.

The first explosion jolted Scott from his self-pity. He watched the fireball in disbelief, as it's flickering tongues spread throughout the hangar, licking at the bewildered work force with it's fiery breath, it's searing heat turning their skin instantly into a rubbery, stinking, melting pulp.

Scott gave out a loud cheer, then cut it short, realising that Karl was in the lead craft. As he watched, the command craft erupted with a second huge explosion, bringing hundreds of tons of rocks down upon itself, and blocking the exit tunnel. Above the catastrophic crescendo, he heard someone calling.

"Scott, come on, we have to get out before the whole place blows." It was George.

"Was that your brother?"

"Yes, come on, we have no time to dwell, we must go now." She begged.

"You are not going anywhere, only to bloody Hell." The voice came from behind her. It was Hitler. He pushed her roughly into his office. "Do you realise what you have done you stupid bitch, the world could have been yours, you could have had anything you wanted."

"But not freedom." Scott interceded.

"Just shut your miserable loud mouth for once, I personally am sick of listening to all your smart-arsed arguments and clever answers. You are nothing McLenan, you were only sent here because they did not want to waste a good agent." Hitler raised his gun, aimed, and shot him. Scott slumped to the floor.

George screamed and pounced on Hitler, kicking and scratching, trying to punch him. Hitler knocked her to the floor with his free hand. Before she could recover, he shot her. George lay still.

Hitler used his remote control to open the door leading to the ancient craft. At that moment Lynn came into the office.

"Oh my God," she gasped on seeing the two bodies, "what have you done?"

Hitler didn't reply, he aimed his gun and shot her, the bullet entering her skull in the centre of her forehead, she was dead before her face smashed into the office carpet. As he turned, Scott stood up and charged at him, sending Hitler sprawling one way, and his gun the other. Scott was on him instantly. He punched Hitler hard in the mouth, loosening Hitler's teeth, but splitting the skin of his knuckles. Hitler fought back, kneeing Scott in the groin, causing him great pain. Hitler managed to push Scott off him, and land a punch on his all ready bleeding eye. He tried to retrieve his gun, but as he stooped to grab it, Scott kicked him solidly in the ribs, winding him. Scott then kicked him in the face, breaking his nose. Hitler collapsed on to the floor, as he did, he recovered his gun. He turned to shoot Scott again, but Scott managed to kick the gun out of his hand, loosing his balance in doing so, and falling over. Hitler saw his chance and took it. Getting to his feet, he gave Scott a resounding kick to the side of his head. Scott's strength seemed to desert him. He could only watch as Hitler made his way to the ancient craft. He lunged for the gun, picked it up, aimed and fired in one motion. The metal door slid shut as the first bullet slammed into it.

"Too late McLenan, this chamber is proof against most things, you can shoot to your heart's content, but now I'm afraid I have to leave you, I hope you will stay to enjoy the fireworks display. You made one other mistake. You forgot, we Germans always have a contingency plan, this is mine. Goodbye." Hitler turned and entered the craft with a final wave.

Scott dragged himself to his feet. He could see that Lynn was dead. He went over to George and felt for a pulse. She was alive, but like him, had been shot through the shoulder. He patted her face. Her eyes opened and she managed to smile.

"Come on George, we have to get out of here before we are roasted alive." He pulled her to her feet. The flames from the hangar licked fiercely at the panoramic window, as if confirming their plight. Explosion followed explosion, in the inferno that had once held the dreams of so many Germans.

They left the office, Scott taking one last look back at the hangar, could see nothing. Thick, black, acrid smoke had drawn it's dark veil over the large window. He grimaced in horror as the screams of the burning people below, reached his ears above all other noises. A series of huge explosions began to shake the complex, as though it had been built on a geological fault line, and was now being rocked by a large earthquake. The panoramic window disintegrated under pressure from the intense, searing, liquefying heat, just as the office door slid to behind them.

"George, you're bleeding badly, you must stem the flow of blood. Try putting your finger into the hole."

"But you are bleeding too." She gasped in pain as he steered her forefinger into the bullet wound.

"I know, don't worry about me, you have got to get us out of here by the shortest possible route, come on George, which way."

In the sealed chamber within the office, Hitler hurriedly worked at the controls of his most treasured possession. He had seen the raging fire engulf the office, and realised that time was running out. Above the craft, a hidden door slid to one side, allowing precious sunlight into the chamber, giving life power to the dormant craft. Hitler sat at the control console pushing an assortment of buttons. The craft began to rise graciously. Hitler laughed out loud, a callous, evil laugh, like the Devil himself. The devastation and loss of life he was leaving behind, meant absolutely nothing to him.

There was a further series of explosions, seemingly more powerful than the preceding blasts. The craft collided with the shaft walls, wiping the smile from Hitler's face. Above the ascending craft, huge Andean rocks dislodged themselves, and came crashing down, their enormous weight forcing the craft downward, blocking the sunlight, robbing the machine of it's power. Hitler issued a string of vitriolic curses, aimed mainly at Scott McLenan. The lights inside the craft dimmed and finally extinguished. Hitler stood alone in the abysmal darkness, waiting for the flames to seek him out. Urine soaked his trousers.

The progress of Scott and George was severely hampered

by their injuries, but despite their pains, they knew their only chance of survival was to keep moving and get clear of the mine. The passages seemed endless, as they slowly filled with the thick, black, acrid smoke from the hangars. From nowhere a guard appeared. Scott shot him before he had the time to reach for his weapon. Scott threw the pistol away, and picked up the guard's machine gun.

They came upon a closed door, but some sixth sense, or instinct for survival, stopped Scott from pressing the remote control. He felt the door, it was burning hot, he knew that fires must be raging at the other side of it.

"Come on George, we will have to go back." He ordered.

"Oh Scott, can you not just leave me, I am so tired, please, save yourself?"

"Don't give up on me now lady," Scott replied, "we've come too far."

They retraced their steps, the passages were becoming like ovens, what little air there was, was almost impossible to breathe. The smoke was filling the passages from the ceiling downwards, causing them to stumble along, bent double. George felt heavy as she slumped against him. He knew she was growing weaker by the minute. They arrived at another door. Scott tentatively touched it. This one was cold. He pointed the remote control at the door, and quickly pressed the button. The door slid open. The two guards failed to recognise him at first, because of his injuries, and also, the smoke had coated him in a black skin of ash and grime. By the time they did, it was too late, the machine gun chattered into life. Both fell to the floor, dead.

"Come on George," he encouraged her, "there can't be far now."

George didn't answer. They clambered over the bodies of the two dead guards. She knew her brother was dead, and believed she was dying, she wanted Scott to lay her down, and let death take her pain away. It was taking all her remaining strength just to direct Scott. By now, she was passing in and out of consciousness.

Scott's body was racked with pain from all of his injuries, especially the bullet wound. It was only his will power that kept him moving, his strength was coming from anger and adrenaline. He looked up as they stumbled along. In the distance, he thought he saw a tiny dot of daylight. By now, they were almost on their knees, trying to keep beneath the murderous smoke, as it funnelled along the passage. The dot of light grew larger. Scott knew it had to be the mine entrance, it was the most wonderful sight he had ever seen. He urged George forward. A searing flashover roared along the passage, forcing Scott to fall to the floor with Shannon, burning the clothes off their backs, blistering their skin. Scott waited as the flames passed over, the pain of fire a new experience for him. He mustered his remaining strength and raised George to her knees.

"Come on George, I'll race you to the entrance." He said, trying to raise her spirits, but failing.

They struggled in the passage for another fifteen minutes, before finally, sweating and gasping for air, barely alive, they emerged into the Argentine afternoon sunlight. Scott could see the main gates of the complex. A large crowd was gathering, assuming that they were witnessing a huge mining disaster. The crowd spotted Scott and George as they struggled out of the entrance, and began shouting encouragement to them.

"Nearly there George, just a few more yards and it's all over." His voice was barely a whisper, his parched throat felt as though he had swallowed broken glass.

George didn't answer. She felt the sunlight as it caressed her face, lifting her spirits, yet she was slipping away rapidly. Blood dripped from her clothing, like a melting icicle.

Scott could feel his strength ebbing, only his SAS training made him persist, where others would yield. The gate loomed ever closer.

From somewhere in the distance, Scott heard the unmistakable chatter of a machine gun. The bullets slammed into George, like a bolt of lightening hitting a tree, causing her to fall on top of Scott. The crowd was silenced. Again Scott thought he heard the deadly chatter of a machine gun, only now there were two. After a few moments that seemed like an eternity, the guns were silent.

Scott kissed George's forehead before slipping into unconsciousness, his blood mixing with George's as it soaked into the Argentine sand. For George, the race was run.

The gates of the mine were forced open as the crowd

surged forward, not believing what they had witnessed. From among the crowd, four men ran over to Scott and George. Picking up their lifeless bodies, they carried them out through the gates to a waiting Range Rover. The sirens of an approaching ambulance could be heard as it rushed to the mine, but they didn't wait. The Range Rover sped away as more explosions ripped the very heart out of the Andes. Massive rocks were hurled hundreds of feet into the air. The crowd of onlookers ran for their lives, but for many, it was too late, as the rocks began too rain down on them as they ran, crushing them, shattering their fragile bodies beneath their unforgiving weight. After a time, a morbid calm descended on the area. Survivors searched for friends and relatives among the debris. It was a scene straight from hell. Bodies were strewn everywhere, engulfed by the massive rocks and thick heavy, choking smoke. In the background, the Andes burned.

The small hospital serving Bariloche had been inundated with victims from the mine explosions. The hospital's staff, had been overwhelmed by the sheer scale of the emergency.

The younger nurses were sickened at the sight of the burned victims, and found it very difficult to cope. Of the two-hundred-and-thirty-one patients brought to the hospital, fifty-eight had already died, seventeen were critical, and five were comatose, the remainder had slowly been attended to, and discharged.

Two weeks had passed since the dreadful day at the mine. One nurse had taken it upon herself to care for one of the comatose victims, staying at his bedside for as long as possible, even during her own free time. She had been attracted to the man, by nothing more, than a feeling of deep sympathy for him. In the two weeks he had been at the hospital, he had not had a single visitor. She would sit and talk quietly to him for hours at a time. So far her patient had failed to respond. She realised she was falling in love with him, although she didn't understand why. She had got into the habit of kissing him every time she had to leave him. Every night she included him in her prayers. She also prayed for the woman who had been brought to the hospital with him, possibly his wife, who had been pronounced dead on arrival. Somebody would have the task of informing him of his wife's death, she hoped it would not be her.

The young nurse arrived at the hospital early as per usual. She had brought with her, a personal stereo and some tapes for her patient, as she had read that some coma patients had reacted to hearing music.

She walked onto the ward and approached his bed. She was horrified. The bed lay empty. She ran to the Sister's office to find out where he was. The Sister informed her that, during the night, an ambulance had come and taken him away, for treatment elsewhere. The devastated young nurse broke down in tears and ran out.

Four weeks had now passed since the battle of Bariloche. Thousands of miles away, at the Military hospital in Catterick, Yorkshire, a young man lay comatose in a private ward. The nurse mopped the beads of sweat from his forehead. He had arrived in Catterick two days previously. Nothing was known about him, but judging from the medical reports sent from Argentina, and the wounds still visible on his body, the young man had suffered terribly. She busied herself tidying his bed, and out of the corner of her eye, she thought she saw the forefinger of his left hand, move. She held his hands in hers, and began to talk to him.

"Hi, my name is Sheila," she said, "I hope you can hear me, I am your nurse. You are safe here, we will look after you for as long as it takes."

She waited for a reaction, there was none.

"There are two other nurses who will be looking after you while you are with us," she continued, "they are not on duty at the moment, they are very nice young ladies, one is called Katie, and the name of the other young lady is Shannon." She felt his hand try to squeeze hers, or at least she thought she had.

"Was it Katie?" There was no reaction.

"Was it Shannon?" She felt his hand tighten on hers again. Tears welled in her eyes.

"I have to leave you for a minute," she said wiping the tears, "I will come back, promise." There was no further response. She hurried to the Sister's office.

"Sister," she said excitedly, "our young man with no name

can hear us, he reacted to the name, Shannon."

The Sister was older and wiser. "I hope you are right, how did he react?"

"He squeezed my hand, twice."

"You're sure?"

"Yes, I think so, yes, I know he did."

"Right, go back to his room and see if you can get any more reactions, talk to him, do not mention Shannon again just yet."

"Yes Sister." She hurried from the office back to his room.

The sister dialled a number she had been given.

"Hello."

"Hello, my name is Sister Jackson, I'm stationed at Catterick Camp, military hospital, we have one of your chaps with us."

"Oh yes, how can I help?"

"I was given this number to call if there was any change in his condition."

"And has there been?"

"Possibly, one of my nurses believes he reacted to the name Shannon."

"Ok, fine, well thank you Sister Jackson. Could I ask you to call again if there is any further change in his condition, and can I ask you to remind your staff, that it is imperative, that his visit to Catterick is kept secret at all costs. It is quite possible that his life may depend upon it?"

"Of course."

"Thank you, and goodbye for now."

"Bye."

She replaced the receiver. Leaving her office, she hurried to the private ward. She found Sheila talking quietly to the young man.

"Anything else?"

"No, not yet, he may have tired himself out."

"Ok, now don't forget, this is all very hush hush, I know it must be exciting, but you must not tell a soul that he is here, do you understand?"

"Yes Sister."

"Good, I will be in my office if you need me, keep up the good work."

Sheila sat with him for two more hours, before Shannon

came on duty.

"Hi Sheila, anything happened yet?" Shannon said as she came into the ward.

"You wouldn't believe me if I tell you."

"What?"

"Come here, and let me whisper," she said turning away from the bed, "I told him your name earlier, and he reacted to it, twice."

"Never."

"Honest, there have been no reactions since, but I haven't mentioned your name again, in case it was upsetting for him."

"Yes it could be, should I try now?"

"If you like, hold his hands, and you will feel him squeeze, if he's listening."

"Ok." She sat next to the bed, and took his hands in hers. "I don't know your name, but my name is Shannon." She felt his hand tighten on hers.

"Look Shannon, look at his face." Cried Sheila.

Shannon did as instructed. As she looked, a tear left a moist trail down the man's cheek. Shannon and Sheila both began to cry with him. They knew beyond doubt, that he could hear and understand them. The joy they felt was immeasurable. When they had dried their eyes, they looked at him again. His eyes were opening. He squinted at first as the light penetrated. When he could focus, he smiled at them. They both began to cry again. So did he. He then tried to speak.

"Hitler." His voice was so weak, that the two nurses couldn't understand him.

"Did he say Hitler?" Shannon asked.

"I'm not sure, I could hardly hear him, I think I had better fetch Sister." She hurried off to the office.

"Sister, we think he is trying to speak."

"Are you sure?"

"Well, yes, but it doesn't make sense, we think he said Hitler."

"Right, go back to the ward, I will be along shortly."

As Sheila left the office, the Sister began to ring the number she had used previously.

"Hello."

"Hello, it's Sister Jackson again at Catterick, your man

has begun to talk, although it may be gibberish, we think he said Hitler."

"Ok, well thank you Sister, I will send somebody immediately, can you ask your staff not to ask any more questions, it is important?"

"Certainly."

"Thank you for your co-operation, goodbye." The phone went dead before she could answer. She hurried to the ward.

"Right you two, no more questions, it's an order from the top, Sheila, isn't it time you were getting off home?"

"Yes Sister, but I wouldn't mind staying a little longer."

"No, off you go, he'll still be here tomorrow, Shannon will look after him."

"Shannon." The young man said

"He said your name, did you hear him?"

"Yes." She said. Turning back to the man she said, "Yes, it is Shannon, what do you want me to do?"

He looked at her. "Shannon." He said before drifting off into unconsciousness.

By morning, a team of minders had occupied the private ward, the nurses were no longer allowed to talk to their patient. They were only admitted to the ward to administer care.

Late in the afternoon of the same day, the man opened his eyes. He looked at the men surrounding him.

"Where am I?" He whispered.

"You're back in Blighty mate." The nearest one answered. "Glad to have you back, you've had us worried."

"Is Hitler dead?" He whispered again.

"Christ Almighty mate, how long have you been asleep?" The guard nearest to the door asked.

"I don't know." He paused as he composed himself. "Is Hitler dead?"

"Listen mate, I haven't a clue what you're on about, you just rest for the time being, we're here to protect you, don't worry, you're safe with us."

Over the next few days the man made rapid progress, even remembering his name. He told his guards his name was Scott McLenan. He suffered tortuous nightmares, often screaming out names that meant nothing to his guards. Within two weeks he was ready to leave Catterick. Sheila and

Shannon were both there to say their goodbyes. All three of them cried openly. Scott kissed them both and left. They still didn't know his name.

Scott travelled to London with the guards, they were a good bunch of blokes, and he found them easy to get on with. He was taken to the headquarters of AI, and over the following weeks was debriefed. They found his story incredulous, but it was given credence by the evidence from Argentina. Scott was informed that the underground workings in the Andes, had been totally destroyed, the explosions causing the mountains to collapse into the complex. He was shown photographs of all the survivors, and all the dead, but Hitler was not amongst them. AI assumed that Hitler had been buried beneath thousands of tons of Andian rock, the Fourth Reich buried forever with him.

Scott had by now recovered from most of his injuries, and looked forward to returning to Preston. Most of all, he wanted to rebuild his life. He had been offered a position with AI, but had turned it down in favour of obscurity.

His first priority was to visit the Lake District. He left London, driving through the night. He changed his mind while driving north, and went on toward Scotland, he wanted to fulfil his promise to visit Angie and her mother. At about seven-thirty in the morning, Scott pulled into a service area, reclined the seat, and fell asleep.

The noise of a car back firing, woke him with a start. He looked into his rear view mirror, and wished he hadn't, he was a mess. His eyes were red, his hair was everywhere, his tongue felt like a dirty doormat. He combed his hair, but he still looked like he had seen a ghost.

He left the service area, and went in search of a hotel. The first one he came to, had an A board outside, advertising early morning coffee and breakfasts. He went in and booked a room.

The hot water of the shower stung his body as he came back to life. He dried himself, and dressed in his new clothes. If Spider could see him now, he thought, he would wet himself. He left the hotel, and resumed his journey, arriving at Angie and her mum's hotel at lunchtime.

He threw open the door of the lounge bar and walked in.

"Tony," Angie squealed, "Oh brilliant, you made it back?" She came running from behind the bar and hugged him with all her strength.

"Careful, I'm still sore in places."

"Oh God Tony, have I hurt you."

"Only when you made me pay for the ale, you can call me Scott if you like, it's over."

She slapped his shoulder. Scott winced. She saw his face.

"What is it Scott?"

"Just an old war wound."

"I'm so sorry, I've heard you've been through hell."

"Yeah, just a bit. I'm ok now though, where's your mum?"

Angie bowed her head and looked towards the floor.

"What is it?" Scott asked.

"She's dead Scott, they killed her while we were out at sea rendezvousing with the sub."

"The bastards," Scott said angrily, shaking his head, "anyway, there won't be any more killing, I think I got most of them." He took her in his arms and drew her to his chest.

"I hope so Scott, she meant the world to me."

"Would you mind if I visited her grave?"

"Of course not, I will come with you, the bar closes at about two-thirty, we can go then, is that alright with you?"

"Yes, that's ok, right, I'm just going out for a while, I will come back for you at closing time, see you later." He said as he turned and left the bar.

"See you Scott." She called after him.

At closing time Scott returned to the hotel as promised. He had been for a walk around the small Scottish fishing village. It seemed so peaceful after the last few months, he had even taken a passing glance at some of the properties with sale boards planted in their gardens. He bought flowers at the local grocer shop. Something had puzzled him as he walked, but he had no idea what.

"Hi Angie," he said entering the bar, "are you ready, or am I too early?"

"No, I'm ready when you are."

"Come on then." He said leading her outside to his car. He waited as she locked the front door of the hotel. He opened the car door for her. "Just a moment, I've left something in the boot." He went to the rear of the car, rummaged around in the boot, then came round to the driver's door, slamming the boot shut as he walked.

"Right Angie, you will have to give me directions."

"Ok, it's right out of the car park, then just follow the road, it's not far."

"How are you coping without your mum?"

"Well, it's been hard work, but I feel obliged to keep the old place running, it was her dream to own a hotel, the tragedy is, she had just got everything how she wanted it, then this happened."

"I'm sorry Angie, it's all my fault."

"Don't be silly Scott, we were all acting under orders, you must not blame yourself."

"Thank you, but I can't help it, a lot of people are dead now, I blame myself for all of them."

"Well you should stop right now, Hitler is the one who should carry the blame, left at the church entrance." She directed.

He drove the car into the car park of the tiny church. He collected his flowers off the back seat. They left the car and walked into the cemetery. He could see that it was beautifully cared for. Most of the graves had had flowers placed on them recently. In the distance, he could see that one that had more flowers than all the others, it was obviously Angie's mum's.

Scott stood in front of the grave, tears welling in his eyes. He had grown to like the old lady, in the short time that he had known her. He went down on one knee and placed his flowers in front of the headstone. It was black, with gold writing inlaid. He read the epitaph.

'Here lies the body of Helen Dorothy Spencer, dearly beloved mother of Angela Marigold Spencer, sadly missed.'

Scott reached inside his jacket and felt the cold steel of his pistol as it nestled in the shoulder holster beneath his right arm. As he stood, he withdrew the gun and turned to face Angie.

"You f.....g bitch, your own mother?" he said shaking his head.

"She had to go, she had suspicions, how did you know?"

"Only the debriefing officer knows about Hitler, and

Marigold is hardly a common name."

"What now then, you won't shoot me?" she sneered. "You are much too English for that, and I have no weapon, I am just a poor defenceless woman." She laughed at him.

The bullet entered her forehead centrally, passing through her brain, and exiting at the rear of her skull, taking a large portion of bone with it as it went. Angie was as dead as her mother, before her body crumpled to the ground.

Scott reached into his jacket and removed the small tape recorder from the inside pocket. He re-wound the tape and played it, it had recorded their whole conversation. He took one last look at Angie, then turned and left the cemetery.

The drive south from Scotland was picturesque. He drove slower than he would normally, trying to understand, trying to figure out people's motivations, trying to put it all behind him. There was one more task he had to face, then he could truly begin again.

As Scott drove beside Ullswater he became deeply morose. He had hoped to be spending the remainder of his life with Shannon. He blamed himself for her death. As he drove toward Watermillock, he couldn't restrain himself from crying. She had been his reason to live. She had kick-started his miserable life. In the few weeks he had known her, he had come to love her deeply. He now felt his guilt more acutely, knowing he had betrayed their love.

Scott brought the car to a halt beside the skip that was blocking the access road to the Rampsbeck hotel. He climbed out of the car, and removed a wreath from the rear seat. He looked out over Ullswater, which lay majestic and calm in front of him. He looked down the narrow little road, half hoping to see the hotel still standing, but of course, it wasn't. He walked slowly down the sloping road, remembering their last night together, when they had walked home from the pub arm in arm. The guests applauding as they had kissed outside the hotel. He remembered his first glimpse of Shannon, wearing her see-through nightie. The first time they had made love. The warmth of her body as he lay next to her in bed. The last time he had seen her, as he left to go jogging.

The Ullswater steamer passed by on the far side of the

lake, as it had on that first morning. Scott watched as it disappeared, just as his life with Shannon had.

Through tear filled eyes, he could see the large mound of rubble that had once been such a beautiful hotel. The yellow tapes of the police cordon, fluttered in the gentle breeze, as it came inshore off Ullswater.

He walked towards the devastated hotel, stooping under the yellow tapes to get a little closer. He bowed his head and began to sob. The sight of the mound of rubble, underlining the reality of his nightmare

Form behind, he heard footsteps approaching.

"Scott?"

He lifted his head, turned, and peered at the newcomer through his tear filled eyes.

"Shannon?"

THE IMMACULATE MISCONCEPTION

A sequel to The Father, the Son, and The Unholy Ghost features Scott McLenan in an international adventure entitled 'The Immaculate Misconception'